# Derra

# Derra

**BARRY F. PARKER**

# DERRA

iUniverse books may be ordered through booksellers or by contacting:

iUniverse
1663 Liberty Drive
Bloomington, IN 47403
www.iuniverse.com
1-800-Authors (1-800-288-4677)

Because of the dynamic nature of the Internet, any web addresses or links contained in this book may have changed since publication and may no longer be valid. The views expressed in this work are solely those of the author and do not necessarily reflect the views of the publisher, and the publisher hereby disclaims any responsibility for them.

Any people depicted in stock imagery provided by Thinkstock are models, and such images are being used for illustrative purposes only. Certain stock imagery © Thinkstock.

ISBN: 978-1-5320-3886-0 (sc)
ISBN: 978-1-5320-3887-7 (e)

Library of Congress Control Number: 2017919072

Print information available on the last page.

iUniverse rev. date: 12/16/2017

for my friend Derra
who inspired all of the good qualities in the title character

# Prologue

The wind disturbed only wisps of her long brown hair. Otherwise, Derra stood unaffected by the cold bite in the night air. Her deep brown eyes showed hints of sadness, moistened slightly either by her mood or the sting of the breeze. She was a vision as she stood alone at the top of the cliff – a phantom from days past, perhaps, or a memory of something eternal. She was tall, but fragile. Although the idea would have been tempting, she seemed too frail to hug, as if the pressure might turn her into dust. Yet the gentle spirit that always pushed through the mysterious cloud in which she was enveloped, begged for the human touch. How she withstood the elements, or why she would even try on such a night as this, was a secret that even her guardian angels could not unravel. But there were deeper secrets: secrets that reached back in time; secrets with which she was endowed even before her unborn flesh took form.

# FROM THE MEMOIRS OF DR. NOAH GILES: NOVEMBER TO MID-JANUARY

I have taken the high road to mediocrity. I am well educated. I have a flair for the arts. But I put neither attribute to any good use. Instead, I surrender my academic title to the public relations department in a position my father would have referred to as "civil service," but what was, in fact, a cushy middle management appointment for a government sponsored organization. I have never married, nor have I built up a core of close friends – though those around me found me personable enough. I approach the black hole of middle age with some trepidation - halted from being wholly consumed by that monster only through a resilient dose of personal vanity. To what purpose I cling to my youth is difficult to describe. Overtly, I could say that I want to remain appealing to the world's unending supply of beautiful twenty-two-year-old women. But even when I had been of age for them, I had never been appealing to them. There was nothing hideous about me. There was just nothing that would draw anyone to me. My desperate need to keep the last vestiges of my youth is rooted more in my desire not to see the last doors of opportunity closed upon me. Opportunity for what? That is more complex. It is certainly not the lost opportunity to ensnare a twenty-two-year-old woman. That door has never been open. And, although I am not launched into a career that I would have chosen, I never had any alternatives in mind. As for fame and fortune, they had their draw, but again it was not something that had ever seemed viable for who I am and for what I have to offer.

As is common for males too long protected from the feminine touch, I have acquired my own set of peculiar habits. I plan my meals a week in advance, and my weekly schedule has few variations. I calculate my grocery budget to the penny – substituting only when special offers make such an alteration practical. I wash my dishes by hand every night, and dry them with a fresh tea towel from the top of a stack neatly arranged in order of last use. I keep one pet – a cat named Bubastes that roams freely in my gardens by day, and warms me in my bed by night. My gardens are my obsession, and I am proud to say that I know the majority of my plants by their Latin names. Of course, I had no one to impress with such knowledge, and on the few occasions when I let slip the less familiar name, I usually find myself as the object of ridicule rather than admiration. Having sought neither to impress nor to be embarrassed, one reaction is just the same as the other to me.

I live in a modest two-bedroom home, purchased more for the garden prospects than any intrinsic aesthetical qualities of the structure itself. And, though the task of upkeep is not particularly daunting, I have a woman (herself secure in her deep submersion in middle age) come to clean for me on Friday mornings. Having opted for ten-hour workdays from Monday to Thursday, Friday begins my weekend for me, and there is something almost festive about beginning a long weekend with a fresh abode. My housekeeper, Lucy, lunches with me when she has finished her work. The menu never varies: coddled eggs, toast, watercress, and a glass of beer. The inclusion of watercress stems, no doubt, from my English heritage. The miracle is that there is actually a shop in the state of Washington that carries it. I grow my own *nasturtium officinale*, but I use it sparingly since I like the impression it creates within my tiny backyard stream. The beer too is English, purchased in large cans, opened fresh for the noon meal. Once Lucy leaves, I sit down by the fire with a second glass and good book. On rare sunny days, I take my second glass into the garden and sit in quiet admiration in one of the lawn chairs accompanied, of course, by Bubastes. Bubastes, however, prefers the rainy days when he is allowed indoors to warm by the fire in the comfort of my lap. These afternoons traditionally ended with both of us falling sound asleep.

My weekends seldom pick up from there. Saturdays are for my garden work, and on Sundays I attend church (Episcopalian, of course). There is little excitement, though my comfort level is high – as witnessed by the ever-increasing ridge around my middle. I am not obese, by any means, and look relatively trim in my clothes, but I can project, in my mind, the pear-shaped shadow that I will cast as the years progress. In all likelihood, I will simply skip over the dreaded middle life and land securely in old age. I am mentally almost there already. Although very much at peace with myself and my world, I am aware that, especially without any heir, I am simply one of the faceless masses filling in space while this world awaits its final destiny. The last project that I ever expected to occupy my time was the recording of my memoirs. What cataclysmic event in space or time could make my very mundane existence of any lasting significance?

St. Paul's Church is a large stone structure. It was constructed with a traditional layout (a must for me) in the later part of the nineteenth century. It has a good coating of ivy on the outside, and large wooden beams on the inside. There are a few minor flaws in the design, and one major one – that being the incomprehensible replacement of the original stain glass windows, shortly after the Second World War, with windows depicting soldiers in battle. Fortunately, the colors distract most visitors from what is being portrayed, and the tall, narrow shape of the windows only allow one or two soldiers per scene. Even that is open to interpretation so long as the glasswork is not associated with the brass memorials at each end of the rows of windows. Yet, despite the irritant (which really only seems to affect me), the atmosphere of the church is what it should be: full of quiet dignity for the majority of the year, and full of timeless festivity during the Christmas season.

It was at the beginning of the Christmas season that I first saw Derra. Even though the church population swelled in that season between Thanksgiving and Christmas, it was not very likely that I would miss the addition of someone like Derra to our congregation. It was my habit, both for selfless and selfish reasons, to examine the inhabitants of any given service pew by pew. The selfless reason was taught to me by a biblical scholar under whom I had studied briefly many years ago. When I had spoken to him about the power and the intellect infused into a sermon that he had just delivered, he gave credit to the fact that, before he preached, he prayed for the congregation pew by pew. It seemed to explain the success he had encountered compared to the faltering efforts I had made in my youth, even with solid material clutched in my hands. (At least, I liked that thought better than the idea of conceding that I had a far inferior mind.)

As a result, I had decided to limit my contributions to future services to a similar pattern of prayer for whomever had control of the pulpit. On the selfish side of things (and I blush to confess it), I systematically survey the congregation for attractive women. I have no hidden agenda in this exercise. I simply find little in life more aesthetically pleasing than the sight of God's more appealing creatures, garbed in their Sunday best, pure as the day they were born, in the divine sanctuary.

Seldom are these women unaccompanied. Young wives come with their husbands, and the unmarried are with boyfriends, family, or occasionally, a small group of likewise unattached women. Derra was clearly on her own. The unlikelihood of seeing such a remarkably beautiful woman on her own, particularly at this time of the year, was almost as alluring as the woman herself. I tried to absorb myself in the liturgy, but I couldn't take my eyes off of her. Of course, I would quickly avert my gaze when she looked in my direction, but she caught me staring too many times to allow for any coincidence. Ultimately, in a manner that I came to know as typical of her, she made a game of it. Awaiting my next visual assault, she flashed a quick smile at me. I was thoroughly embarrassed, and resolved to keep my eyes on the Book of Common Prayer until it was time to exit the service. I failed in my resolve, however, and on several occasions I was caught by my prey – her smile broadening with each subsequent success.

My inclination was to skip the post-service buffet so that I would not further disgrace myself should this woman be present. But, slave to my habits that I have become, I could not depart without my food. I convinced myself that she would not be there, and that, even if she were, she would be oblivious to my presence. My conclusions seemed solid enough, even though both turned out to be wrong. Not only was she present, but she wove her way through the gauntlet of drooling young men and planted herself securely by my side. I wondered, initially, if she had done so simply as a means of discouraging potential suitors. But I soon learned that she was oblivious to these assaults. She would smile sweetly, and respond politely, but her manner in doing so seemed to discourage further advances. Being myself fully subject to the urges of my gender, I have never been quite sure how this worked. I have known, too, many a beautiful girl who, despite Herculean efforts, was given no respite from the endless lines of men who were slave to such urges. Yet Derra, offering no outward signs of rejection, managed to deflect such attention, or at least, transform it into some brooding admiration that, contrary to all nature, kept its distance.

Derra greeted me as if I were a long lost friend – again, typical of her with people she has decided she might like. I was rather taken aback by her familiarity, and was even less coherent than I usually was in the presence of a beautiful woman. She didn't seem to notice. She sipped thoughtfully on the eggnog, expressed mild surprise that it was actually laced with rum, and watched the crowd from my side. Although she seemed to drink in the scene, her gaze was almost playful – as if everyone there, youngest to oldest, were a schoolmate. Rather than losing herself in thought, as many do when they contemplate a busy scene, Derra seemed almost released. It was like prom night for her. Still, despite the festivity, there was a ghostly aura around her. I filled my eyes with her, then withdrew my gaze to see what vision of her I could conjure in my mind. I could see her, more than a hundred years back, waltzing carefree around the ballroom, suitors in long black coats lined up around the room waiting for those few precious moments at her side. Yet the music in my head distorted, and the unsuspecting dancers dissolved into dust as the eerie tune played on. This vision was so realistic that I snapped my head to the side, to see if Derra was still there. The violence of that motion startled her slightly and she turned to me with a look of deep concern.

"Are you all right?" she asked.

"Someone just walked over my grave?" I said as a shudder ran through my body.

"*Your* grave?"

She asked her second question as if she knew something. Of course, that made no sense, as even I knew very little of my vision. I just smiled blankly. I knew then, though, that my existence would be totally subsumed by the mystery of this woman. The feeling, I guess, was much akin to being in love. Not one hour of my life has passed, since that time, when Derra has not filled my thoughts or dreams. But the sensation is not so much one of yearning as it is of distress. I am old beyond my years in my mind, and she is to me like a daughter that I have lost and somehow found again through an appeal to the occult. Again, I do not draw my analogies from experience, but from dark corners of my mind where

Derra has somehow shone her light. Even as I write, knowing all that has passed since that time, my words seem unreal and beyond the scope of credibility – perhaps formed only through the power of hindsight. Yet I believe that, had I written of that time while it was still fresh in my mind, I would have done so even more graphically. Hapless wooer that I have been throughout my life, I stood tall beside the loveliest of God's creation in the full knowledge that we would not be parted in this life unless God chose to part us. This I knew within minutes of meeting Derra, and after only a handful of words had been exchanged. If love is half so profound as this unexpected meshing of unlikely souls, then the poets craft empty words. The logistics of planning a single date have eluded me all of my life, yet Derra and I were constant companions for those few weeks, and whether or not in each other's company, I have sensed a nearness to her from the moment that we met.

**T**he ease with which we enjoyed each other's presence that season was uncharacteristic of both of us. At a superficial level, I was all right with some people, but that certainly never had included beautiful young women. Derra, too, although friendly with all living creatures, had a shyness about her that kept her from becoming engaged with particular individuals. She lounged comfortably in my kitchen though – a zone that had seen no lounging prior to her. She chided me as I puttered about, fixing us a cup of tea. She preferred not to partake of my refreshments beside the warmth of the fireplace, claiming that it made her too drowsy, and that such an atmosphere was much better suited to Bubastes. She was particularly amused by the neatly arranged plates of biscuits (my gourmet selection transcended the more usual epitaph of "cookies") that I placed on the kitchen table, and on more than one occasion suggested that I was just one apron short of a Broadway musical.

Our conversations were highly animated, and consumed hours as if they were minutes. Yet as I look back on it, we talked very little about the details that had brought our lives to the current point in time. We discussed religion extensively. She was amused by what she considered the quirks in my theology, but she was receptive of my perspective to the extent of adopting some of my views – at least, I would like to think so. My politics, however, were a harder sell. We agreed to disagree on a lot of those issues. On one occasion, I remember her telling me that my prematurely aged mind, though of great value in unraveling the intricacies of the divine perspective, kept me out of touch with the human perspective – bogging me down with idealisms rather than practicalities. She was probably right, though I was reticent to concede it initially. When I suggested that her perspective was, perhaps, the product of youth, and that she might someday grow out of it, she flared uncharacteristically. *I would sooner be dead*, she blurted, *than to grow cold to the world around me.*

Another omission in our conversations, obvious now that I look back on things, was a description of our activities when we were apart from each other. Naturally, if anything exciting happened in my life (a rarity to say the least), I would tell Derra about it the minute that she walked in the door. But she never asked questions beyond what I would tell. She never had much to say about what had happened to her in her absence. And any questions that I directed that way were simply deflected in that same gentle manner that she deflected most anything or anyone that was probing in areas that she wished to keep secret. I don't remember ever being particularly irritated by this. The important thing about my relationship was simply being with her in the present. Whatever stories she might have regarding her private times, although subject to some speculation while we were apart, were not a matter of concern for me once we were together. If we were not immersed in a dialogue on religion or politics, we would talk literature and movies. Our tastes meshed nicely there. Art in general was our one springboard to more personal conversations. Those were precious moments in which we explored the hidden recesses of our souls. Through those moments, without knowing her past, or even very much about her present, I came to know Derra intimately. I think, too, she came to know me in a way that I might have once feared.

I did not see Derra at any point on my extended weekends until our paths crossed at church. I didn't really think about it. I was pretty much set in my weekend routine. I would certainly have welcomed such an intrusion, but when it didn't come, I was not overly disappointed. Derra and I rarely scheduled any time together. It just happened. And, when it didn't happen, there was no sense of broken engagement or neglect. Again, I probably should have noticed that she consistently avoided the weekends with me, but if I ever did think about it, I would likely have attributed it to her respect for my routine. There was nothing mysterious about it – at least, nothing *uniquely* mysterious about it. Everything about Derra was mysterious. On one level, right away I think I knew her as well as any human being could know another. On another level, she was a total stranger to me. The more I knew her, the deeper the mystery grew to be. There was no inherent contradiction in that for me, but I can see the paradox. With Derra, everything was a paradox. But I have long believed that the secrets in this life lie in paradox. Derra was a key to the secrets of the universe. Once I had adjusted to that concept, I was hardly surprised at the numerous paradoxes with which she presented me.

Despite her absence from my weekends, I was continually anticipating her appearance. Had this anticipation not been such a pleasant sensation, I would suggest that it was much akin to an anxiety disorder. I never felt that there was a time when she might not appear – even as I slept. Indeed, many a night found me wakened by a tapping at my bedroom window. If the tapping itself did not cause me to stir, it was sufficient to inspire Bubastes to position himself on my chest and voice a less subtle alert directly into my face. There was nothing overtly sensual about these visits, though my mind has often replayed the vision of Derra hopping adeptly through the window flushed from the chill night air. She never strayed from the bedroom on those occasions, and exited just as she had entered – providing choice gossip, no doubt, for neighbors who might have cared to watch. Certainly there had been no interested surveyors before Derra had entered my life, but I would not be surprised to learn that I had become an object of fascination once someone had spotted this goddess in my vicinity. The nighttime visits were surreal. Once she left, I was never quite sure whether she had been there at all. My dreams only added to the confusion. The morning absence of Bubastes, who often made use of the open window to join his friends in a skirmish and a prowl, provided the only physical verification that the stillness of my slumber had been broken.

**4**

O ur Christmas together is frozen in my memory as a perfect moment in time. We were, in our own ways, two lost creatures who had been continually disappointed by the season, despite our childlike anticipation of the day. Derra had told me as much, but she had not provided any specifics. For my part, though I had gladly partaken in the seasonal events year after year, my spirits were usually as soggy as the weather by Christmas Eve. Annually I vowed either to fill my small home with the needy or to take myself away to some snow laden community for some aesthetic relief, but I followed through on neither. My heart for charity, to my shame, reached no further than the body in which it was encased. I wanted to share the event with someone closer to me than the temporarily displaced. Who, in my imagination, this person might have been I could not say. (I had most certainly not been so bold as to imagine Derra.) As for travel, I was psychologically incapable of making plans that would take me away from home for Christmas. It was ridiculous considering the solitude of my adult living situation. But the concepts of Christmas and home were irreversibly linked through the agency of my childhood memories.

I wonder why it only seems to snow at Christmas when we are young? It is, perhaps, a byproduct of global warming. Maybe, someday, there will only be memories of white Christmases in our collective minds. From my childhood in the eastern reaches of the continent, I remember cold, clear nights when the snow was sealed in a crusty layer so unlike the soggy mass that lands in those rare late West Coast winter downfalls which serve only to unsettle the hordes of mindless motorists. The sky would be full of stars, not clouds, and the shimmer presented that magical quality that I came to associate exclusively with Christmas. I would gaze endlessly at the stars, convinced (in my ignorance of both Middle Eastern climate and the Mithraic roots of the December 25<sup>th</sup> tradition) that it was on such a night as this that the Christ-child was born. My other recurring Christmas fantasy also came from such nights. I was in my home town, back before the town was subsumed by malls and strip development. The wisps of sprayed snow on the inside of multi-paned shop windows added to the whole Dickensian atmosphere – an atmosphere that seemed no less central to Christmas than the virgin birth.

With each passing year, my ability to recapture this special mood waned. I had reached point where, contrary to my hopes, Christmas had become a dark, dank, lonely time brightened only by the occasional visit with a neighbor, and a shared cup of eggnog. I had even taken to skipping the church services, partly because they seemed to mark the end of the season for me, and partly because I hoped that something better would befall me before I was finally struck with the realization that yet another uneventful year had passed. I couldn't have said exactly what I was expecting. I wanted something magical to happen, but I couldn't have defined it. In retrospect, it's easy to say that I was waiting for Derra. But my imagination could not have stretched that far before the reality of Derra came into my life. She was Christmas for me whether that meant the crisp snowy atmosphere of a fictionalized nativity scene, a medieval church and Good King Wenceslas, nineteenth century London and figgy pudding, or the warm selective memories of my youth. We ran the gambit together, and it sticks in my head as a template for the new heaven and earth.

We were a few weeks into our friendship when she suggested that we do some Christmas shopping together. I was rather reluctant. Our relationship was not one that would likely benefit much from outside expeditions – especially such expeditions as seemed contrived to move us away from the cozy atmosphere of our regular tête-à-têtes. Besides, my Christmas shopping list was, to say the least, short. I had stockings to fill only for myself and Bubastes – the former being on the practical side and the latter being on the diminutive side. I took some small delight in finding one or two treats for each us, but as is plain to see, such a peculiar pleasure borders on the pathetic. My resistance, however, was quickly overcome when Derra informed me that her main purpose in proposing this expedition was to find presents for my stocking. I was inspired, not by the prospect of having an unexpected cache of Christmas goodies, but by the enchanting idea of creating one for Derra.

The long awaited magic of the season finally began just two days before Christmas. The elements conspired in our favor by producing a light covering of snow on the morning that we set out. Like me, Derra preferred to avoid the more commercial, less expensive centers in town, and we settled into the old section that included my watercress shop. We spent some time together initially, but since we were essentially shopping just for each other, we decided to separate until noon when we would meet for lunch at an agreed location. I had visited all of these shops at some time during the previous year, and not once had I lingered. Even when I entered for less practical reasons, when my curiosity had been piqued, I was quickly satiated and quickly on my way back home. Externally, the circumstances appeared no different as I stepped once again, a solitary creature, over the thresholds of these private businesses. Yet my lightness of heart must have been evident to all as I worked my way around, examining items that I had never dreamed existed, crying out with joy (in my very reserved way, of course) when I found something that seemed right for Derra. My allotted time for each shop was woefully inadequate, and the one regret that I suffered from my morning adventures was that they were not extended further into the afternoon. This disappointment, however, was more than compensated by the nature of the appointment that curtailed my activities.

As I approached the restaurant wherein Derra and I had proposed to meet, I saw Derra, a few blocks away, engaged in an animated discussion with an unpleasant looking fellow barely five feet in height. I briefly considered coming to her rescue, but it was not clear to me that she needed rescuing. Hence, I opted for discretion, and entered the restaurant to arrange for a table to my liking. I was still conferring on the arrangements when Derra joined me. I was quite relieved that her conversation with the little man had not been extended. It's hard for me to say, now, whether my relief came from knowing that she was not in any danger, or from more selfish issues – a jealousy perhaps. We were centrally seated, but with a good view of activities both within and outside of the restaurant. This was agreeable to both of us. I did venture onto the topic of Derra's companion, but she brushed it aside quickly as just a matter of someone trying to pry a telephone number from her. It seemed reasonable enough at the time, and certainly the man in question fit the mold of someone brazen enough to make such a move.

Again, it is only the power of retrospect that allows me to see the inconsistencies in her explanation. As appealing as she was, Derra never needed more than minimal effort to deflect unwanted attention. Although it is reasonable to assume that most beautiful women might have occasion to fight off potential suitors with some degree of force, Derra was not most beautiful women. Although her eyes often betrayed a heavy heart, there was no sense that she could be disturbed by such trivial matters as she had portrayed to me. I suppose I knew that even then, but I was glad to let logic win over feelings when logic presented the more appealing scenario. In any case, there was no issue at the time. Our meal was perfectly supplemented by a bottle of Pinot Noir, and the delights of the season infected our spirits.

The snow continued to fall, and songs of the season filled the air. The lunch extended well into the afternoon, and we were among the last to leave the once busy restaurant. Our final project in town was to find stocking stuffers for Bubastes – who had been neglected in my morning expedition. To me, the idea seemed to highlight the silliness of my lonely existence, but to Derra, it was an ideal way to conclude an ideal day. Naturally, I let her way of thinking win me over. We took our time, and allowed the early onset of nightfall to catch up with us. As the tiny specks of snow flowed out of the blackened sky, the fullness of the season filled me then in a way that I thought had been lost forever. Parting was bittersweet in that I wanted our time together to extend, unbroken, into eternity. Yet tomorrow held its own promises, and I was not about to complain.

Even as a child, Christmas Eve was more special to me than Christmas morning. The anticipation ran high, and although I was never disappointed by my morning stocking or the presents under the tree, the unwrapping of gifts forewarned that the day would come to an end, and that the majority of a year must pass before the spirit of the season could be recaptured. Of course, the turkey dinner provided one last vestige of the event, though I stumbled to it barely awake, and filled myself so full that the rest of the evening was essentially lost. On Christmas Eve, however, I always had enough energy to take me well into the night.

I am not sure whether or not, during our shopping expedition, Derra and I had arranged to spend Christmas Eve day together. I think that we just assumed. She arrived in the late morning loaded down with parcels. Some contained the gifts that she had purchased the day before. Others contained wrapping paper, ribbon, tape and scissors. Yet others contained large jugs of Burgundy wine, spices, and recipes for creating hot mulled wine. She essentially moved in, and the pajamas that she brought confirmed that she would not move out until our Christmas celebrations were complete. She ran a checklist by me concerning the turkey dinner, and was reasonably satisfied with my answers. She stationed herself in front of the couch, and she stationed me behind. With the instructions not to peek discharged with implicit warnings, we began wrapping. I tended the mulled wine, which was soon ready, and we both kept a mug in hand throughout the process.

We talked sparingly, as we worked our way through the bags of gifts. We filled the stockings with the ones that fit, and left the larger gifts on their own beneath the sad little imitation tree that had been erected as part of my Thanksgiving Day ritual. It suffered a degree of good-natured sarcasm from Derra, who missed the smell of fresh pine in the house, but I pleaded allergies and assured her that we would both have our fill of genuine pine scent at the church service that evening. She pouted a little, but her mouth soon returned to the broad smile that seldom left her face in those days. Our project wound slowly to an end, and we crawled to either side of the couch, drowsy from the wine, and fell asleep to the faint refrain of traditional carols flowing incessantly from the Christmas music channel on the television.

Derra drove us to church in her car that evening, being somewhat more refreshed than I after our daytime activities. We left a little early, and she wove her way up and down the more lavishly decorated streets between my home and the church. As a result of the recurring snowfall that had, by now, left its mark everywhere with a promise of more to come, there was a stillness about the town, and the roads were less busy than they might have been. From time to time, I noticed a vehicle behind us, but I had no reason to suspect that it might be the same one that I spotted each time. We were late for the service, and there was one car behind us, but again, it did not seem suspicious – though I was slightly surprised that no one followed us in through the front door. Such things stand out in my mind now, but they may well have been ordinary events without a trace of ominous undertones. Even if they weren't, what could I have done? At best, the phantoms that chased her remained vague and unapproachable.

The service fit perfectly into our day. The festivity of the carols was nicely tempered by the solemn atmosphere and the brief, yet resounding, message of peace on earth. Unlike our previous times together in church, when we consistently broke the worship with whispered asides, Derra and I remained silent. I felt then, and nothing has transpired to make me feel any differently, that this was because our minds were one. Indeed, in this unspoken bond, we seemed more deeply connected than we had ever been in any of our animated conversations. There was a timelessness in this moment of worship that rightfully belongs to any moment of true worship. Yet the quality of that moment that Christmas Eve stands out, likely because the season fed into our state of mind. That our souls were united in this moment, I have no doubt. It was a marriage of sorts, but not an earthly marriage. Our bond was not carnal – though I confess to my physical attraction to her. And I do not suggest that our union was higher because of the absence of that element. But it was a high union nonetheless. And, in that wonderful swirl of festivity and solemnity, we rose above the chaos of this world and borrowed the divine perspective. At the end of the service, as we made our way, still wordless, to the impressive array of Christmas baking that awaited us, the temporal and the timeless merged into the perfect Christmas moment. I filled my plate almost exclusively with mince tarts, thus adding an Epicurean component to the mix. It didn't destroy the moment, but perhaps stretched it a little unnaturally.

As we made our way to the car after the service, I could feel many eyes resting on me – perhaps curious, perhaps a little envious. My pride swelled to think that some might even be presuming a romantic link between us. Derra glanced sideways at me as she edged to the car door. Tall and lean, with her hair pulled up loosely, in her long black dress she still brightened everything around her with her Midas touch. Her smile had a quizzical look to it, as if she were waiting for something to happen. She landed in her seat with a carefree bounce, and we drove away to quieter scenes. The route we took was usually free of cars, though I do remember seeing headlights behind us once or twice. I thought nothing of it. Derra had my full attention, and I was in her hands. The ride had that quick yet endless aura to it that is so common in dreams. Indeed, my entire existence had assumed a dreamlike quality, and I had no desire to awake.

Bubastes greeted us at the door, clearly upset with the offering of snow that had settled into his thick fur coat. Derra laughed a little as she knelt down to offer succor to the distressed creature. There was no other sound except the distant hum the occasional car that still braved the roads. If one of those cars was just then departing from my neighborhood, I didn't notice. And, if Derra noticed, she showed no concern as she wrapped Bubastes in her arms, and waited for me to unlock our door. I did so and we were swept inside with a snowy gust. I reheated the wine, and poured our cups in anticipation of a night of Christmas movies. We made it through neither the first cup nor the first movie. I have only a vision, locked in my memory, of Derra gently ordering me off the couch to my room as she stood waiting, her hair down now, and clad in striped flannel men's pajamas, with a blanket and pillow in her arms.

**M**y sleep lasted until the first rays of the morning sun broke through my bedroom window, but I think it was the smell of bacon that was ultimately responsible for waking me. Bubastes watched, stretching as I wrapped myself in my robe, and slid my slippers onto my feet. He followed me reluctantly as I made my way down the hall towards the kitchen. Derra stood there, still in her pajamas, proudly displaying a frying pan full of over-cooked bacon. There was a bowl of scrambled eggs already on the table, and she signaled for me to fetch the orange juice. The meal, though not necessarily scoring high on the gastronomic scales, was decidedly one of the most enjoyable that I have ever had. It undoubtedly pushed my cholesterol levels to new heights, but the sacrifice in health was a fair trade for the satisfaction it instilled at so many levels. Even Bubastes, in advance of his usual Christmas can of gourmet cat food, shared in the moment with some scraps of bacon. He, too, was uncomplaining regarding any damage to his system.

It was the first Christmas when I had ever opened my stocking on a full stomach. As a child, my stocking had been pinned to my bed, and was completely ravaged before my parents entered my room. The delight, then, was in showing them the many ways that Santa had been good to me. As I grew older, and the selection of gifts under the tree grew more refined, the stockings moved to the fireplace and became part of a shared ritual – after which we partook of our breakfast. On my own, I have upheld pretty much the same pattern, though my only company has been my cat. On occasion there have been visitors, but they have usually appeared in the late afternoon, after both stockings and presents, and in advance of my Christmas dinner. I have had my regular share of dinner invitations, but have never come to terms with the idea of intruding on someone else's family on such an occasion. Thus, the simple introduction of a solitary soul into my Christmas ritual produced a much more radical revision of the day than any of the subtle changes that she brought with her. A sense of well-being enveloped me as we settled down with our Christmas stockings. It stifled the protests of my stomach – which was not coping overly well in its battle against mass forces of an unwelcome acid.

I had forgotten the sheer joy of watching someone open a gift that I had chosen especially with that person in mind. I admit, with some pride, that I had been quite successful in my selection for Derra. Had I thought about it more, during the purchasing process, I am sure that would not have been true. As it was, I had bought instinctively – grasping at anything that spoke to me of her. She was particularly thrilled with a silver locket that I had found and had engraved with her name on the spot. She slipped it around her slender neck and patted it gently – as if to say that it had found a permanent home. Likewise, she had managed to find simple things for me that touched me deeply. We had only discriminated by size as to whether the gift was placed in the stocking or under the tree, but nonetheless took a break once the stocking items had been unwrapped. We were tired, though not hungry, and spent the time preparing for the evening feast. I also brewed a fresh pot of hot mulled wine for us to share while we opened the presents and waited for the turkey to cook. Our afternoon did not have the spurts of frenzied excitement that filled our morning, but our enjoyment was no less for that. The warmth of Derra's smile as she soaked in the day was the greatest gift of all, and has surely sustained me ever since.

Christmas dinner, though traditionally marking the dénouement of the Christmas celebration, sustained the good spirits that had filled us for the past few days. We over-ate. We supplemented our mulled wine with one or two goblets too many of a Chardonnay that I had chosen to complement our turkey. Our level of conversation seriously declined. Still, it was the right fit for the moment. The table was a horrible mess by time we were finished, but we left it pretty much as it was – protecting only the turkey from possible assaults from the ever-hopeful Bubastes. Still in our pajamas, we each claimed a corner of the couch and tried once more to work our way through some Christmas movies. This time, despite the exhaustion, we met with more success. I lasted right through the first one, and part way into the second. Frequent visual checks on Derra confirmed that she was also surviving well. Sometimes, I would just watch her as she as she focused on the movie with such sweet expectation. I was caught in the act, occasionally, and she would give me a look of mock distain. I'm not entirely sure that, despite her concentration, she was ever unaware of my gaze – anticipating it as she had done in church when I had first seen her. Perhaps allowing my gaze to linger a little without chastisement was just another one of her many gifts to me. I cannot say where my eyes were ultimately resting when they finally surrendered to the relentless downward pressure of my eyelids.

I must have been asleep for some time when I was suddenly awoken by the closing of the front door. In my haze, I saw Derra pressed against the door. The door seemed to be supporting her, and she looked loath to move until her eyes caught mine. She immediately stood herself up, and smiled sweetly, before telling me that she had just stepped out for a second to clear her head. The glow on her cheeks belied her words, but I had no reason to call her to task. It was true that her eyes had lost some of the ease that characterized her past few days with me, but I naturally attributed that to the waning of the day and the season, rather than to dark unseen forces. Still, I do not consider myself blameless in letting this issue rest. The lie itself, accompanied by a sudden uneasiness, was as red as any flag could be. Yet, perhaps, I reasoned thus far, and simply attributed her uneasiness to having told the lie. If so, it was circular reasoning at best, and I am haunted by the thought that I might have been of more value to Derra if I had been less forgiving. At the time, however, all was lost in her smile. I led Derra to the guest room, folded back the sheets on the bed and told her to lie down. She agreed, reluctantly, only after I promised that, in closing up the house, I would leave the majority of work for the next day. I pulled the blanket over her and fought the urge to kiss her forehead as I said goodnight. She probably would have understood, but in her childlike repose, the eternal innocence that was inspiring the paternal kiss was also warning me about giving it. I have learned (through the wisdom that I have acquired in the vacuum of time in which I live) that inaction is the best solution to that type of paradox.

Derra was asleep in minutes, and I returned to the living room. I paused, once the lights were dimmed, to peek through the curtains onto the street. Something was not right, but since it was nothing that I could identify, I chose to go to bed. I was exhausted, but with willing flesh and weak spirit, after several futile hours, my restlessness drove me once again to the front window. It had stopped snowing, but the layers that had been deposited over the past few days shone brightly under the clear sky. The illusion of peacefulness, bolstered in my mind by the day I had just spent, and by the sermon of the previous night, remained, but there were hints that it was breaking down. The hum of some early morning traffic could be heard in the distance – a faint echo of the summer rush that also started up at that hour in its season. A dog barked, and either alerted by that dog or in response to the same prey, others joined into a growing chorus. I knew that my perfect moment was passing, that it would drop from my life as surely as the snow would drop from the branches in the glare of the morning sun. I held on as best I could, not knowing what lurked out there under what sparse cover such a night could provide in its dying moments. I looked once more into the guest room where Derra lay so peacefully. I envied her gift of being able to shut the world down so completely. There was a rumble of unsettledness that began to stir in me forewarning that, even yet, I would not find rest even if I slept. I was thankful then, however, and infinitely more so now, that Derra was spared such rumblings once those lids fell softly over those beautiful brown eyes.

I missed the light of morning altogether, having fallen into a fitful sleep that even drove the ever-faithful Bubastes from my bed. Once again, I was greeted by the sight of Derra in my kitchen, this time laboring over some turkey sandwiches. She wore tight fitting jeans that sat low on her hips, offering a brief glimpse of her belly when she stretched enough to separate the precarious line between the pant top and the lightweight blue sweater that she had chosen. In protest of the chilled atmosphere that marked my home when the fireplace was still, she also wore a long tan jacket with fringes that reached down to her knees. She was a fetching sight, but then, I suppose that I always thought so. I did, however, feel a twinge of disappointment when I saw her bag packed and ready by the front door. It was not unexpected, but I had hoped to stretch our time out just a little longer. Still, the sandwiches were good, and though the day had the aura of being the hangover after a time of festivity, our spirits were still high and we relaxed, as usual, in each other's company.

Parting felt harder than it should have been. After all, it had never been an issue for us at other times. Of course, we had never spent such a concentrated amount of time together, and then there *was* that whole Christmas thing. I don't think either of us wanted it to end. Nonetheless, parting seemed to represent some sort of a shift in our relationship, and not an altogether good one. Enlightened as I am by retrospect, it is easy to say that there were forces at work, even then. But that merely gives substance (of sorts) to what I clearly sensed at the time. Our hearts should have been lighter. Our time together was surely a precursor of many more such times. I was not afraid of losing her. Certainly I had conceded, from a practical vantage, that a younger man might come into her life. But I also knew that it was only an exceptional man who would win her heart, and that she would not be conquered by deceit. If the idea made me jealous at all, it was a paternal sort of jealousy, as a father might feel at handing his daughter to the chosen suitor. And I trusted her choices. But this was not the issue at hand. The point is that there was a degree of misgiving in saying good-bye, and it stemmed from no logical source.

I watched her as she backed out of my driveway. Her jaw was set, as it always was when she was concentrating, and I don't think that she was aware of my gaze. Once she was ready to drive away, however, she looked at me with her wide smile and waved vigorously as she left – another shot for that camera that I have locked in my head. But I didn't know where she was going. As always, I presumed that she was going home. I had no idea where that might be – as strange as that might sound. It was just never an issue. On the few occasions when I had asked her whether or not she wanted me to contact her, she had simply replied that she would contact me. And so it was. With the weekend upon us, and with Lucy due within twenty-four hours, I thought nothing of Derra's absence over the next few days. Of course, most garden duties would not be possible for me that weekend as a result of the snowfall, but there would be snow to move and debris to clean up in the areas where the snow had receded. And, beyond that, I had another full week off of work, and all the opportunities that afforded me to be with Derra before I resumed my duties. I didn't see her at church that Sunday, but she had not attended every Sunday even in the short time that I knew her. I only started to wonder about her on Tuesday (that being New Year's Eve) assuming that, if she did not plan to spend the evening with me, she would at least call in advance of any other plans.

By ten o'clock on New Year's Eve, I was well settled by the fire, with Bubastes on my lap, in anticipation of another uninspired introduction to the new year. I did miss Derra then, despite my confidence in our more enduring, unseen bonds. It had been a good year, though (at least since Thanksgiving), so I had few regrets and a certain amount of excitement as I watch the clock tick away the final hours of the year. Indeed, it seemed likely that I would miss the moment altogether as my head kept nodding forward, lulled by the contented purrs of my feline companion. I awoke with a start, however, when a sudden rapping on the door, beginning within minutes of the approaching midnight hour, sent Bubastes scurrying for the far corners of the house. There, looking flushed and out of breath, stood Derra, with a bottle of champagne in one hand, and her other hand patting her chest. There was no car around, and I asked her how she had come. She hurriedly told me that she had been dropped by taxi in a spot where she felt feet would take her quicker than the vehicle (a debatable calculation at best), and that she had run from there. She was very anxious about the time, however, and was relieved to discover that it was sufficient to allow us to uncork the bottle, and to settle in comfortably before the striking of the hour.

We had only time for a few sips before the moment arrived and our glasses were raised in a toast to each other, and to the new year. We stood, facing each other. I noticed then that beneath her coat, which she had kept on, she was dressed, contrary to her nature, in a short black dress. The novelty of seeing her in a short dress, I must confess, caught my attention. It worked well on her, her legs (as I had suspected) being perfectly suited for display. It gave her an air of sophistication, too, and I wondered, for one brief second, if it meant that she had plans for the rest of the night that might include me. But that thought (along with many less pretentious ones) was quickly shattered when she announced that she had to leave. Numerous protests, mainly focused around the fact that she had not stayed long enough even to finish one glass of champagne, arose within me. But she silenced them before they were spoken with a gentle kiss upon my cheek. She told me that she would not be leaving had it not become absolutely necessary – that she just wanted to make sure that she was with me as the old year ended and as the new one began. I asked how she was going to travel, and she told me that the cabdriver had promised to wait where he had left her. When I suggested that I should accompany her to that location, she simply said *better not*. It felt like a warning, and it was against my better judgment to acquiesce.

She left. The touch of her lips still burned sweetly on my cheek.

*8*

I confess that I felt like I had betrayed a confidence when I followed Derra that night. My reasons, though, were purely precautionary. The route to the main street was isolated, and certainly not a good one for a woman to walk alone – especially one so appealing as Derra. A level path of a few hundred yards began beside my house. At the end of that stretch it ran up then down a small hill. An old cemetery lay on the other side of the hill, at the far end of which was the main street. It was a quaint walk in the daylight, but had a sinister air about it at night. I was shocked when I discerned that this was route that Derra had taken to my house that night (– though the initial joy of seeing her quickly pushed any concerns to the back of my head). I was not, however, willing to let her return by that route unescorted. If she forced me to proceed by stealth, then I would proceed by stealth. Still, I was uncomfortable allowing even a necessary element of deceit to enter our relationship.

I kept well back during the first leg of the short journey since I would be easily visible should Derra decide to check over her shoulder. The path bent to the right though, behind a small clump of trees, as it reached the bottom of the hill. I had to move quickly at that point to keep up with the pace that she had set. As it was, she was already at the top of hill by the time I had reached the base. I climbed quickly, uneasy that I could not see her once she headed down the other side. I had a good vantage when I arrived the top of the hill, but I did not linger there since it would have been easy to spot me against the cloudy sky. As a result, I had considerable trouble picking up her trail as I descended. There were a few options that she might have chosen, depending upon which gate was her destination. Being an older cemetery, many of the gravesites were accessible only by foot. Over the years, a variety of footpaths had sprung from the road that encircled the perimeter. They wove in every direction, determined by the terrain rather than by convenience. The pastoral aspect that this conveyed by day bore no resemblance to what I saw as I surveyed the horizon.

Patches of snow spotted the landscape. Otherwise, the earth had a dark gray aspect to it. The black outline of leafless trees on the horizon reached down towards the murky ground with long gnarled fingers. A shudder ran through me as I thought how Derra had traversed this scene alone, and had returned without accepting my offer of company. I looked for some sign of her, only to be distracted as small gusts of wind would alternately bring life to random corners of this desolate vista. I was ready to surrender to my despair when I caught sight of a black silhouette moving behind the branches of a distant tree, like someone walking across a room lit only by a strobe light. The roads were still quiet in the lull of the midnight celebrations, but I could see the lights of one vehicle approaching the gate to which Derra was headed. I said a silent prayer of thanks for the taxi driver who had remained true to his word, and I was ready to make my way back to the warmth of my fire.

As the car drew near to the gate, however, the roar of the engine suggested to me that this was not a taxi – or at least not one like I had ever encountered. A pang of fear shot through me as I considered that this might in fact be someone simply cruising with trouble on his mind. Indeed, as I looked more intently, even from several hundred yards away, the distinct outline of a Corvette was apparent. Derra continued to walk in that direction. I was about to shout a word of warning to her when I realized that she would be even more cognizant of the fact than I that the vehicle she was approaching could not be, by any stretch of the imagination, a taxi. Instead, I decided to take my chances that she might spot me, and cut directly towards the gate as quickly as I could move. I stumbled more than once, and received several scratches at the bottom of my legs both from brambles and twigs that were protruding from the uneven ground. I had closed the distance between us considerably when I watched Derra walk through the gate and saw the car door open for her. She had settled in, and closed the door behind her, by the time I reached a safe surveillance point behind one of posts that supported the heavy wrought iron gates. I was ready to pounce if she was in danger, but my brief sighting of the driver gave me pause.

I knew I had seen him somewhere before, but it took me several seconds before I could place him. It was the swarthy little creature that I had seen in animated conversation with Derra on the day that we went shopping. My first thoughts were that he had simply been successful in securing her number, and that he was her date for the evening. I was certainly uncomfortable with that thought. Although I had reconciled myself to the idea that there would be men in Derra's life, I could not come to terms with the idea that there should be ones such as this. His character was all too transparent in his demeanor, and even with that unfortunate blind spot that is inherent in so many beautiful women, I could not believe for a second that Derra would be gullible enough to give him a second look. But, there she was, at his side – undeniably familiar with him. It did not, however, look like there was any romantic connection between them. Of course, that may have been wishful thinking on my part, but subsequent details bear me out on that. Nonetheless, it was with a very heavy heart that I trudged back home that night. I ran theories through my head as I sat by the fire with Bubastes purring contentedly on the back of my chair (choosing that location in preference to the continual agitation of my body). This was all rather cloak and dagger, I concluded, and the secrets that Derra was concealing from me likely extended well beyond this little rendezvous. That was hardly any comfort, but there was nothing I could do for the moment. We would talk when next I saw her. Undoubtedly, she would throw some light on this mystery.

I touched my cheek where she had kissed it. I felt warm in the memory of that kiss, and in the thought that, whatever her situation, she had made the effort to greet the new year with me. *It would all sort itself out tomorrow.* The next day, however, brought me no news of Derra – nor did the next day nor the next. By mid-January I despaired that I would ever see her again. My first news of her did little to quell the despair.

*9*

**N**ear the middle of January, a letter arrived from Derra:

*My dear Noah,*

*I'm so sorry to have disappeared so suddenly. On New Year's Eve, I would have said something had I known that I would have to leave. I guess I knew it was a possibility, so I do feel a little guilty. Hopefully, beginning the new year with you is a good omen for both of us.*

*I have passed a lifetime since we last talked. My days are long and dreary, and I have been plagued by age-old questions about the meaning of life. I have drawn some strength from the memory of our conversations. I just wish that you were here with me now so that you could provide some ready answers for some of the issues that I am facing. I often think about our deep discussions at your kitchen table. I can almost see Bubastes, tearing himself away from the warmth of the fire to join us, looking for a little food and a little attention.*

*Unfortunately, there are few details of my circumstance that I can relate to you. You will have to forgive my secretiveness, and just trust that my silence is in your best interest. It is contrary, I know, to the openness and honesty that marks most aspects of our relationship. You have respected my privacy, and I am thankful for that, but I fear that you would not have been so patient with you if you knew how much I am consumed by private matters. It is rather embarrassing to confess even this much to you – knowing how important it has been for both of us to speak from the heart.*

*My letter to you will arrive without a return address. The postmark will be of little help to you since I will have moved on by time you receive this. Again, I apologize, but beg you to understand that I have my reasons for keeping you in the dark. I'll ask you my questions, though, in the hope that, as you formulate your answers, something inside of me will hear what you say. I am surely being unrealistic, yet hope, however faint, sustains me. Even the very act of writing my questions may bring us closer. I trust that this is true.*

*Let's begin with the eternal questions. Why is there suffering? What is the point of existence? We've dealt with these I'm sure – though not so starkly posed. I remember the conventional answers, but I am not altogether certain of the twist that you might insert into the explanations. Let me try to piece it together from what I can remember.*

*Suffering is the result of the fall, right? The question is not why we suffer, but why we should have any relief. And the answer is: though we all deserve suffering and condemnation, we are spared through the grace of God. (How am I doing? I think I have it down.) And your twist on it all would be to say that we are* all *spared – or something to that effect. I just remember it being of great comfort to me the way you told it. Right now, however, it doesn't seem to have any practical application to my situation. I don't mean to make my own suffering special. If it were mine alone, I think I could bear it. But I suffer because I see the suffering around me. I see so many instances where just a touch from the divine hand could make things so much better for so many people. And I don't know why God withdraws his hand. Is it because he has used up his grace somewhere else? I think that I, with my limited mind, could chart out a more equitable dispensation of grace. The existence of grace is hardly a defense of divine justice if you cannot see that grace in anything around you. Yes, I know what you would say: our very breaths of life are evidence of*

*God's grace, and if we just concentrate on our blessings, we can see how God has touched our lives. If I were with you now, I might be convinced. As it is, I am angry, though I am silent in my anger to everyone but God – and now you.*

*That brings me to the related question about existence. The standard answer, as I remember, is that we are here to glorify God. Your twist? I'm not quite sure on this one. I think it relates to having moments when you know, whatever your circumstance, that God is there and that there is something perfect about life that we are blind to in much of our daily existence, and that it will all sort itself out in the end. Even though we have shared moments like this, I still have trouble with the whole concept. I have seen too many endings that are not all sorted out. I fear that the only sorting out in my own end will be through the fact that it is an end. And, if that's the extent of it, why bother with the beginning? I'm sorry. I'm being unnecessarily morbid. But that's my mood these days. I have comfort only in memories. Your role is prominent in providing me with such comfort. Even as I write, as depressing as my philosophy must sound, I am heartened as my mind creates the dialogue that I might have with you.*

*There are other issues, too, that I can't write to you without compromising you. But these will have to wait, perhaps indefinitely. Although I will not be able to write to you again, I want to send this to you without delay in the hope that your forgiveness might be felt that much sooner. I know that I am undeserving, but I know that you do not judge as others do. Your perspective is more divine, or if that sounds too grandiose, it is based on your judgment of the inner person – in this case a person who has bonded with your own soul. I hope that I don't overstep to claim that.*

*love,*
*Derra*

I was flooded by a confusion of emotions once I read what she had written. It was hard to believe that so much of her life had been hidden to me. I have to confess that I felt a little betrayed by that. I could not conceive of anything that she could have told me that would have been compromised in the telling. The fact that major aspects of her life had been deliberately concealed was hard for me to accept considering the depth of our relationship. On the other hand, her confidence in us, and her need to open even a one-sided dialogue with me, was touching. Mostly, however, I was worried. I had always known that there were shadowy corners in her life that she did not want me to explore, but I did not suspect that they touched on her current life, I was content to let them rest undisturbed until an appropriate time might come to bring them to light. I would not have been offended if Derra had determined that there would never be such a time. The dark mood of her letter, however, hinted at how black those shadows might be. The fact that they were very much a part of her present life frightened me. After all, what evil could compel her to hide such things from me *in my best interest?*

Suffice to say that I could not let matters rest. Lucy would arrive to clean house for me the next day. With a sad heart, I would assign her the singular responsibility of caring for Bubastes. My routine, designed to carry me safely into my old age, was about to undergo a severe remodeling.

’m not sure that I would have thought to have taken note of the postmark had Derra not drawn it to my attention as a futile means of tracking her. It may or may not have been her way of suggesting it to me as a viable means. Or, maybe it was a subconscious appeal. In any case, it was all I had, and the location was specific enough to provide me with a good start. It seemed a much better idea than simply waiting for a letter that might never come.

I boarded a flight for Boston on the evening of the very Friday that I had surrendered Bubastes to Lucy. I had never been to that part of the world, and I was sorry that I would not be exploring it in the more traditionally tourist sense that I had, for a long time, hoped. The city of Boston itself, however, with all of its historical highlights, was of no interest to me on this trip. More pressing was the need to find immediate transportation several miles east to where Derra's letter had originated. I presumed that I could catch a bus or a train that night which would bring me to Fitchburg, within a few dozen miles of my destination, and that I would have to find a motel before completing the rest of my journey. I was correct in the first part of my presumption, but due to the lateness of the hour, I could find no place to rest once I had reached the end of my night's travels. So, on top of having disoriented myself with a cross-country flight, and having made myself positively ill with a bus trip that must have detoured to every corner within ten miles of its direct route, I was left to ponder the awakening of a new day freezing from the discomfort of a park bench. In retrospect, it would have made perfect sense to rent a car from the airport to save myself the ordeal of public transportation. At the time, however, it seemed more practical to place myself closer to my destination before I attempted a navigation that would be seriously impaired by my sense of direction.

As it was, I had a difficult enough task making my way from Fitchburg, in the car that I rented that morning, to the town of Middlemore that was named on the postmark. Having spent most of my life on the West Coast, I had an innate fear of snowy roads and icy patches, and my extreme caution was more of handicap than an advantage. It took several near mishaps before I convinced my right foot that sudden strikes on the brakes might be counterproductive. The mystery surrounding Derra's relocation was not lessened as I wove my way into the isolated reaches of this corner of the world. If it were simply a matter of hiding, the city would be a more logical destination – where perhaps even Derra could be lost amidst the faceless masses. I certainly could not imagine any such possibility in a town where the population numbered only in the hundreds. Strangers of any sort must be a novelty – let alone one so striking. *How hard could it be for me to track down where she had stayed, and to pick up the trail of her recent travels?*

The town of Middlemore was as pretty as the postcards that filled the racks outside the solitary grocery store in the town center. The store housed the village post office – the very place where Derra must have ventured to mail her letter – so I felt as if I was off to a good start. I asked the proprietor if he remembered such a girl, but he merely responded that many pretty girls came through year round, and that it would be hard for him to place one or the other. He had a gruff demeanor, not well suited to business I thought, but there wasn't really any competition for his services, so I suppose that wasn't a factor. His response sounded weak to me, but then, I had to admit the possibility that maybe it was my own prejudice that made Derra stand out among the other pretty girls of her age. I was given directions to a nearby inn, and again had hopes that this might provide me with further leads. In any case, I was dead tired, and I realized that any search would be futile unless I could revive myself. I was delighted to discover that the inn, known as the George, like everything else in Middlemore was picture perfect. It crossed my mind, as I wandered into the rustic lobby, that there must be something very sinister afoot to fill Derra's mind with such depressed thoughts in such an idyllic setting.

The words of the storekeeper gained some veracity when a parade of very attractive young ladies marched through the lobby and outside to a waiting bus as I made my way to the reception desk. It was, in fact, a little surreal. I wondered if there were a beauty pageant in town – some snow queen contest, perhaps. Certainly the quality of woman with which I was confronted exceeded even that of the sororities that had so terrified me throughout my university years. Possibly, this was some tight knit clique that had bonded on the basis of beauty. It was clearly not a random collection. They came and went like a vision, or a daydream. Naturally, they all ignored me, and I did my level best not to look star struck. The innkeeper looked up at me with a friendly smile, and I couldn't help asking him if this was a fair sampling of the local residents. He laughed and told me that, believe it or not, it was relatively common to have such an unusual concentration pass through. In the midst of this onslaught, it seemed pointless to ask about Derra – at least, not right away. I retired to a delightfully colonial room, and although it was only late afternoon and I hadn't eaten in recent memory, I slept straight through to the morning.

Church bells rang in the distance, and they inspired me to ask at the front desk if there might be an Episcopalian church in the vicinity where I might be early enough to catch a service. I felt that I might do better in my search by delaying it a while in favor of a little divine counsel. It seemed providential to discover that the church I sought was only a mile or so away, and that I had plenty of time to walk that distance if I so chose. It was a luxurious option, that kept me on several well-marked trails traversing this earthly paradise. My mind was filled with peaceful meditations that offered thoughts of Derra in prayer, and lifted the burden of my search from my shoulders for the first time in days. I arrived at the church (a quaint wooden structure well in keeping with everything else that I had seen in Middlemore), and I seated myself at the back of the small congregation moments before the clergy paraded to the front of the sanctuary. The service was brief, and the sermon was anecdotal. Nonetheless, there was a profound sense of worship, and I felt extraordinarily refreshed and ready to begin my search.

My search was actually given some new life when the rector greeted me as I was exiting the building. On the off chance, when he asked me why I was in Middlemore, I told him that I was looking for a friend. When I mentioned Derra's name, his face clouded, and he told me that he had, in fact, spoken to her (the name and description being too coincidental to suggest someone else), and that he would be very interested in talking with me about her later that day if I had time. Of course I readily accepted, thrilled with my good fortune, and the invitation was extended to the dinner hour at the rectory adjacent to the church. I decided that I would use the intervening time to explore Middlemore as best I could. In browsing the pamphlets in the lobby of the inn, I discovered that the Historical Society kept Sunday hours for the benefit of the tourists (mostly skiers, I determined), and I decided that this might be the best course for gaining a feel of the place. Besides, most of the other options took me away from town, and it made the most sense to begin on home turf. The sooner I began thinking like a local, the better.

The history of Middlemore turned out to be so fascinating, and I became so involved in the study, that I was late for my dinner appointment. I discovered that the land grant for Middlemore was issued in 1676, although the town was not chartered until 1734, taking its name from an English Earl (who was an alleged illegitimate son of Charles II and his mistress Nell Gwynn). This, in itself, was an interesting sidetrack for me – being the child of English-born parents, and being a bit of an English history buff. But I stayed focused on the topic at hand. In the middle of the century, it seems that Middlemore was at the center of abolitionist activity, and possibly a link in the underground railroad. Of course, by the time the village entered the 1770's, fueled by high taxation, dissatisfaction with its English connection was at its height, and the town soon became embroiled in the fever that sparked the Revolutionary War. The tavern that housed the meetings at that time already had a history to it, however, that extended back to a time of considerable unsettledness at the beginning of that century. This is the period that caught my attention.

The problems arose on two fronts. First, contrary to most records in the surrounding area, there were apparently problems with the Indians that the settlers had displaced. Graphic stories of torture and burnings at the stake were preserved in many of the documents. A second problem, which might somehow have been tied to the first, was even more intriguing. Despite a fair distance in both space and time, there seems to have been a connection between the activities that ignited the Salem Witch Trials of 1692 and the Indian rampages of around 1720. Some of those awaiting trial or execution in Salem, who were set free by the Superior Court of

Judicature in October of 1692, made their way inland to Middlemore soon after. Conditions were rife for continuing the dark tradition of devil worship which had actually only involved very few, if any, at Salem. The religious atmosphere in Middlemore was, by most accounts, fanatical. Disease and distrust of both fellow settlers, and the natives from whom they had seized their land, created an environment of fear. This scene was familiar to those who had brought their nefarious practices with them from Salem, and they proceeded cautiously in order to prevent a recurrence of the events that had almost cost them their lives. Young girls were prominent in their rituals, and the rituals themselves only faintly resembled that which was alleged to have taken place in Salem. In fact, it was reported that the group existed in much the same form that it had first existed in Middlemore, well into the twentieth century. At no time did this group claim any allegiance to witchcraft or any variation of Wiccan practice, though it did claim to be a modern example of fertility religions that had existed since the beginning of recorded time.

The subject, as fascinating as it was on its own, caught my attention because, as steeped as it was in the tradition of this region, there was a sense that it was deliberately downplayed. Certainly the records were there for anyone to read, but nothing in the town reflected it in any way. One would expect a witches' museum, or at least a section within the Historical Society, as a measure to increase tourism. There were, I discovered when I asked, files and other records available at the local library. So, nobody was trying to hide the existence of this cult. I wondered, too, whether my own fascination had been unduly enhanced by the seductive drawings of the young women who had been among the first participants. Still, this was surely a goldmine of untapped resources for any researcher who was looking to make an original contribution to the field of social sciences. Yet, it sat there, hiding in plain sight, not far from the greatest scholars in the world. Surely I was missing something. After all, my own scholarship had not continued much past my terminal degree. I was lost in such thoughts as the hour arrived for my meeting with the parish rector.

11

I was not entirely comfortable with Father Luke – as the church rector was known. I detected some irritation over my tardiness, but he was a congenial enough host to be sure. He welcomed me with a glass of strong red wine, and bade me to sit with him in conversation while the church sexton prepared the table. The rector was a man in mid-sixties, single, and fit. Although his hair was completely white, it was thick and was not receding, and therefore framed his head youthfully rather than lending credence to his age. The conversation was awkward, and I wasn't quite sure whom to blame for the long periods of silence. His questions seemed to be standard issue small talk, but they evoked little in response from me. I was not, to my knowledge, being deliberately obtuse. I simply could not find a way to extend my answers into anything that could be transformed into a dialogue. We did not initially broach the topic of Derra. That seemed to be something that he had reserved for a deeper part of the evening.

The meal was excellent, and the wine flowed freely – though our conversation still did not. Father Luke seemed intent, not on enjoying himself, but on observing whether or not I was enjoying myself. This did not seem to be out of any natural gregariousness so much as something calculated – for what reason I could not tell. But, if this was a trap, then I was easy prey. The trauma of Derra's letter, my travels, and a sad separation from my constant companion Bubastes, all weighed upon me as the evening wore on, and relief, courtesy of Bacchus, was more than I could resist. Surrendering to such a pleasant escape transformed the silent spells from blank spaces into moments rich in memories. Derra hovered above me – my guardian angel – scolding me with a glance, then breaking into one of her winning smiles. I'm sure that the dumb look of satisfaction on my face caught Father Luke's attention, for he moved into my thoughts without missing a stride.

"How do you know Derra?" he asked.

The question was simple enough. But the thoughts upon which he had intruded complicated the answer. *How did I know Derra?* Maybe I didn't know Derra – at least, not in the sense that I thought I did. We had a perfectly happy relationship. We were very much like two children, playing games and discovering life. We had tucked the darkness away, and had lived in the light. I should, perhaps, have explored the hidden Derra, but I knew that such gifts as she were rare, and that it was not wise for one such as I to look too carefully, and upset the balance. Thus, deliberately, I did not know Derra. Yet I could not take a breath of air without Derra filling me – even then as I found myself chasing her shadows.

"We met at church," I said simply.

"She's a lovely young woman," Father Luke began. "She stood out – a rare combination of such mature beauty and purity."

It was an accurate description, yet he seemed to defile her simply by voicing it. My mind fought against the clouds that encumbered it to determine what motive Father Luke might have in discussing Derra at all. By speaking of her in the past tense, he showed that he knew that she had left Middlemore, and yet the letter that Derra had sent me from town was still only a few days old. Clearly he was still fascinated by her. Whether this reflected a more lecherous side of the rector, or a simple curiosity, I could not determine. In any case, I felt that I should try to discover what he knew, though it seemed that he was trying to position himself in control of the questioning.

"Do you know where she is now?" I asked bluntly.

"No," he replied quietly, leaning back in the chair, and at the same time signaling the sexton to enter with a carafe of brandy. "She told me last week that she was leaving Middlemore, but I didn't inquire as to where she was going."

The answer conveniently explained how he knew she was gone, but raised the even more contentious issue as to why he had not asked what he would surely ask any other parishioner, let alone one who had so apparently captured his imagination. My brief look of incredulity must have caught his eye, however, and he quickly tried to cover his error.

"Well, of course, I *asked*," he said with a smile, "but she was not forthcoming in her answer. I didn't press her."

I debated confronting him with a barrage of questions, but there was a sense that, even if he knew something, he would not be accommodating. I decided that I might learn more by making myself vulnerable to his queries, since there was little of value that I could offer him. Certainly there had been some purpose in inviting me to his home, and it could only benefit my search to learn what that purpose might be. I would do my best, in the face of his questions, to convey that I was not revealing all. If he uncovered me for what I was – a friend who had traveled across the continent on a whim in pursuit of his friend – then I was convinced that he would dismiss me out of hand. So I played my cat and mouse game with him well into the night. Neither of us surrendered more than basic information. It was not until the matter of my daytime research was broached that he perceived that I might be onto something.

"Everyone thinks that New England breeds witches, and such a reputation has lured any number of crackpots," he said. "But every village has its story, whether of witches or ghosts or Indians, and it would be a waste of effort to try to tie such tales to anything of historical value. It's fascinating reading, to be sure, but it's like junk food for the mind. An educated man like yourself should find more noble pursuits than reading scary children's stories. Wouldn't you agree?"

The wine and brandy had done their work on me, and I was almost drowsing as he moved his face close to mine with his final question. Yet, as foggy as I was, I still noticed that he had, once again, given himself away by trying too hard to cover himself up. His strong protests against my afternoon studies were out of proportion. And, moreover, his desperate attempt to make me stop had inspired me to resume my efforts – this time with a purpose. I left his question unanswered, and rose to leave. Again, my response (or lack thereof) seemed to show him his mistake, and he laughed as though his entire line of questioning for the evening had had no serious direction, and was simply a matter of casual conversation. When he asked me if he would see me at church on the next Sunday, I immediately answered yes, though, at that moment, I was not at all sure what my plans might be.

decided upon an extended stay in Middlemore within twelve hours of taking my leave of the rector. I spent a restless night at the George, and could only cure the empty feeling that I experienced that morning with a good dose of resolve. Although I was pretty sure that Derra would never grace the town's streets again (certainly not in the foreseeable future), I was equally confident that there were secrets to unravel in Middlemore, and that such secrets might eventually lead me to her. It was presumptuous, of course, and I am not altogether sure that my motives were as simple as I suggest. I was long overdue for a break. My excuse had always been that there was no place to go. But, now that I was there, it made no sense for me to leave.

It was not as difficult as I might have guessed to call my office in Washington State and to inform them that a personal matter required that I take a short vacation. I had no idea how long I needed, but I now had a few days before I had to make that call. Financially, it was not a big issue. A solitary and frugal lifestyle, combined with careful retirement investments, had provided me with enough resources to keep me afloat indefinitely. Lucy's initial disappointment with my news was quickly overcome when I suggested that she accompany Bubastes back to my home and stay with him there. Having been confined to single room apartments and converted garages most of her life, Lucy could not resist my offer. Thus having so easily settled my simple affairs, I prepared for my adventure.

In the excitement of rearranging my life, I forgot, for the first time, the sorrow that had driven me to this circumstance. When my thoughts inevitably returned to Derra, I felt rather guilty, initially, for having deserted her so. Nonetheless, I reasoned that good spirits and restored energy would not hurt my cause – ultimately, *her* cause. For both of our sakes, I was anxious to begin as soon as possible. So, having negotiated a slightly less exorbitant weekly rate for my stay in the George than had originally been proposed, I proceeded without further distraction to the Middlemore Public Library. I was unprepared for the volume of pertinent material that was at my disposal. Even more shocking was the nature of the assistance that I was to receive – both its source and its scope. The scope was unlimited. When I described that nature of my research, it was suggested that I enlist as a short term volunteer in the library. Thus, no area would be out of bounds for me, and I would have, by way of helping other patrons, a means of learning the various nuances of such an old and irregular depository. This opportunity was presented to me by the Library Director – a woman who was the very antithesis of the usual caricature of the typical librarian.

Jessica Burke was, perhaps, in her mid-twenties, but certainly no further along. My initial thought, upon seeing her relay directions to the circulation desk as I entered the library, was that it seemed that all of the world's finest women must have, at one time or another, passed through the town of Middlemore. Her hair was dark – I think what they call *raven*. It was full and really quite luxurious. Her eyes were dark, too – almost black – and her skin was deeply tanned. I suspected that there might be some Native American blood in her. Her dress was short, and well suited to her long thin legs. She looked every bit the dream coed, totally devoid of the professional aura that would mark a regular librarian, let alone one with authority. Her manner was friendly enough, but a smile never crossed her lips. Instead, there was a permanent pout there – seductive enough in its own right, but countered by a warning glare from the depths of those endless portals to her soul. I confess that I felt both drawn to her and frightened of her, and I suspected that I was not the first mortal to feel so conflicted. Had she not offered to help me, I doubt very much that I would have found the courage to speak to her. But, in some preordained roll of the dice, she was destined to be my benefactor. Thus my research began, and I thought of nothing else – except, of course, the one whose fate had brought me to this time and place.

THE EVENTS FROM JANUARY THROUGH FEBRUARY RECONSTRUCTED BY DR. NOAH GILES FROM THE RECORDS AND CONVERSATIONS WITH DETECTIVE JOHN STURGESS

**S**inister events in my hometown cast a new light on my search for Derra, and ultimately lead Detective John Sturgess to Middlemore, and launched me into worlds I had only ever imagined.

Detective Sturgess was fifty-six years old, and he had spent his entire life in Southern California before moving to Washington State. The last thirty-three years had been with the police force. Although he had been stationed far enough outside of Los Angeles to avoid some of the really ugly crimes, his last case there had been ugly enough, and rather than retire early with the taste of that lingering at the back of his throat, he had decided to make the move up to God's country to see if he could recover a sense of what had drawn him into police work in the first place. He was a teddy bear of a man, both physically and emotionally. Although he was overweight, his gentle features made him look younger than his years. Unfortunately, the good that his natural appearance did for his presentation was undone, in part, by the cheap cop-look of his attire. It was as if he had never owned a new suit – that everything had to appear as if he had walked a beat in what he was wearing for the last twenty years. But John Sturgess had not walked a single beat in almost three decades. As a young uniformed officer he had excelled, building trust with the African American community, and bridges to white residents who were initially more than a little wary to welcome a heavy six foot four black policeman into their world. He had donned the thick mustache only after he made detective, at the age of thirty-three – convinced that it gave his youthful face a little more credibility. It became a fixture, along with the cheap suits, as he continued his distinguished career. John Sturgess had never married – probably because he was too involved with his work. He seldom thought of his cases as *cases*, though. *It was people*. His compassion fueled his determination, and many a fine woman could have done worse than to siphon off some of that compassion as his wife. But it never happened, and Sturgess suffered no regrets over his solitary social existence.

He never spoke to me about the case that had driven him north, beyond telling me that a beautiful young woman had been murdered. Apparently many of his colleagues had suggested he had fallen in love with her– *post mortem*. He had brooded over the case right up until the time of the move. It seems that the circumstances were highly unusual, and something about the whole process had stirred eternal questions within him for which he could find no answers. Rather than live with these ghosts in perpetuity, Sturgess made his move. It was simple enough, and though Seattle did not hold the city-terror for him that Los Angeles now did, he nonetheless requested to be put on cases in the neighboring towns, where he could work in cooperation with the smaller police units. As a result, there was little action for him in his first few months. As the new year dawned, however, a case came across his desk that seemed to fit. Sturgess wondered aloud to me whether maybe this case fit just a little too well.

I t was murder. The body of an unidentified woman was found in a park atop a small pile of snow, her throat slit – possibly ritualistically. *Another Jane Doe*, Sturgess would have thought as he read the report. Only a receipt, found pressed tightly in one of her pockets, suggested that she had been in Boston as recently as that past summer. Further inspection of her personal effects had led to the conclusion that she had actually migrated from that part of the world, and probably fairly recently. That complicated the identification. And, the idea that there might be a cultic element to this made him shudder. It was New Year's Day, in the afternoon, when this case opened. A couple of kids had stumbled across her when they were taking their dog out for a run. There were pictures. She was pretty – *very* pretty. Sturgess groaned as he looked. She was about twenty years old. She was a blonde haired, blue-eyed beauty. Her complexion was pale, but that was likely exaggerated by the fact that she had been draining blood for twelve hours – or however long it took. She didn't die right away. Maybe that was intentional. Maybe it was just her bad luck. But she was immobilized – lying there waiting for it all to end, or for unconsciousness to spare her that last horror.

This was exactly the type of case that Sturgess did *not* want, but he was hooked from the moment that he opened the file. He had the skills to find out what could be found out about this girl – probably even trace her last few hours. But, in immersing himself in the person, he knew that he would develop attachments. A girl, who would never have crossed his path while she lived, would, in death, dictate his days and haunt his nights. As a dating system, it was pretty sick. For cop work, however, it made Sturgess a cut above the rest. He would have no excuse for begging off of this case. He wouldn't look for one. If he could offer the smallest grains of hope in a hopeless situation – to her family, to girls like her that he would never meet – then he was bound to his duty. Duty, for Sturgess, was mixed with a strict moral code that defined his life. It was this unwavering need for moral order that filled his personal life, and had driven him to his professional life. He could not leave Jane Doe lying there, on a melting mound of snow, for some bungling detective to try to explain. It was the type of case that marked his impressive career. But it was also the type of case that was destroying him as a human being. Yet there were no mind wrenching decisions to make. It was a no-brainer. He would start on the case right away.

On the bright side of things, the crime took him out of the city. That was not a knock against Seattle. As far as big cities went, he saw Seattle as the best. It was green and fresh. There were reasonably few dark corners. And there was a quaintness about it that was rare in Sturgess' experience. But a big city is a big city. A short drive in any of the non-ocean directions, though, and the city was gone. A smattering of bedroom cities, and pleasant little residential towns, marked the way to his destination. It would have been a more enjoyable trip if the rain had been a little lighter. Sturgess was prepared for that, though, and had been sorely tested in the fall. It seemed a shame to wash away most of the Christmas snow and to bury the rest in mud. Still, it was good to smell the pine mixed with the pungent farm odors. And it was such a reasonable commute from the city. As he drove past the houses towards the town center, Sturgess tucked the idea of moving here in the back of his mind. It was not such a farfetched idea. Most of the inhabitants worked in the city. Traffic bogged down a little during the rush hours, but it was nothing like LA. Of course, Sturgess had never commuted a day in his life, and he had chosen his current residence for its proximity to the station. But moving a few miles inland was nothing compared to the move up the coast that he had just made. He felt pretty confident that he was not too old to try one more new trick.

The police station in town was even more laid back than his old post in suburban Southern California. The detective who handled murder investigations in that town was a go-getter, but he was eager to learn from Sturgess' experience. It was unusual to pull someone in from the city, but not unprecedented. The case was so lacking in clues that a little expertise was more than welcome. In the sleepy atmosphere, Detective

Graham Kennedy seemed a little out of place. He was bursting with energy, bouncing from his chair to Sturgess' shoulder as he they reviewed the case. Kennedy was the physical antithesis of Sturgess. He was fortyish, but looked a little older. He was slim – almost gaunt. His thinning head of hair was still mostly black, with just a few traces of gray, and the remnants of an Irish accent added a sense of urgency to his many questions. Sturgess, deliberate by nature, was like an old bulldog, with a Chihuahua at his heels. Yet the contrast was not unpleasant for either of them. They moved from the paperwork to the morgue. When the girl's body was brought out for inspection, Sturgess asked to be left alone with her. It was an unusual request, but Detective Kennedy was not about to question his methods. Alone with the lifeless shell, Sturgess allowed the case, *the person*, to consume him.

She was prettier than her pictures – if such could be said about a corpse. Cleaned up, there was no sign of a struggle or unusual bruising. She had likely met her fate unaware. Someone she knew had stood behind her, and simply slipped a knife across her throat. She probably never even saw the weapon in that hand. Logically, this was a boyfriend, or some sort of paramour. Uncovering her identity would certainly the narrow the list of suspects. The absence of trauma to the body suggested that, after slitting her throat, he must have laid her gently in the snow. On the one hand, this was not a frenzied killing or a crime of hate. On the other hand, knowing that she was still alive as he laid her down, he must have taken some perverse delight in her terror. *Psychopathic*, Sturgess thought. No other sort of creature could have acted in such cold blood. There were signs of sexual activity on the girl, but no indication that she had been forced. Perhaps the secluded rendezvous in the park had been planned at an encounter earlier in the night. It was a strange place to meet, though, on a party night where they had been such active participants. The killer's purpose in choosing the spot was obvious. More helpful would be some indication as to why she had agreed.

Sturgess and Kennedy made their way to the site of the crime. The rain had let up, but it had done its job in washing away most of the distinguishing features on the scene. There was just a strip of hard dirty snow left, and the blood was gone. Even the police ribbons had taken a beating, mostly torn from their stakes – ready for removal. Sturgess walked purposefully over what must have been the poor girls last steps. It seemed an awkward angle, and must have been more so climbing onto the bank of snow that remained at the time. But, as he reached the fateful spot, Sturgess realized why it had been chosen. It was a narrow plateau on the slope, but it provided a rather spectacular view of the horizon. Trees, both below and above that spot, would obscure the view. Sturgess asked Kennedy if he recalled the New Year's Eve weather.

"Cloudy," Kennedy replied without hesitation.

"You're sure," Sturgess said – more of a statement than a question.

"We had the Christmas snow," Kennedy explained, "and I remember thinking, seeing those clouds on New Year's Eve, that it would be gone soon – and being glad that the rains had held off until the partying was over."

"What would the view be like from this spot on a night like that?" Sturgess asked, backing up a little so that Kennedy could join him on the plateau.

Kennedy knew, even before he reached Sturgess' side, that there would be little if any view at all, but he proceeded in order to find out what Sturgess was thinking.

"Well the trees, of course, would stand out against the gray sky. But that would be about it."

"No mountains? Lights? Anything else?" Sturgess asked.

"Nothing."

"Then why would someone scramble up to this particular spot on a night like that?" Sturgess inquired.

"No reason. It's a great spot for a view most of the time, though."

"Have you got a picture of the girl with you?"

"In my car," Kennedy replied. "Why?"

"Just meet me with it by the gate to that apartment complex."

It was a small brick building, maybe twenty apartments, probably forty or fifty years old. It stood out a little among the mixture of single owner dwellings that had developed across from it over the years, but it blended nicely with the park, being surrounded by large trees and being partially covered with a long established growth of ivy.

"We checked here," Kennedy said as they made their way around to the front of the building. "Nobody saw anything."

"I expect not," Sturgess confirmed.

"Would you mind explaining, then," Kennedy asked politely – though with a trace of irritation in his voice.

Sturgess smiled. He was happy to explain.

"The girl lived here."

"The only place we could link her to was Boston," Kennedy observed.

"Undoubtedly, there's some connection there. She's probably from there. But she was living here."

"Because?"

"Because she was familiar with this park. She knew where the best viewing spot was and instinctively went there. She wouldn't have found it that night otherwise. She had been there before – maybe it was a sort of refuge for her."

"Maybe it was the boyfriend's spot?" Kennedy suggested.

"I doubt he was aesthetically inclined."

"Why this apartment complex?"

"She's young – probably new to the area," Sturgess continued. "Unless she was visiting an aunt or something, she would not be living in one of these houses. She couldn't afford it – there wouldn't have been time if she had just moved from Boston. And a relative would have reported her missing. From here, it would have been the easiest thing in the world just to wander into the park – become familiar with its nuances. So, I'm expecting that either one of these apartments has been empty since New Year's Day, or even better, that there's a roommate around who, for some reason or another, has not reported our girl as missing."

Kennedy, Sturgess told me, was still a little irritated. He was, by nature incisive, and would likely have reached these conclusions on his own. The speed at which Detective Sturgess had put it together, however, probably impressed him – TV detective stuff. Kennedy's irritation, however, would not be directed at Sturgess so much as with himself. This was a standard to which he hoped to attain. Five apartments into the search, a very pretty girl in her early twenties opened her door to Kennedy and Sturgess. Before she even saw the photo, she guessed the nature of the inquiry and passed out on the spot.

I t was a great relief for Sturgess to be able to give a name to the face, even if the identification brought grief to someone else. Mandy Endicott, having recovered sufficiently to provide answers for the detectives, was well poised with her responses. Mandy was very similar in appearance to the victim. Her hair was a shade darker, and her eyes were more of a gray color, but everything else lined up well. It would have been quite a vision to see the two of them enter a room together, Sturgess told me – pausing in his narrative, and leaning back in his chair with a wistful look, Undoubtedly, a lot of eye shifting would have taken place on such occasions. Sturgess was somewhat taken aback by the similarities, and the vision of the young woman in front of him, and his prolonged silence with her may well have been the result, in part at least, of how this new scene had stunned him. Graham Kennedy began the questioning:

"Why did you faint when you saw us?" he asked.

"I didn't know where Sarah was. You looked very official. I put two and two together."

"Still, not the conclusion that I would automatically reach in your position," Kennedy noted.

"Perhaps not," Mandy said, "but there were things in her past that made her…nervous."

"Like what?"

"I'm not sure."

"But you were worried about her?"

"Yes."

"Then why didn't you report her missing?"

Mandy hesitated.

"I was gone over the holidays," she began. "Sarah was planning to stay here. She has a boyfriend. I just figured that something went wrong and maybe she headed east after all. It wasn't until I saw you at my door that I thought the worst."

"The boyfriend?"

"Horrible little creature," Mandy observed. "His name is Leo. I don't know any more than that."

"But you were her roommate."

"I wouldn't talk to her about him. He was only here once. He hit on me and I didn't like it. They would meet at other places – I didn't ask."

Sturgess, who had remained silent up to this point, asked his first question.

"Would you mind telling us anything you remember about him, or what he said to you?"

"Sarah had told me that she had met someone. But she was kinda guarded about it. I thought it was a little strange because, even though I hadn't known her that long, she was always very expressive – over the top – when it came to talking about the men in her life. At first, I figured that maybe she was in love or something – you know, being more reserved because she thought she had met *the one*. Well, when he arrived at the door, I have to say that I was shocked. I don't mean to be shallow, but Sarah is… was… a beautiful girl, and the few guys she had been with, even briefly, since I have known her had reflected that in some way. In comes this guy, not much over five feet with a receding hairline – though I don't think he was over thirty. But that wasn't the worst of it. He wore this shirt, open to the navel, and he had all of these gold chains around his neck. And his chest was really hairy – a pet peeve of mine – all of this black curly hair hanging out over his shirt. He had this smile pasted on his face. I think it made him feel endearing. It made me feel creepy."

"Why do you think Sarah was interested in him?" Sturgess asked.

"I have no idea. I figured maybe money – some very hidden quality. I was ready to give him a chance. I have some very attractive friends with some strange looking boyfriends, and some of those guys are real gems. But, when she left the room, any illusions about him disappeared."

"How so?"

"Well, right away, he moved in close. He put his hand on the small of my back, and asked me where Sarah and I had met. I started to answer, and he slipped his hand downward. I grabbed it and pushed him away, but he just laughed – more of a low chuckle actually, as if he knew something that I didn't know. Then he started to talk about me, my body actually, using all sorts of obscenities – I don't have to repeat them do I?"

"I think I get the picture," Sturgess said. "Was there anything else about that first meeting?"

"Well, he kept moving towards me – like I was just playing some sort of a game with him. He didn't try anything else, but something about him scared me. I was glad that I wasn't alone, but I was worried about Sarah."

"Did you talk to Sarah about him?" Sturgess asked.

"I tried, but she wouldn't hear anything negative about him. I think she knew what he was like, but didn't want to deal with it. She was like that – always assuming the best even when the worst was obvious."

"Did you think he might harm her?"

"I don't think I ever thought about it in that way. I mean, he was already with her. I figure, what more could he want?"

"Yet you concluded that something had happened to her when you first saw us?" Kennedy interjected.

"Yeees," Mandy replied thoughtfully. "It was Leo, combined with the other things."

"Other things?" Kennedy pushed.

"There was nothing specific. She would get calls – from back east I think. And she would get all silent, like she was scared. This happened from the time that I met her – before she knew Leo."

"When did you meet her?" Kennedy asked.

"Last summer. I saw her at the university. She was looking for a place to stay. I talked to her a few times first. We had a lot in common, so it made sense to invite her here to share the rent. I liked her a lot."

Reflection on her last point caused Mandy's eyes to water. Sturgess offered her his handkerchief (which was always clean, pressed and ready in his jacket) before taking over the questioning.

"I can see your concerns," he said, "but I don't see any link between this Leo and the calls."

"I guess that it's just that she often got the same way after he called," she said. "When she started acting like that, I thought that maybe she had known him from before, but then I remembered that, when she had first talked to me about him, she was pretty clear that they had just met. She seemed to recover pretty quickly from his calls – I guess because he was good at groveling. At least that's how it sounded when she was still talking to me about him."

"And you don't know where we can find him?"

"I don't know where he lives, but there was a club where they used to meet – initially, anyway."

Kennedy wrote down the details.

"What about family?" Sturgess continued.

"She never mentioned any. That was part of what worried me. She was so ready to talk about *everything* – everything except home and family. She never mentioned parents or brothers or sisters. *Nothing*. When I asked a simple question, or when our conversation seemed headed that way, she would just freeze. That scared me too. But all I had was a bunch of vague fears that I figured were made worse by my imagination. But I never imagined the worst – not until I saw you at my door."

The detectives did not feel that it was necessary to question Mandy any further at this point. She had done well, but she was starting to crumble under the pressure. As an afterthought, though, as he was about to step out of the apartment, Sturgess decided to confirm one point that had been inferred from the beginning of the investigation.

"She was from the Boston area wasn't she?"

"Not exactly," Mandy replied. "I don't where she was from originally, but she talked about a small town, quite a bit east of Boston from what I gathered. Middle something. Middleton? No, Middle... Middlemore! That was it, Middlemore. Does that help?"

Sturgess assured Mandy that this was, indeed, helpful information. The detectives provided Mandy with their cards and told her that they would likely be speaking with her again. She nodded gently, her sweet face forming the perfect picture of pathos.

**S**turgess, in preparation for a night of clubbing (the thought of which frightened him more than confronting a killer), booked himself a room in a local motel. He filled the intervening time (except for a fifteen-minute hotdog break) on-line at the police station trying to gather information about Middlemore. Apart from finding its exact size and location, most of the facts that he gathered were relatively useless.

Sturgess was actually relieved that previous commitments kept Graham Kennedy from joining him. It was nothing personal. Kennedy was just exhausting, and Sturgess had a preference for doing field research on his own. The distraction of a highly-strung assistant would have prevented Sturgess from communing with Sarah to the extent of seeing what she might have seen in her last hours. It was important to keep his focus in such situations as he would face that evening, for there would be no disguising who he was. He was every inch a cop when he was around people of his own age. A nightclub filled with young people would only broadcast that fact with neon lights. He had done his share of time in like places, and had become good at not making people unnecessarily nervous, but such investigation was nonetheless an art form that required a delicate touch. His mental preparations began from the moment he entered the taxi outside the police station (a police car would have been overkill), and were fully set by the time he could hear the pulse of the throbbing nightspot breaking apart the otherwise tranquil sky.

The logic of such a high decibel of noise had always escaped Sturgess. It was hard enough to order a drink, let alone carry on a conversation that would allow a person to find out something about someone. His ears would ring for days as the result of a single visit. He couldn't imagine the long-term damage on someone who frequented such a place – or worked there. His mind, he knew, was partially closed to explanations as the result of his age. In his youth, he too had liked loud music and was not averse to cranking up the car stereo. Still, he couldn't remember trying to engage in meaningful dialogue under such circumstances. Maybe that was the key: deliberately keep it meaningless. He did well with these kids, but often wondered if he would have such patience with kids of his own. Probably not. He would be too worried about their minds, their hearing, and the like. It was hard enough not to become emotionally involved with young people he met on his cases – especially the dead ones.

A pretty waitress took his order. Sturgess made a point of being friendly, even though the small talk required considerable energy in that atmosphere. She could tell that he was a cop, but that was not a problem for her. She wondered what would have drawn him into the club, though, and she took the fastest route to finding out:

"You here on a case?" she asked.

"I'm looking for someone," he replied, able to continue this conversation due to the temporary replacement of the painfully loud live music with the moderately annoying taped music. "Are you familiar with the regulars here?"

"It depends on how regular," she said. "Do you have a picture?"

"No, but I could describe him."

Sturgess proceeded to describe the man that Mandy had described to him earlier that day. The waitress listened passively, with no sign of recognition.

"There's a few like that here," she observed. "Do you have a name?"

"Leo."

At the mention of the name, the waitress's eyes grew wide.

"Leo!" she exclaimed. "Why didn't you say so? He's here all the time. He loves to dance and he's always hitting on the girls. He hit on me once, but he either didn't like the rejection or the way the owner looked at him when I brushed him off. I can't say I see the appeal, but he's been with a lot of girls here. Maybe it's the dancing."

"Are there any particular girls?"

Sturgess did not want to show her the picture of the dead girl. Apart from making the crime obvious, he felt it might prejudice her answers.

"Yeah, there is one – at least, in the last little while, anyway. She was really pretty – a lot classier than what he would usually pick up. I couldn't figure that one out at all. She could have had any man in the place. Why would she waste her time with a loser like Leo?"

Sturgess shrugged. The live music had started up again, and it was hard to speak.

"Did you know her?" he shouted.

The waitress shook her head.

"How about him? Do you know his last name?"

"It was something Italian. Magini or Magroli – something like that. *Mussolini?*" she added with a quick laugh – and the first smile that she had managed since Sturgess had arrived.

"Do you know where he lived? Where I might find him?" Sturgess asked, making himself hoarse in the effort.

Again she shook her head.

"I've only ever seen him here," she said. "I really wasn't interested in knowing anything about him. You might catch him here sometime. What's he done? He hasn't hurt that pretty girl has he?"

Sturgess just waved his hands, signifying that he couldn't hear her. He handed her his card, shouting that he would welcome any further information or persons who could provide any. He really didn't want to bring Sarah into the conversation. When the waitress returned with his drink, he gave her a big tip, but did not ask her anything further. She had probably provided him with all of the information that he could hope for – short of having Leo personally enter the nightclub. It was pretty clear to Sturgess that Leo was not the sort to cultivate friendships. There was nothing to do but to sit and wait, trying to figure out exactly what it was that was going through Sarah's mind that would link her with this unsavory character.

After a few drinks of scotch, Sturgess found himself a little more in touch with what the club was all about. The music mattered much less than the primal beat that it sent shooting through one's system. The dance was the mating ritual. The women were all aware of this, but not all of the men understood. Those who didn't hovered around the bar, hoping to pick off the stray women that wandered that way – isolated from the herd. The men in the know, however, gladly abandoned their inhibitions in order to harvest from the rich crop on the dance floor. Leo, no doubt an accomplished dancer, gave himself an edge there. His stature and his appearance would be largely forgotten in the spell that his dancing would allow him to cast over the already highly stimulated participants in this ceremony. In fact, he would become a desired entity quite unlike the repulsive creature so easily discarded by the waitress, and by someone he might approach completely out of context – like Mandy. Of course, someone like Leo counted on percentages. He would hit on every woman he saw in the knowledge that, after a certain number of rejections, he would eventually find someone agreeable to his advances. If the chances were one in ten, then he would hit on ten women. If they were one in one thousand, then he would simply hit on one thousand women. Whatever the odds were off of the dance floor, he narrowed them considerably when he was on it.

Sarah, as the chosen one on the dance floor, would be the object of envy for the other girls in this ritual. Psychologically, she would become possessive of Leo – whatever the logic of the situation might normally have dictated. He would have known that, and he would have used it to his advantage. The abusive calls, and the groveling reconciliation would have kept her emotionally on edge. She would see his faults, but his actions would suggest to her that she could reform him. And, of course, all sorts of female emotions would kick in that Sturgess could make no pretence of understanding. As a result of it all, however, she would be intolerant of those who wanted to criticize her man, but very trusting towards a creature who had not warranted an ounce of trust in his life. And, as had been Sturgess' experience far too many times, trust in one such as Leo could be fatal. That was what Sturgess discerned as the dead girl's story.

The story of the living provided fewer answers. In similar cases, death was almost always the result of passion: the woman sees the light, and the man would rather see her dead than not with him; an argument sparks something – or the woman ridicules him. Sometimes it is nothing more than a display of power – a wife-beater mentality. Yet, always, *always*, there is an element of passion. Sarah, however, had died as if there had been a contract on her life. Leo (Sturgess was convinced that he was the killer) had acted in cold-blood. It doubtless excited him to watch his victim die – to see the confused look on her face as she wondered why he had done such a thing. But he did not let this pleasure interfere with his business. There was something outside of Leo that had prompted him to act – possibly from back east. Mandy's insights may well have been right on target. But that only complicated the question about who would want Sarah dead.

Sturgess could almost find some appeal in the nightclub by the time he had consumed his fourth scotch. But there were no further conversations, with the waitress or anyone else, and it soon became apparent the Leo was not going to appear, and that apart from a stray dancer or two (who would have settled for one good dance from pretty much anyone), no one really cared at all. Over the next few days, Sturgess waited patiently, for one of the leads to develop into something useful. Despite further interviews with Mandy, and even the waitress, all evidence of Leo's existence had disappeared. It was clear that he was no longer in town, and that the investigation would have to be taken elsewhere. Even the ever-excited Graham Kennedy had shifted his focus elsewhere. It was decision time for Detective John Sturgess.

February, still a week and a half away, must be the month when the most Seattle residents contemplate moving elsewhere in the country. The skiing is still very good, and there aren't the numbers of winter storms that assault most of the rest of the country to endure, but the drawbacks are more evident than at any other time of the year. There is a hard, cold rain that has been in place forever, and will seemingly never end. The illusion of color has not been evident since the dawning of the new year, and the lush greenery (the reward for enduring year round precipitation) has a gray luster to it. Even the evergreens look like they have surrendered to the oppressive skies. Colds and flues run in a perpetual cycle, enhanced by the weather and prolonged by the depression which, too, has become epidemic. Football season has ended and baseball season, though technically on the horizon, seems even further away.

Sturgess' frustration with the pending month was certainly tied into his feelings about the case that suddenly consumed most of his time. He had heard about the Seattle rains, but thought that he had been coping pretty well – until he was introduced to Sarah. The relentless showers offered no respite from the tedium of the daily routines that had led him nowhere. February promised more of the same, and Sturgess was not at all certain that he could last into that month. His options were limited. He could drop the case altogether. At such an early stage in the investigation, however, Sturgess did not even consider this to be a viable choice. More reasonable would be the option of shelving the case temporarily in the hope that, given time, something new about this Leo character might surface. This was no more appealing to Sturgess than the first option. The only thing that could possibly frustrate him more than expending his efforts ineffectually was the idea of sitting around doing nothing and allowing his case to become cold. The move from Southern California was beginning to look like a mistake. At least, in Southern California, Sturgess could count on sunny days to help dissipate the clouds that would engulf him. His status there, too, might have made it easier for him to press for his one remaining option: an out-of-state search for the man that he believed had committed the crime.

Sturgess was ultimately granted his request, but he was put on a short leash. Normally, someone in his position would have been rejected out of hand, but Sturgess was persuasive in his argument that a visit to a small town drastically limited the parameters of his search. In the end, he was allowed two weeks in which to conduct his investigation, but apart from airfare, accommodation, and car rental for that time period, he was on his own as far as other expenses were concerned. Sturgess did not feel slighted. At his worst, he was not extravagant. If there were out-of-pocket costs, he would be well able to absorb them. The two-week time limit was not at all disconcerting. He knew that departments could be flexible over such matters – given a good argument. And, even if they weren't, a little leave time was not going to affect his financial status. The prospect of pursuing some fresh leads in his case, combined with an escape from those damned rains, seemed almost too good to be true. Even before his plane had lifted into the dark skies that enveloped SeaTac International Airport, Sturgess felt his spirits rise. So much more hinged on this case for him than a simple call to duty. Sarah was a symbol of all that was important to him in his work. And his work had been the driving force of his life.

The perversity of human nature had always preoccupied John Sturgess. He might just as easily have become a psychologist as a police officer. In many ways, it might have been a more satisfying career for him. As a psychologist, Sturgess might have been able to stop some crimes before they happened. As a cop, he was always looking backwards. Along with the *why*, there was always the *what if*. There could be no possible explanation for the untimely death of a young woman like Sarah. Sturgess was obsessed with the idea of making that fact known to her killer, *or killers*. If her death was the result of some intrigue into which she had fallen, then what were the steps she could have taken to avoid such a pit? What sick and twisted road would lead anyone to the point of wanting to see this beautiful girl dead? Although not an advocate of the death penalty, Sturgess firmly believed that there were people who just never should have been born. Perhaps this belief might have handicapped a career for him in the behavioral sciences. The deserved fate of such creatures, however, having indeed been born, was a more complicated issue for Sturgess. In moments when he was overwhelmed by emotion in a particular case, he wanted them dead. But, at other times, the philosophical Sturgess would kick in, and he would take into account environment and genetics, and he simply would want to make sure that these predators were permanently de-clawed. In the present case, having not yet encountered the perpetrator(s), Sturgess' mind wavered. Justice could wait. The all-important issue was uncovering those who were responsible.

Although uniquely suited by nature to his occupation, Sturgess' sensitivity also worked against him. The intrigue that such victims as Sarah generated within him, although pushing him to solutions, also played havoc with his emotions. He was a wreck. It was not simply a preoccupation with his job that kept Sturgess single. In all likelihood, he was emotionally incapable of handling a long-term relationship. In fact, he was not very good at the short-term ones either – with the living, at least. That was a shame. In a world half-populated by the male gender, where a good half of them could be rejected as possible spouses out of hand, and where more than half of what's left would not fare terribly well under further analysis, Sturgess would have made an excellent family man. His love for wife and children would be unparalleled. But he would never have survived the intensity of his emotions. On the job, he was always borderline breakdown, though his demeanor concealed his condition from even the most astute.

Sturgess' sensitivity might well have been used against him in any number of the cases he had worked throughout his career, yet no one had ever really used that option against him. For all intents and purposes, he was the model of stability. His deep concern for the victims and their families was often apparent to those close to him, but it read more like a character strength than a character flaw. An urgency, too, could be seen in his actions, but no one saw the compulsiveness that bubbled over into gnawing obsessions that emptied him of all but that one resolve: to unmask the guilty. To what lengths he might have gone under deliberate pressure is hard to estimate. People are never sure of their limitations until they are pushed. But Sturgess may have had a better perspective on his own limitations than some, seeing as how the pressure on him was almost always internal. He may have even been frightened by the knowledge of how close he was to the edge in cases such as these. If so, he never showed it.

# 6

The local police force in Middlemore was not terribly receptive to the idea of Detective John Sturgess poking around their backyard. So far as they were concerned, anyone from the West Coast was from Hollywood. Undoubtedly, Sturgess' Southern Californian ties bolstered that impression. In addition, there was nothing in Middlemore, so far as they could see, that bore any relation to the crime that had been committed. Sarah's name had been run through the computers and nothing had emerged. Perhaps she had come there on vacation at one point, but if that were the case, surely Seattle's more extensive databases would be a more logical resource. If local authorities could find no trace of this girl in Middlemore, then it was not likely that some big city cop would do any better. Nothing suggested that the killer would be in Middlemore either. If Sturgess was so intent on chasing his own tail, then maybe he should focus a little more on the crime scene.

The station itself is not very extensive. There are only a couple of cells – probably because there is remarkably little crime. Most police action would involve traffic violations – the worst of which would usually be drunk driving. The violators were almost always either kids from the high school, or tourists who had overindulged. Seldom was anyone kept locked up longer than overnight. On the rare occasion, when longer incarceration was necessary, the prisoner was shipped off to Fitchburg. After that, the Middlemore police themselves were never sure what happened to them. In any case, murder is not a crime that was in the collective memory of the current population of Middlemore. There is one full time secretary at the station, and she keeps pretty busy with paperwork. But, apparently, when she is on vacation or away sick, the station muddles through without any replacements. As a rule, anyone who walks through the station doors is well known to those who are already inside. Sturgess stood out, and no one was particularly interested in helping him feel at home.

Unless there was some sort of conspiracy afoot, it was likely that, if Sarah had been a permanent fixture in Middlemore, the local police would have provided that information. As a result, Sturgess focused his questions on what the police knew about the tourist population.

"Are there any long term residents at the inn?" he asked.

The officer on duty shrugged.

"You'll have to ask Tom."

"Tom?"

"Yeah, Tom Monroe, the innkeeper at the George. He's been there forever. I doubt that he has any long term residents there, though – not at those rates."

"Do the tourists stay anywhere else?"

"Like where?" the officer laughed – as if Sturgess had asked the most ridiculous question.

"I don't know," Sturgess replied, a little perturbed. "That's why I asked you."

"Look," said the officer, already growing tired of the questioning, "you're the big city detective. You tell me where this town can hide someone. I've been on the force here for ten years. I went to high school here. I know everyone who lives here. I know nothing about your victim or your killer. Like everyone else, I just want to know why the hell, of all the godforsaken corners of the world, you think you'd find out something here."

"The victim had been here. – for how long, I don't know, though long enough to make some contacts," Sturgess explained impatiently. "Somebody here knows something about her. If your department doesn't want to help beyond the standard checks, fine. You've done your work. But I'm tired of being told that I have no business here. I'm a detective, and I am here on the worst of business. I would appreciate it if you would maybe lend a hand before you try to rush me back home."

The officer just shrugged. Sturgess had tried not to let the complacency of the local police affect him, but he could not understand it. Sure, he was an outsider, but that didn't mean that the case that he brought should be of no interest to them. *In a one-horse town like this you think they'd welcome a little investigative work,* he thought. Clearly, police work took on a different definition here. It was more social and less practical. Patrol cars, as far as Sturgess could tell, were used for cruising more in the manner that teenage boys cruise for girls. There were regular stops, but such stops were dictated more by the quality of coffee and conversation than by any possible criminal activity. Crime, if it wasn't a matter of chasing down a couple of punks for fun, was viewed mainly as an inconvenience. They had apparently never known it any other way, and were not receptive to the idea of advancing their department in a manner that might incur more work.

Sturgess trudged dejectedly to his rental car. The prospect of driving around on these snowy streets had little appeal to him, but the town was small enough that a quick tour of the business section could be completed in a matter of minutes. Sturgess wanted imprint this place on his mind. He wanted to be able to picture things in his mind as he questioned the locals. This was always his method. It would be remarkably easy in a place like Middlemore. There were a few shops, catering to the tourists, downtown. More prominent, there, were the library and the historic tavern. There was one grocery store, and it housed the post office. Outside of this small core were the inn and a chalet at the base of the ski slope. Although it was not a huge detour, Sturgess decided to forego a visit to the chalet in favor of sticking to less snowy roads and returning to the George. As a pretty regular hub of activity, the inn would be his main resource. The innkeeper had not been present when Sturgess checked in, but he would be a logical starting point once Sturgess returned.

As picturesque as Middlemore is, Sturgess had a vague sense that something was not right there. Yet, as he ran events and people through his mind, there was nothing that he could pinpoint as being out of the ordinary. Still, it was a limited playing field. Although he had not uncovered anything yet, his investigation had only just begun. Sturgess was confident that, given just a little time, he could uncover most any secret that this town might have to offer. A humble man by nature, Sturgess was not so humble that he did not, at least, recognize his own skills – though he underestimated them by far.

# 7

Tom Monroe had inherited the George from his father, and his father from his father before him. No one is better known to the community than Tom, and Tom knows the community better than anyone. Although his occupation had fallen upon him simply as a result of the circumstance of his birth, he is well suited to it. He is gregarious by nature, quick to laugh, and with an infectious charisma that endears him to most who know him. An automobile accident had orphaned him when he was in his early twenties. He had been rather wild in his youth, with little interest in the family business, but the death of his parents had a sobering effect. Long nights at the tavern, followed by various misadventures, came to an end – at least, as a regular part of his routine. He started rising early, tending to business, and being around to wish the majority of his patrons a goodnight. It had been this way for close to thirty years now – though, in a dim light, Tom himself didn't look much over thirty-five.

Sturgess had not yet met Tom Monroe because Tom had been tending to a vendor when Sturgess checked into the George. There was a casual diligence in the manner in which Tom conducted his business. Nothing was left to chance, and Tom put in long hours. But there was a certain flippancy in his manner – like it was all really just a game that was being played for his convenience. Undoubtedly, there was a touch of arrogance to the man, but it was easily forgiven when all things were considered. He was, after all, perpetually good-natured. He was a responsible citizen and would be a great catch for any of the single local women. That he remained unmarried raised few questions. Most people, however, wrote off his prolonged bachelorhood as the symptom of a Peter Pan syndrome. The volume of beautiful women that apparently passed through the inn reinforced the idea. After all, why would he want to be tied down to one woman when he could live in such a Never Never Land? It was a question with some weight.

Tom Monroe was at the desk when Sturgess arrived back at the George after his day in town. The innkeeper extended his hand, and offered Sturgess the usual warm welcome. A few pleasantries were exchanged. Usually that was all that it took to win someone over to Tom, but Sturgess was a hard sell. Years of detective work had taught him to look beneath the surface before drawing any firm conclusions about the people he met. There was nothing negative about Tom that jumped out at him, but on the other hand, it was remarkably difficult to see anything at all beneath the surface. Of course, this might have been nothing more than an indication that Tom's public persona was rather firmly entrenched – which it most certainly was. Still, Sturgess never quite trusted what he never quite knew. Mysteries irritated him. He was good at his job because he did not like mysteries. The satisfaction for him, unlike most of those with a leaning in that direction, was not in the solving, but in the total annihilation of the mystery. The methods of a Sherlock Holmes (more akin to Detective Kennedy), where the delight was in the deductions, bored him to tears. *Know the territory. Get inside the heads.* That was Sturgess' philosophy. When he encountered a head with no apparent entrance, it irritated him – no matter how appealing the outer presentation might be.

Whatever the character of the inner Tom Monroe might have been, the outer Tom Monroe was congenial, talkative and more than willing to answer Sturgess' questions. Although not committing himself to any firm assessment, Sturgess found himself begrudgingly liking the Tom Monroe with whom he was in conversation. Word of Sturgess and his mission had already reached Tom, through the police, of course – all of whom he had known since childhood. As for long-term residents in his inn, there were a few long-term guests, but the groups that came through never stayed longer than a couple of weeks. Tracking down a beautiful girl who might have stayed for a couple of weeks was more complicated than it would be at most inns. In the first place, the volume of beautiful girls that flowed through the George was much higher than might expected when considering usual percentages of the population. There were a variety of groups and clubs that had regularly been staying at the hotel even before Tom had taken control. Exactly what these groups were, he didn't know. *Beauty clubs? Models in training? Were there even such things?* Tom neither knew nor cared – so long as they kept coming. However, he declared himself willing to help Sturgess trace some of these groups through whatever records were available. As for individual names, that would be even less productive. The rooms associated with these groups were paid for in block, and the individual occupants never showed up on the register. It had always been done that way, and considering the paperwork that it avoided, Tom had never had any reason to change it. If, however, the parties that Sturgess was seeking had come on their own, then their names would be on the register. Sturgess was most welcome to check.

If Tom Monroe had anything to hide, then he was acting with the utmost of cockiness, and Sturgess had no reason to suspect that. Secretly, though, Sturgess wished that it were true. Cocky people always slipped up. There was some consolation in knowing that, if indeed Tom were hiding something, it would eventually become evident. How long that would take didn't matter. Sturgess was in this till the end. If, on the other hand, Tom was simply the forthright person that he appeared to be, then Sturgess was confident that it would not be very long before he knew all that he needed to know about the town of Middlemore Still, Sturgess did not feel great about the prospects. Tom Monroe had that same indeterminable aura of mystery about him that disturbed Sturgess about the town in general. It may be nothing, but as long as it was a mystery, Sturgess could not relax.

Investigation of the various group registrations was an intriguing process for Sturgess if nothing else. The records were as Tom Monroe had represented them in his conversation. There were certain patterns, but there was nothing overtly unusual in those patterns. Longtime affiliations were prominent, and many could be traced back to almost the earliest accounts that were readily available. (The very earliest documents, prior to 1960, were housed by the Historical Society.) There seemed to be some sort of standing arrangement, as certain groups claimed certain seasons – one beginning in mid-December for the Christmas season, another at the end of January, another in mid-March, another at the end of April, another in mid-June, another at the end of July, another in mid-September, and another at the end of October. If these groups were interrelated in any way, it was not apparent from the register. The connection was that they were all comprised of women – or so he was told. Tom Monroe had offered no explanation for this, and seemed to be as perplexed about it as was Sturgess – though not wanting to look too deeply into the gift horse's mouth. Given the age of these affiliations, Sturgess surmised that these groups might have had a common origin, say, a girl's school or some other such segregated institution. But that was difficult to tell on the basis of the register. Sturgess made notes, mostly comprised of the dates and times that the groups arrived, the names that the group signed under, and the names of those who signed into the George on behalf of the group.

The exercise of wading through the registers was, in itself, not highly productive, but it offered a wealth of information that, if researched from the appropriate sources, might provide some telling information. Still, it was a long shot. At best, Sturgess hoped to gain some insights into the real nature of this town – the secrets that only the residents seemed to know.

From there, he might discover the best means of conducting his search for Sarah's connection. What these secrets might be, he could not even guess. They might simply be dirty little secrets common to any isolated location, ranging anywhere from an underground business to a hidden crime of violence. Sturgess was more inclined towards the former, presuming that it would be easier to enforce a community pact of silence if there were a vested interest in the outcome. He had only encountered a small sampling of the town perspective, but nothing led him to believe that there was anything particularly sinister being concealed in Middlemore. Still, one person's indiscretion is another's mortal sin. Some may well have a much more vested interest in silence than others. But all of the speculation in the world was not going to solve anything for Sturgess. He needed facts.

It was late when Sturgess finally closed the hotel registers. His last several hours of contemplation had brought him no further in his thought processes than the first few. There was something suspicious taking place, but not overtly so. Uncovering anything from the leads that he had gathered that day was going to take work. Tom Monroe might be able to offer some shortcuts – if he were willing. He was still lurking around the lobby, so Sturgess decided to try his luck.

"There seem to be certain patterns of bookings for different groups," he observed. "Has it always been like that?"

"It seems to be," Monroe acknowledged. "Usually, one group has me block of the same dates a year in advance. It makes sense considering how limited we are for space – especially at Christmas time. I've actually refused bookings that other groups want to set up more than a year in advance in deference to my regular customers whom I usually expect to rebook at the time of their arrival."

"But you're not overbooked right now," Sturgess noted. "I was able to get a room, and I noticed that there were a number of new reservations made over Christmas."

"That's true," Tom mused. "I guess it's because we don't advertise the inn. Between the group bookings and repeat customers, we do good business. We're not under pressure to keep the rooms full – three quarters will cover us most of the time. There's no real reason for outsiders to stay here. Our attractions are hardly unique to the area. The skiing's good, but not anything that you couldn't find fairly easily anywhere else in this part of the world. It's a one-horse town. It gets boring pretty easily."

"Yet you have decades of groups that apparently have never stayed anywhere else?"

"It's the isolation as far as I can guess," Monroe offered. "If there are workshops or anything else happening, I can't think of a better place for privacy."

"Do they hold workshops here at the inn?"

Tom Monroe laughed.

"We're hardly equipped for that. It was just a 'for instance.' I don't know what they do or why. They stick to themselves, and the ability to do so is probably one of the main reasons that they return. As I've said, I haven't looked into what they do, and it wouldn't make sense for me to do so. Besides, they're good people. I've never had any problems with any of them. I can't imagine that they would do anything to warrant your investigation."

"Have you addresses?" Sturgess asked.

"What? What do you mean?"

"The group leaders. They sign in and apparently pay with credit cards – but I couldn't see any specific addresses. It looks like the same people signing in for each group over the past several years. They must be good businesses."

"Huh?"

"No turnover," Sturgess explained. "And, as far as I can make out, it seems that there is remarkably little turnover in who signs in throughout their histories. All the groups are like that. It's just unusual. That's all. Do you have personal addresses?"

For the first time, Tom Monroe looked a little flustered.

"That's private information, isn't it?"

"Yeah," Sturgess agreed, "but so's the register – and that didn't seem to be a problem for you."

"I know," said Monroe, laughing a little once more. "I could probably find out something – though I'm not sure where to start. Addresses were never an issue either. I'm sure it's bad business on my part, but I just let most of this stuff go on as it had for years before I took over. I'm not breaking the law am I?"

"No law that I know about, but then I don't know about that type of law. I'm just surprised. It seems to make good sense to get addresses just to cover yourself. – especially when a new guy comes through. Don't you keep anything to confirm bookings – or even for sending out Christmas cards?"

Tom's boisterous laugh returned.

"They just keep coming and I've never thought beyond that. And I haven't sent a Christmas card to anyone in my life."

"And if you could look into finding out those addresses…" Sturgess said as he turned to make his way towards his room.

"I've got some ideas already," Monroe offered good-naturedly. "But I trust you'll be discreet?"

"Discreet is my middle name," Sturgess called back, stretching his hand behind him to wave goodnight as he began to ascend the stairs."

After spending the better part of a day sifting through the George's register, the ski chalet was a logical destination for Sturgess' investigation on the next day. As far as he could deduce, the most recent group of beautiful young women must have spent their daylight hours there, or on the adjacent hills. A warm trail was welcome after ploughing through the seemingly endless history of group after group checking into the George. Despite the apparently steady flow of women passing through Middlemore, the visages of the most recent crops might still be fresh on the minds of those that worked at the chalet. Hopefully, too, Sturgess might discover something useful about the manner in which the ladies spent their days.

The chalet was alive with those who were anxious to make an early start on the slopes. There was no accommodation for overnight guests, but there was a restaurant and a coffee bar which were both brimming with customers. The corridor on the main floor led to an open museum-like display of the wildlife in the region, and to a small theater. The lower level housed an auditorium and several conference rooms. A group of twenty or thirty young ladies would not be invisible in this setting, but there were places to hide – if need be. Sturgess estimated that there were easily a couple of hundred people milling about as he surveyed the area. And this probably wasn't even the peak time. A combination of local residents and guests from the George would only make up a small portion of the crowd. Likely this spot absorbed visitors from a fairly wide radius of neighboring towns.

Sturgess ascertained that a lot of the holiday help at the chalet was provided by university students – most of whom had long since returned to classes. There were, however, others in that age bracket who stayed for the full skiing season. They were all aware of the girls to whom Sturgess referred. It did not surprise Sturgess that the males were acutely aware of the group, but he was surprised that the females were able to offer more useful information about them. For instance, almost all of the female employees noted that these girls were seldom, if ever, on the slopes. The male employees seemed to be aware of the girls while they were in the lobby or at the coffee bar or restaurant, but had no clue where they spent the rest of their time. From his conversations with the female employees, Sturgess determined that a lot of that time was spent in conference – in the daytime, at least. The girls were gone most evenings, but it was simply presumed that they returned to the inn. More than one male employee, however, had ventured to the George to try his luck only to find that the girls were not present – or, at least, not visible. One had been about to give up and leave the inn late one night when a bus arrived depositing all of the girls outside of the lobby. They appeared to be highly chaperoned, however, and he decided not to try to risk approaching any of them.

The management of the chalet was less helpful in providing information regarding the activities of the group. Pressed, they did confirm that the group made use of the conference rooms, but could not provide any details on how much time was spent there since the rooms were not formally booked, but instead, made available by request no more than a week or two in advance of the needed time. Considering the number of available rooms, and the relatively small number of requests, overbooking had never been a problem, and a room, once informally booked, was available for the entire day if necessary. As for outside activities, no one had anything to say. It was pointed out that traffic through the chalet in the holiday season was in the thousands, and that it was pretty much impossible to track a small group when everyone had so many job-related responsibilities. The explanation was reasonable enough, but Sturgess wondered why the comments were so consistent with all the managers – especially when the temporary help was able to provide so many more details. It was if there had been some sort of meeting, warning them in advance of Sturgess' visit, and providing answers in anticipation of his questions. If that were true, however, then it raised a couple of important questions. First, who forewarned them? Sturgess had only been in town for a couple of days, so there were limited answers to that question. It could, of course, have been Tom Monroe. The timing on that, however, seemed rather tight. He and Sturgess had only talked the previous day. It seemed unlikely that Monroe would have been able to convey the nature of his conversation with Sturgess to the chalet in time for the upper management to convene a meeting with all of its full time employees before Sturgess arrived. But it was not impossible. The local police were more likely suspects in this conspiracy, having been aware of Sturgess' arrival in advance, and being the first to ascertain the details of his investigation. Either way, the more pressing question was *why*. Certainly, the police had been uncooperative, but why would they want to hide facts? Why would anyone want to hide facts? It could relate directly to Sarah's death, but it could just as easily relate to something much more trivial. Sturgess didn't want to jump to conclusions. How many times had government institutions messed up investigations by withholding information directly related to cases simply for the purpose of covering up their own, totally unrelated, foibles? The really bad news in all of this was that it might take much more time than is usually helpful in such cases before Sturgess even came close to finding out anything about Sarah.

Middlemore, being such a small town, could hardly keep two persons with similar missions, such as Sturgess and myself, separated for very long. The few locations that housed Sturgess on any given day, also housed me in a similarly exclusive manner. As fate would have it, I was also looking for information on a beautiful young woman – though I had hopes that the object of my search was still alive. On occasion, Sturgess and I had seen each other at the inn, but there had been no real meeting there – perhaps a nod of the head. Our paths had also crossed, once or twice at the Historical Society, but we had been too absorbed in our projects at hand to speak. Even in the library, though browsing through similar sections, we had not spoken during our first encounters. It was only when Sturgess realized that I actually worked for the library that he proffered a question. Excited conversation blossomed once we realized the common nature of our research.

The coincidence of our situations was mind-boggling for Sturgess. Of course, as a detective, Sturgess did not believe in coincidence – at least, not in the sense of pure chance. Chance might account for the timing of our searches, but not for much else. There was nothing of chance in the fact that two beautiful young women had gone missing from the same Washington town, and had been traced to the same obscure Massachusetts town – a town which, incidentally, seemed to draw beautiful young women like a magnet. Both of us, being of analytical minds, had greeted the dead ends of our research by wading through the unique history of Middlemore in the hope of uncovering some current secret that might bring fruition to our quests. Discovering each other brought new hope to our searches, though I was understandably upset to learn that Sturgess' search was initiated by murder. Our exchange of information was a lengthy process.

I had uncovered volumes of historical data, and had time to speculate on the implications of that data. Sturgess' focus was more on recent history. It was an interesting meshing of minds: the philosophical and the practical. We took an instant liking to each other.

Oddly enough, the one practical lead from our initial discussions came from me. The concept of exploring the churches had never occurred to Sturgess. His faith was nominal, and he certainly would have had no idea which denomination might provide answers for him. Considering the origin and nature of my association with Derra, however, it was not unexpected that I should have stumbled into her church. There were not necessarily any implications there for Sarah, but Sturgess was certainly intrigued by my description of Father Luke.

"Do you think he knew more than he was saying?" Sturgess asked.

"That was certainly my impression," I admitted. "I can't say that there was anything specific to confirm it, though."

"I get the impression that you didn't like him much?"

"Well, I was *uncomfortable* around him. His public persona and his personal persona seem to be at odds. He's very gracious at the church. His sermons are humble, and often profound. At his home, he's distant. There are awkward silences – like he really doesn't want you there. I don't know. Maybe it was my problem. Maybe it was the nature of meeting."

"So I presume that you haven't been back to the church?"

"I go regularly," I countered. "It's a good church, and a very pleasant walk from the inn. And, as I said, he does a good job in the public setting."

"But, knowing about that man, isn't the service tainted by hypocrisy?"

"We're all hypocrites," I explained. "Yes, it is more serious when you have seen the hypocrisy in someone who is supposed to be a spiritual leader, but you can look beyond that depending on how it affects you personally. And, to be honest, I have thoroughly enjoyed my church experience here in Middlemore – from the walk to the church right through to the walk back to the inn."

"I'd be inclined to be a little more skeptical, I'm afraid," Sturgess said with a wry smile. "Still, I'd be very interested in attending a service with you if you wouldn't mind."

"I'd enjoy that," I declared. "I usually start out from the inn around ten. The service starts at ten thirty."

The brisk walk across the snowy fields put Sturgess in a good frame of mind for the services at St. Jude's Church. A sense of *something* came over him as the worship began – *nostalgia* perhaps. His parents had rarely taken him to church when he was young, and when they did, it was nothing like this. His memories were chiefly of noise. I have some experience with those types of services. No one is quiet. The organ blares, and hands clap in rhythm as the congregation jumps from its seats. Even the times of prayer are filled by shouts from the pulpit, and echoed by loud cries of "amen" or "hallelujah" from the four corners of the building. Sturgess remembered, too, the strange sensation of seeing his parents in full participation, crying out on cue, raising their arms, with hands cupped, high above their heads. St. Jude's bore little resemblance to anything that Sturgess had experienced. Soft classically-inspired tones from the choir preceded the traditional processional music that accompanied the clergy in their march to the pulpit. The liturgy, sung weakly (poorly even) from the pulpit, and answered more powerfully from the congregation, somehow filled the building with something unique, something holy. Despite himself, Sturgess felt mesmerized by words that Father Luke spoke, and by the steady pace of the service – culminating in the serving of the Eucharist. Sturgess did not partake, but did accept a blessing at the hands of Father Luke.

As Sturgess exited the church, Father Luke clasped his hands around his. I offered a brief introduction, but Luke was already aware of Sturgess' identity. Sturgess looked for a trace of deceit on Luke's face, but could detect nothing. *Either this man is the consummate actor, or Noah is simply mistaken*, he must have thought as he surveyed the rector's face. The latter probably seemed more likely, yet not in keeping with what Sturgess had learned about me. The issue, however, was given a unexpectedly quick opportunity for resolution when Father Luke invited Sturgess, along with me, to join him for lunch. There was no delay in accepting. Sturgess, of course, looked forward to what might be a unique angle for uncovering some of the town's secrets. I, along with hoping that I might discover more about Derra, was eager to resume my conversation from the safety of Sturgess' side. I did not fear Luke physically, but nonetheless, a chill ran through me as I recalled the intimidating mental power of the man. Of course, the question as to which Father Luke would make an appearance was one of great intrigue to both of Sturgess and myself.

Once the worshipping parishioners had departed, Father Luke led us to the rectory. It was plush and warm inside, and Sturgess almost immediately felt drowsy. Luke's public persona (if that's what it was) was still firmly intact. The smile seldom left his face as he showed Sturgess and me, first to the living room, and then to the table. He presented both of us with goblets of rich red wine, without asking, almost before we had settled into the soft lounge chairs. Sturgess had half a mind to refuse the drink, already fighting drooping eyelids, and still conscious of his need to be alert, but the vision of the dark red fluid cast its own spell, and the journey from cup to lips was irresistibly short. Similarly, at the table, the wine was poured without question or ceremony.

"The sexton is away this week," Father Luke offered by way of apology as he poured more wine. "I'm afraid that the meal is very basic."

It was true that there was nothing complicated in the preparation of the food, but the volume and variety was remarkable. Apparently the sexton had left the refrigerator well stocked. There was a selection of breads, meats and cheeses, as well as a choice of green salad, fruit salad, or jellied salad (meant to supplement the obligatory potato salad and pasta salad). Father Luke arranged it all strategically on the table, smiling broadly all the while, and never neglecting to top off the waiting vessels with wine. So far, there was nothing for Sturgess to dislike about our gregarious host. I watched, curiously – wondering where all of this might be leading. I felt none of the discomfort that I had experienced at their previous meal. The conversation flowed freely, too, interspersed by loud laughter – usually originating with Father Luke.

Ultimately, the discussion focused on Sturgess' investigation. Father Luke was not familiar with Sarah, but acknowledged with another loud laugh, that Middlemore could become the tourist capital of the world if it advertised the number of beautiful young women that passed that way. Luke listened intently as Sturgess explained why his search had led him to Middlemore. Father Luke cocked his eyebrow in genuine surprise when he heard that Sarah had been killed in the same Washington town where I had met Derra. Sturgess decided to press a little by offering to Luke that I had told him that he had been rather disparaging of the historical search that I had begun (though this was the same route that Sturgess has decided upon subsequently).

"I think that Dr. Giles misunderstood," Father Luke said, leaning forward across the table, still chuckling – though with, perhaps, a trace of irritation in his voice. "I suggested that the folklore here is rather contrived. If an historical study can shed some light on the current state of affairs, then I might even be able to provide some sort of assistance. I simply didn't want Dr. Giles to put any hope in chasing phantoms. To be honest, I am convinced that there is some innocent explanation for where Derra is right now, and despite the remarkable coincidence of locations, I doubt, and sincerely hope, that your searches have nothing else in common."

I thought that Luke winced as he mentioned Derra. Of course, I realized that I might be reading into Luke's reaction – misled, perhaps, by the now grogging effects of the wine. When I shared this observation with Sturgess as we left the rectory, Sturgess confessed that he hadn't noticed – being too focused on what Father Luke had to say about Sarah.

"You have a detective's eye, though," he said to me by way of consolation. "I would not be surprised if you caught what I missed. What would you make of it then?"

"I still think he knows more about Derra than he's said," I explained.

"But what about his manner?" Sturgess asked. "I didn't detect anything of that private persona that you spoke about."

"My guess is that he doesn't know anything specific about Sarah. He was comfortable talking about her because he had nothing to hide. But, when you linked her with Derra, he seemed genuinely surprised – and, perhaps, a bit uncomfortable."

"Well, again, you seem to have been the better detective at this meeting," Sturgess said. "I don't doubt what you saw – even though I missed it. The problem is that it puts neither one of us any further along in our search."

"That's what I'm thinking," I said dejectedly.

Both of us hung our heads in silence for the remainder of the walk to the inn. Our minds were whirling, but a subtle element of despair had entered our thoughts and made conversation impossible.

His job had trained him in the art of dissociation, but Detective John Sturgess was, in that sense, a poor student. While most of the rough and tumble street stuff had no effect on him, he was plagued with moods of tenderness over the occasional victim when some aspect of his usually dormant paternal nature was somehow tapped. He knew for certain that, only a year previous, Sarah had gazed out across this frozen landscape. Sturgess watched as the snowflakes landed softly on the rooftops, giving a false sense of peace and well-being for all of those falling under this gentle blanket. Even from a cynically critical point of view, Sturgess had trouble imagining that all was not well in this town. The local police, with their adolescent arrogance, were perhaps the only unpleasant experience of his visit, and that could be written off simply as abuse of authority in a town where little authority was needed. It was certainly an idyllic setting – especially with the little whiffs of smoke that rose from the chimneys of the quaint little houses scattered at the base of the hills. God had no doubt erected this little scene to show us all how life could be.

The unlikely dose of personal optimism that graced the detective was no doubt partially instilled by his personal motto: *Today is the best day of my life.* On bad days, he would chuckle to himself at the thought – wondering how much his life must have sucked for it to be true. On most days, however, he started fresh, excited by the opportunities that lay before him, with no sense of nostalgia or regret. He sat outside, working his way slowly through a thermos of coffee from a location that he had found that provided him with a panoramic view of the town and the surrounding districts. He waited there for me (having my own morning routine) in anticipation of a mutual expedition to the library. Although we had shared our research, we had not yet done any research together – with the exception of our visit to the church and Father Luke. I had become familiar with the library, and was aware of its hidden resources, so it made sense to bring Sturgess' fresh eyes to view what I had discovered.

I had insisted on walking to our meeting spot, but we departed together in Sturgess' car. Apart from arranging this meeting, we had not spoken since church. Neither of us felt inclined to begin a conversation as we drove, and nothing was spoken until we had settled into one of the obscure corners of the library. The first question from Sturgess was unexpected.

"Who was that remarkable woman that greeted us when we arrived?"

"That's Jessica Burke," I answered. "Why do you ask?"

"Well, for starters, in a town that we have established as brimming with beautiful women, this is one of the few that I've met."

"Ah, yes," I reflected, "I'd forgotten that you missed that last group. There were some at the chalet, weren't there?"

"One or two. But have you noticed that there is something mysterious about the beautiful women who pass through this town?"

"Well, certainly the two that we are seeking," I acknowledged, "but how so the rest?"

"The groups themselves…" Sturgess began, "notice how they are reputed to draw beautiful women like a magnet, yet we hardly see any outside of these groups – especially the young ones."

"I've seen other attractive women in town," I protested. "And, at the chalet, they are mostly college age."

"I suppose," Sturgess mused, "but they are few and far between. And, with all due respect to your judgment, there's been no one out of the ordinary – except this Jessica Burke. That's why I ask."

"I could ask her to lunch with us," I suggested.

Sturgess was pleased with the idea, so without another word, he plunged cheerfully into the pile of books and papers that I was piling on his desk.

The morning passed quietly, interrupted only by the occasional grunts from Sturgess when he was struck by an oddity in the information that he was perusing. As excited as he had been about beginning this research, it was the pending lunch hour that preoccupied his thoughts. Research, for him, was a necessary evil. He didn't hate it altogether. He enjoyed the moments of revelation that it often provided. But Detective Sturgess always preferred the personal contacts. Such an intriguing contact as Jessica Burke had him positively giddy. Of course, the pained expression on his face as he waded through the material looked more the product of boredom than of an over-excited schoolboy who could hardly contain himself.

Jessica reinforced Sturgess' opinion of her as she strode to the lunch table. There was something undeniably sexy about her – though, somehow, not overly so. Certainly there was nothing of the library director about her. She looked every part the coed, or better still, the barfly. Her short skirt exposed long well-toned legs. Her low-cut tank top sat several inches above the skirt, thus highlighting two other exquisite portions of her body. Her dark hair was straight. It framed a pretty face, with dark eyes and fine features, yet the focal point was the pouty mouth. As I explained it later, it enhanced her sexuality yet, paradoxically, averted leering eyes by creating an aura of disinterest around her. No doubt, though, that secret glances were continually cast her way as she sat with the two gentlemen who had summoned her. Sturgess, out of habit, began the interrogation.

"How long have you lived in Middlemore?"

"All my life," she said distractedly – as if she was already bored by her company.

"Would you mind telling me how you managed to rise to such a responsible position so quickly?"

"Not much to say," she said (sounding not at all like anyone with any responsibility). "After high school, I started working there. The director died, and I took over."

"So you have no degrees?"

"None."

"Isn't it a little unusual – no one with any library training in your library? I mean, I'm sure that you could advertise a position, and bring someone in with no problem."

"Maybe."

"Do you have any idea why not?" Sturgess asked – pushing for something more than one word answers."

"There hasn't been any real need," she said, relenting to the pressure. "I was trained on the job by a qualified librarian. It isn't exactly brain surgery. I haven't really needed much help since she died, but there is lots of intelligent help around. Dr. Giles is a good example."

The explanation seemed reasonable to Sturgess. Despite its simplicity, he could detect from it that quite possibly this girl had the brains to match her beauty. Her nonchalant, detached attitude was likely more of a defense mechanism than an indicator of ignorance. This was clearly a person who was more complex than she appeared. The contradictions intrigued Sturgess. On the one hand, she was an efficient businesswoman, yet on the other, she cultivated the impression of a disinterested kid. She dressed convincingly as a woman on the make, yet there was every indication, in the way that she lived her life, that she was destined to become the stereotypical librarian spinster. This was all readily apparent to Sturgess after seeing her at work for just a few minutes, and after only having just begun a conversation. The obvious dichotomy suggested to Sturgess that she had made some definite choices. What lay behind these choices was what was of particular interest to him.

"Do you have any family in Middlemore?" Sturgess began once he had determined the nature of his new tack.

Jessica shook her head.

"My birth parents lived on the Hassanamesit reservation."

"I'm sorry, the term is new to me, is that a Native American tribe?" Sturgess interrupted, casting a glance at Noah, who seemed equally baffled.

"The Nipmuc Indians were the original inhabitants of this area. Only two groups of Nipmuc Indians have survived. My parents belonged to the Hassanamisco Nipmuc. Actually, my birth mother was the only blood Nipmuc. There are not many left – maybe a thousand. I'm surprised that you haven't come across them in your research."

"I have encountered the Nipmuc in my research," I said, "but I am not familiar with any of the groups. But, I confess, I have not spent any time researching Native Indians in this area."

"You should," Jessica asserted. "Not only is it interesting, but I suspect it might be vital in filling your history of this area."

"I was hoping to get to it," I said sheepishly.

"In any case," Jessica continued, "my parents died when I was a baby – car accident. I was in foster homes here, initially, and I ultimately ended up with Mrs. MacDonald."

"Mrs. MacDonald?" Sturgess asked. "Is she still around?"

"No. She was the librarian."

"Would you be able to direct Dr. Giles to some of library resources on the Nipmuc tribe?" Sturgess asked.

"Sure," Jessica said, fully recovering her disinterested tone.

"So, let's eat," Sturgess said, drawing the investigation conversation to a close. "We've got work to do this afternoon."

Conversation was sparse for the rest of the meal, but it was friendly. On one occasion, a smile even crossed Jessica's lips. *She should do that more often,* I thought. *It's absolute dynamite!*

Although the plan had been for us to do our research together, Detective John Sturgess and I had taken diametrically opposite routes from the very first day of our proposed project. The research that I had done was quickly digested by Sturgess, who grew weary of focusing on someone else's work within a day. It was not that what I had done was unhelpful. On the contrary, the history of Middlemore was rich and fascinating, and the various threads of my work showed good promise for sorting out some of the mysteries of the current town. But Sturgess knew how long it had taken me to piece things together. Moving things forward would be a similarly tedious process, akin to watching paint dry from Sturgess' perspective. For all of his thoroughness, Sturgess needed to see things happen. The good news was that the research could now be left in my hands. The bad news was that, despite our efforts, there were no new starting points for Sturgess. I, at least, by studying the Nipmuc Indians in the area, was working on a fresh thread of research.

In removing himself from the resources of the Historical Society and the library, Sturgess felt, with some justification, that he was wasting his time in Middlemore. Putting his optimistic spin on things, he preferred to think that he was *biding his time*. He could not, however, put any clear vision into what exactly he was hoping to happen. Both he and I were solitary sorts. We were by no means anti-social, but on the other hand, we were total disasters as far as small talk and casual friendships. We encountered each other numerous times over the course of a given week, but unless there was something new to communicate about our investigations, our conversations seldom extended beyond a greeting. I didn't say much about my research, though. I preferred to have a complete package to offer before I shared information. So, in fact, Sturgess was waiting for my full report – but he couldn't really say that he expected anything that might break the case open.

Thus Detective Sturgess took the time to do in detail what he did so quickly in his first days in Middlemore: explore the town and meet the people. The geographical boundaries of this exploration were not very extensive. As well, everything that could be discovered easily about Middlemore had pretty much been covered in his first days of investigation. Still, it couldn't hurt to know where each street lay and where each building could be found. Likewise, there could be no harm in coming to know the regulars in the café, or what the general store/post office kept in stock. Of course, such knowledge would not read well on his reports. Such knowledge did not exactly inspire Sturgess himself, and having already extended his stay beyond what the department felt necessary, he was on the verge of just giving up. There was one byproduct of becoming a part of this small town, however, that offered Sturgess the necessary inspiration to re-energize his search. He was about to enter café, when a familiar figure caught his eyes. In disbelief, he turned so quickly that he lost his footing. The cry that left his mouth, however, had nothing to do with pain that he had caused himself.

"Mandy!"

The young woman, herself caught off guard, maintained better balance as she returned his cry.

"Detective Sturgess!"

He had time to return to his feet before she reached him, though she almost knocked him over again as ran straight into him with a giant hug. He was a little embarrassed, not having spent more than a few minutes with her in his entire life. Nonetheless, both recognized the bond that brought them together, and both recognized the disproportionate relief that came from finding each other in this distant locale.

"Why are you here?" she asked.

"I suspect it's the same reason you are," he replied.

"No, I didn't mean that," she explained. "I mean…I guess…I'm just surprised. I don't mean to be rude, but I didn't think that the police would go to such lengths to solve a case. I mean, I can't believe you are still here. Or have you been somewhere else? Or have you come up with some answers?"

Her voice grew more and more excited as the idea that Sturgess might actually be making some headway entered her mind. His look, however, told her the story before he even had a chance to answer.

"I guess I meant why are you *still* here?" she said quietly when she realized that he had gathered no new information in his first days of investigation.

They entered the café together, and Sturgess told Mandy what he could. He presented the conclusion of his story honestly, saying that he was quite out of resources, and that the idea of just giving it up had crossed his mind.

"You need a new perspective," she said, simply, when he had finished.

She seemed remarkably perky considering what she had just heard.

"Have you got any suggestions?" he asked.

"As a matter of fact…" she began with a big smile.

"Yes?"

"Well, forgive me, but I think you need to see things through…er… *younger* eyes – if you don't mind me saying so."

"I don't mind at all," Sturgess said, smiling broadly at her. "But I'm not sure what you mean."

"Have you had any help?"

Sturgess spoke a little about the disinterest of the local police, and then told her about me, and about the research that I was doing with regard to a similar case.

"I'm sure you are doing a great job," Mandy said, when he had finished, trying her best to tread carefully. "And I'm sure that this Dr. Giles is too. But I'm thinking that you have both come into this…well, *old school*."

"Old school?"

"Right. I mean, if Sarah had been *old* – forty or fifty – then I'm sure you would have found out something by now. Have you even talked to anyone under thirty?"

"Actually, there were a number of young people that I interviewed at the chalet…."

"Where do they usually go on the weekends?" Mandy interrupted.

"What do you mean?" Sturgess asked defensively. "They are working at a ski chalet in the heart of the most beautiful, peaceful…."

Mandy burst out laughing.

"What's the matter?" Sturgess asked, more embarrassed than irritated.

"Have you *ever* been young?" Mandy asked, still laughing, but not pausing for an answer. "*Peaceful?* Since when has anyone under thirty wanted a *peaceful* existence? I'll bet you didn't even ask where they lived?"

"I guess I assumed that there was some sort of arrangement."

"With the cost of things around here? Even a discounted deal isn't going to help a busboy survive."

"Well, I survive," Sturgess argued. "And the groups of girls that come through all do."

"These girls are all sponsored – or maybe it's a special vacation. Only the rich and the, forgive me, *elderly* can do that."

"But I'm pretty sure that Sarah was a part of one of those privileged groups," Sturgess said, feeling a little more justified in his methods."

"That may be," Mandy reasoned, "but that group has been and gone. If you want to find out anything about her from the people that are left – *the young people* – then you need to find out where *the young people* stay."

"And you know that?"

"You never asked me where *I'm* staying."

"I assumed…," Sturgess began before realizing the error of his way. Smiling broadly, he began again. "*Where* are you staying?"

"Funny you should ask," Mandy said, smiling smugly in a manner that quite won over Sturgess for life. "I'm staying at a hostel out Fitchburg/Leominster way. And… *where* are *you* staying?"

"I'm at the inn – with the old people," Sturgess laughed. "But I drove in from that area. Isn't it a long commute?"

"For *old people*," Mandy smiled. "Seriously, Boston isn't really *that* far from here."

"And you think that other young people from Middlemore – say from the chalet – might be living out that way?"

"I know it for a fact. I've met some of them."

"And you found the same accommodation? Isn't that a little coincidental?"

"Think young!" Mandy shouted in mock anger. "I came here. It took me about thirty seconds to realize that I couldn't afford to stay here in town – wouldn't want to anyway."

Sturgess looked surprised.

"Yes, I know, it's beautiful and all that," Mandy continued. "But like every other person under thirty that must have landed here, I saw right away that, unless you were going to be on the slopes for every single waking hour, you'd be bored to death. So I headed into the more populated regions."

"And you happened onto the hostel?"

"You're getting ahead of yourself old man," Mandy joked. "I wanted to see people – people within twenty years of my age. I hit the clubs. I met the people. Someone knows someone knows someone who works in Middlemore. I found out where they were staying and *voila*."

"I haven't felt this stupid in a long time," Sturgess conceded.

"We all need to feel stupid once in a while," Mandy said cheerily.

"So, have you discovered anything?"

"Well, I think that I have played all of my cards, and shown you the extent of my detective skills," Mandy said. "So I guess that's where I start feeling stupid. I thought that maybe, if I came out here, and just went where she might have gone, I might find someone who knew her. I haven't had any success at all, though. Maybe this is where the *real* detective comes into play."

"Maybe *old school* can help us out now that you've got us back on track," Sturgess acknowledged, "but there is no doubt in my mind who is the *real* detective – and it's not me. Do you think maybe we could hang out tonight? I'll keep my distance. No one will need to know that you are with *an old guy*."

Mandy laughed.

"I'm sorry," she said. "You've taken quite a beating from me. Personally, old guy or not, I think you're adorable. I'd be thrilled to have you escort me."

By now, Sturgess had been totally disarmed. Making plans for the evening with Mandy made him feel twenty again. This was, indeed, the best day of his life.

The ride towards the cities, with Mandy at the wheel, was much shorter than Sturgess remembered. Of course, in that relatively short span of time, on the treacherous roads, his life flashed before his eyes at least a dozen times. She offered friendly chatter along the route, but Sturgess was not anxious to say much – lest it took her mind off of the road. She detected his apprehension half way along, smiled to herself, and made a conscious effort to eliminate some of the more terrifying moves. He didn't seem to notice, and she half expected him to kiss the ground once they came to a halt at the club.

"What am I looking for?" she asked.

She had offered the same question when they had first begun to make their plans, but Sturgess had only told her not to focus on Sarah. He said that she was probably right in assuming that no one in her circle really knew her. If he was right in his deductions, Sarah had probably kept close to the group with which she had arrived, and had been pretty inaccessible to any of the more permanent residents. Nonetheless, he had hopes from what she had told him. Her job was simply to take him to the liveliest spot that she knew – the spot with the greatest number of pretty girls – and to ignore him beyond that. He expected to stay until closing, but she was free to leave whenever she wanted. There were quite a few motels in the area, and he figured to stay at one of them. If the club that she chose seemed like it was having a slow night, and she had an idea of somewhere where there might be more action, only then should she speak to him. He could always make his way back to one of the motels if somewhere else was a better location. This latter contingency, however, was not going to be necessary, as from all appearances, the first stop was the best option.

As Mandy went towards the action, Sturgess instinctively headed to a corner where he would be least conspicuous. It was not too hard here. Unlike some of the other clubs in which he had found himself, this club did not cater exclusively to the young. The bar was dotted with what Mandy referred to as *old people* – mostly men, probably hoping for some leftovers once the young men had finished their prowl. Sturgess did not look out of place there, and he found himself a good spot from which he could survey the dance floor. He sipped his scotch slowly. This was not an occasion for trying to put himself in the mindset of the patrons of the establishment. He needed to be alert in order to act at a moment's notice. This might not be the night, but *something* was going to happen here. *He knew it.* So he sipped slowly on his drink. And he watched.

Sturgess' eyes remained focused on the dance floor – except when he took the time to question his waitress. The employees of such establishments had always been a good lead for Sturgess. This time, however, he didn't probe. He gathered a general sense about the crowd and the typical evenings. The specifics of his search, however, were not mentioned. Nor had he mentioned them to Mandy. This was not an occasion for gathering leads. Answers might actually get in the way at this point. Sturgess did not want to know anything beyond what Mandy had told him. He would allow his mind to drift, a little, but he would be ready to strike when needed. *Float like a butterfly; sting like a bee.* He watched Mandy in her element. She sat at a table of about seven or eight, drinking ice water. She took turns dancing with the young men at the table, gliding across the dance floor like she was skating on ice. Other men, whom she apparently did not know, approached her – drawn, no doubt, by her enchanting movements. Sturgess was impressed by the way that she politely declined outsiders. *Those in her group,* he thought, *must have worked hard to win her confidence.* He watched her as if she were actually his date. It made for a pleasant evening. It felt nothing like a stakeout.

Shortly after midnight, Mandy and her crowd rose from the table. She glanced at Sturgess, not sending any hidden message, simply letting him know that she was calling it a night. He detected an appeal in her eyes, though. She no doubt wanted some sort of confirmation that she had done well, and that he was still optimistic about the possibilities of leads. Sturgess merely nodded, simply conveying that it was fine for her to leave, and that he was comfortable on his own. The club was becoming livelier.

It was exactly what Sturgess had hoped it would be at this time of night. There were no guarantees – he knew that – but he felt good about what had unfolded as a result of his contact with Mandy.

The dance floor was packed. Sturgess wondered how they even managed to move. Still, he could see the appeal. Body pressed against body. The heat was palpable. Sweat glistened on the young flesh. The music roared, yet was only the incidental background to the sensuous gathering. The ritual was timeless, primeval. Sturgess himself was stirred as he watched from the sidelines. Most of the other men of his age had left their stools, and had edged towards the dance floor – drinks in one hand, swaying easily with the rhythm. They smacked their lips, with whetted appetite, as they gazed at the feast before them. They cursed the gods of time, who had made them unfit, both in body and mind, to partake in the festival.

Sturgess had almost slipped into the ceremonial trance that had fallen upon the room when his eyes caught a vision more appealing than the nubile young women who graced the room. A solitary man, rather homely by conventional standards, had moved himself into the center of the dancers in exactly the same manner that Sturgess had pictured that he might – though Sturgess had never seen this man before. But Sturgess needed no confirmation. He was, in fact, glad that Mandy – the only one he knew who could confirm this finding – had opted for an early night. Sturgess raised himself majestically from his stool. He then took his first steps in the direction of Leonardo Mascagni.

# III

## THE INTERVIEW WITH LEONARDO MASCAGNI AS RELATED TO DR. NOAH GILES BY DETECTIVE JOHN STURGESS

I awaited Detective Sturgess's description of his meeting with Leonardo Mascagni with great anticipation. He seemed a little flustered when I first saw him, but was quite willing to tell me about his encounter. He spoke in measured terms, much like one would expect from someone in his profession, and he trimmed the profanities from his account – which, according to him, surely halved the length of his narrative.

"It was surprisingly easily to gain an interview with Mr. Mascagni," he said. "Although he has a gift for keeping much of his dark business (whatever that might involve) underground, he has an affinity for the limelight, and an ego that makes him believe that he can impress those around him without compromising his own secret activities. While this is not entirely true, it is, sadly, true enough from a legal standpoint."

"Nonetheless, I for one was not impressed. My own experience as a detective has brought me into contact with more psychopaths than I would like to count. All of them believe that they are above the law, and are firmly convinced that they can charm their way out of – or into – any situation. And, although I do not count myself among the number that can be easily charmed by the likes of them, I concede that they are successful enough among the general populace, and to my own shame – and despite my experience – occasionally with me."

Sturgess paused, allowed his body to emit an exaggerated shudder, and then continued with his report.

"Leo did not fool me for a minute. It is true that my opinion of him was already prejudiced before I saw him on the dance floor. Watching him ooze around the room, however, was a sickening experience that told me all that I needed to know about him. Although not, by any stretch of the imagination, an appealing man, many of the beautiful women at the club were drawn to him. His dancing skills were the first point of attraction. A straight male dancing partner with an advanced ability to dance is a rarity in a place like that. There was a rush on his attention for that alone"

"My initial approach was greeted with the disdain that such creatures greet any male contact in a situation where beautiful women are present. Nonetheless, my age worked in my favor. And he felt even less threatened when he discovered I was a cop. I don't doubt that he has flirted with the law all of his life – aware of his own acts, but firmly convinced that the legal system employs no one clever enough to convict him of his crimes. The opportunity to taunt a detective on his trail was too much for him resist. I wondered, initially, if my presence might cause him some fear, and force him into hiding. That might have been the case had he noticed me before I noticed him, but with all of my cards laid on the table, and his freedom still intact, he decided to play a different game. Besides, it would have been difficult on him to be forced to flee. He had established himself in the region, and there were too many attractions for him there simply to leave. His employment may have had some roots there as well, and leaving might have caused some unwanted complications. I wondered that Mandy had not encountered him by now since he would likely, indeed, inevitably – considering where I found him – haunt many of the same locations where she and other young women might be drawn. It is remarkably fortunate that their paths didn't cross. The only explanation that I can offer is that Mandy, while clearly young and attractive, is nonetheless quite modest in her behavior, and does not like to remain in places once the action becomes hot and heavy – precisely the point when the likes of Leo arrive. Still, given a little time, I fear that their paths would have undoubtedly crossed, with possible dire consequences. Leo, unlike Mandy, only wanted the spotlight, and felt that he could control any fallout from making himself so public. I believe that he agreed to meet me, and kept his appointment, solely on the belief that he was so intellectually superior to me as to make me give up on my case against him altogether. To a certain extent, he was correct in his assumption."

Sturgess's demeanor changed drastically when he recalled Leo's own words

"'Yes,' he finally admitted with a sneer on his face, 'I remember Sarah well. She was a great....'"

"I interrupted him before he could spit out the vile word that was on his lips. I had trouble enough dealing with what had happened to Sarah. I was not willing to let him defile her memory so blatantly. In the beginning, he was reluctant to tell me too much about the relationship. He admitted that he had been at the same clubs that she had frequented, and of course, could not resist bragging about several relationships that he had had with women that he had met in those clubs. When pressed, however, he realized that it would be futile to deny knowing her after admitting to everything else that I had asked. His confidence grew, too, in the realization that, despite what I knew, I had no case. As Sarah's boyfriend, statistics made him a prime suspect. But there was nothing else in the case against him, except my gut – and that was not admissible in court."

"His mouth curled into an arrogant sneer when he slandered Sarah. I tried not to show any expression. I knew that he was trying to provoke a reaction. Either I was unsuccessful at maintaining my poker face, or he simply guessed how he was making me feel. His laugh sounded nervous, but he used it freely to flaunt his control of the situation."

"His words word meant to provoke me. He said things like 'Women are naturally stupid. They believe anything. Sarah would do anything I told her to do – right to the end. I mean, she wasn't any more stupid than any other woman, was she? I liked her – in a way. Too bad about her. Do you have any suspects?'"

"It was frustrating – listening to his misogynistic rants," Sturgess continued. "He was playing with me. His words were loaded, but they were no help to me. I already knew that Leo hated women. I knew, too, sadly, that Sarah would have done anything that Leo wanted *right to the end*. The phrase, I knew, was a little ironic. Its impact was underscored by Leo's question about suspects. He knew that I wouldn't have chased him across the continent if I had any other suspect. He knew that there were no other suspects. My goal was simply to let him talk about the murder – hypothetically. If he were bold enough to paint an accurate picture, he might trip and hang himself. But he was skillful enough to dance around the edges of anything clearly incriminating."

"When I mentioned the park where Sarah's body was found, Leo's eyes lit up. 'There was a park there?' he asked, acting surprised and laughing. 'Sorry, I didn't notice. I'm more of an *indoor* person. I was much more interested in what was going on inside Sarah's apartment than outside – if you know what I mean.'"

"I knew what he meant, and I was not impressed. Sarah or Mandy or any other attractive girl that might be found in that apartment – it didn't make any difference to him. Mandy had told me about his advances, so I decided to lead him down a different track, and asked him if maybe his interest in Sarah's roommate made him want to get Sarah out of the way."

"The question did catch him off guard. He looked surprised, at first. Then, as if he were slowly digesting the implications of such a question, a smile of triumph crossed his lips. I knew what he was thinking. He was wondering how anyone could be so stupid as I was showing myself to be by asking such a question. In a normal mind, my question might have raised a red flag. In the psychopathic mind, however, I knew that something else was happening. I knew that his enormous ego was basking in idea of how much more superior he was than I. He was no doubt chiding himself for giving me more credit than I deserved, and simultaneously forgiving himself for making such a miscalculation considering the extent of his presumed superiority.

"The condescending sneer returned, and he began is sarcastic little dialogue, saying 'it was necessary to get rid of Sarah because it would have been *so hard* for me to have taken her slut of a roommate with Sarah around. And *what if Sarah found out*? Maybe she would have *shouted* at me!'"

"Leo ended his sarcastic little monologue with a peal of laughter. I was unnerved, not by the tack he had taken, but by that nervous laugh. It just sounded wrong. The contradiction of that uneasy noise escaping his lips, at a moment when he was confidently displaying his superiority, was unnatural to the extreme. I played along, though, desperately hoping for him to provide me with just one opening."

"I asked him if he was confessing to the crime. 'I am confessing to your great ignorance,' he shot back. 'Sarah suited my taste for the moment, but there were many more – before and since. Mandy wanted me, and I wouldn't have her. Oh, I might have taken her, too, had the mood struck, but I had more than enough going on. You need to know that, not only could I have had Mandy, I could have had her with Sarah's blessing. If I wanted, I could have had then both at the same time, and dumped them both the next morning. And what could they have done about that? Maybe they could have tried to drown me in their tears!'"

"Again, Leo seemed to have amused himself disproportionately to anything that his words might have even suggested. The eerie laughter again echoed in my ears. But I was able to shut him up by noting that he seemed to have remembered Mandy's name – even though he had trouble even recalling Sarah's name."

"Leo's face grew grim when I said that. I had struck a blow, not to his defense, but to his ego – which was much more important to him. Despite the abnormally high number of female conquests that could likely be attributed to the hideous creature, the number in his head was undoubtedly significantly higher. Over a period of months, to have remembered the name of one woman, with whom he had admitted having no relationship, was totally contrary to the image that he tried to portray. It was in his defense of image that I hoped to catch him for the crime, which I suspected was simply a matter of business for him."

"He tried to compose himself. 'Was that her name?' he asked, as if surprised at his own memory. 'It was really just a guess. I seem to remember meeting other whores with the same name. I guess I subconsciously made the association. What of it? Do you think that, because I accidentally remembered the roommate's name, I killed the girl? I have no feeling for either of them. If you are looking for a crime of passion, you are looking at the wrong person. I save all of my passion for the bedroom, and it's gone by the time I close the door behind me. You are looking at things backwards. If anything, it is they who would want to kill me because they couldn't have me.'"

"I smiled, and simply asked: So, you are saying that you killed Sarah in self-defense?"

"Leo's patience was wearing out. On the one hand, my contention that I was looking at a crime of passion fed into his defense – since that clearly was not the case. On the other hand, it was insulting to him to think that I believed that he had resorted to such a crime over a girl who was nothing more than an assignment to him. Despite his dispassion over the crime that I was convinced that he committed, his passions ran high in just about everything that had to do with him. In his own mind, he was the ultimate savior and the ultimate victim. He could easily laugh over the injuries that he inflicted, but he would pour tears of self-pity when he felt the slightest twinge of injustice. My line of questioning suggested that I thought that he was inferior – the sort to suffer a broken heart at the hands of a mere girl. It is, of course, not unusual for these sorts to act violently over a woman who caused them humiliation. And, in erasing the humiliation from their minds, there is a tendency to erase the memory of their own violence. But it is inconceivable to them that their hearts could be broken by any being that is beneath them – and that includes pretty much the entire population. The suggestion that he might act on such an imagined slight inflicted more injury on Leo than any physical assault that he could imagine. Thus he began his self-defense, providing me with more of the details around the murder than I expected, but still not enough for me to hope to bring this sick joke of creation to any justice."

Sturgess leaned back in his chair, exhausted by the final words of his diatribe. It was hard to read the look on his face. I thought, perhaps, he had exhausted his anger over Leo, and might be wondering if he had shared too much of his professional investigation with a civilian.

Although I was probably just as keen as Detective Sturgess to see Leonardo Mascagni brought to justice, details uncovered about the society to which Leo claimed to work were much more relevant to my search for Derra than were the details of Leo's alleged crime. So when my conversation with Sturgess resumed later that day, I was not displeased when he directed the conversation away from the murder investigation, and towards *the Society of Diana*.

Leo apparently called it a charitable organization that provided less fortunate women with scholarships, so that they could find opportunities that they might not otherwise find. He claimed that Sarah *was* his business, along with several others. It was just a follow-up. She had skipped out on her scholarship, and they wanted to know why.

Sturgess resumed his narrative.

"He told me he liked to work quickly, but that there was a certain *tenderness* that kept him there a little longer.    I knew that Leo had never had a tender moment in his life – especially in so far as such a moment might relate to another human being's needs. I suspect he prolonged the relationship because he was particularly proud of his conquest. If there were no one to whom he could brag, there were plenty who would watch him parade around with his trophy in tow. There may well have been some of that envy that he so coveted, but there was likely a great deal of bewilderment, disgust even, from those who saw this unlikely couple. Leo's ego, however, would not even have conceived of this alternative reaction. I asked him how this Society of Diana felt about him mixing business with pleasure."

"'I wouldn't know – since I never told them,' he gloated. 'I was asked to find out if there were some particular reason why she ran out on her scholarship and I found out.'"

"When I asked him what he found out, he sneered, and said 'nothing.' And when I asked him if he was paid well for 'nothing,' he laughed and told me that he was paid very well to find out nothing, because if he found out nothing, there was nothing to find out."

"I pressed him on the Society of Diana. I doubted he knew much about them, but believed that if he knew anything at all, he would want to impress me with his knowledge, and how invaluable his services to them were. He told me that he had a reputation for getting thing done, for finding answers. He insisted that they helped young girls with scholarships, and that sometimes need answers when someone leaves, or that they sometimes needed him to watch over someone – to keep them safe."

I had listened to the account impassively to this point, but those last words caught my attention. Sturgess noticed my reaction right away – anticipating it I'm sure. The relationship that Leo had with Derra was nothing like the one he had with Sarah, and seemed to fall logically into the category of being watched over. This gave me hope. Sturgess had no doubt reacted the same way when he heard the words from Leo, and he brought Derra into the discussion, though not by name.

"The cop in me came to the forefront," Sturgess confessed. "Oddly, Leo was less forthcoming with me about Derra – he surely knew I meant Derra – than he was about the girl that I was suggesting that he had murdered. I explained to him that this other girl was surely no student like Sarah, yet they had both traveled between the suburbs of Seattle and the town of Middlemore, Leo muttered that he wished he could help me with this particular coincidence. I leaned into his face, in full bad cop mode, and barked, *I don't believe in coincidences. I certainly don't believe in the number of coincidences that seem to involve you in this case.* Leo's response was measured, but emotion-packed. 'Then maybe you should back off until you find something you believe in!'"

"Leo's face distorted horribly as he spoke. If there had been any trace of doubt, that I was addressing Sarah's killer, it was totally removed in that moment. His eyes, which seemed to sparkle from a distance, were lifeless – despite the passion in his words. That same emptiness must have terrified his victims – for I was certain that there were many more than Sarah – in their last moments, as the realization of their fate overtook them. I must have at least flinched as his spat his words at me. I have faced all sorts of terrors in my career as a detective, but there is nothing more unsettling than a thinly veiled threat, spoken in cold passion, by a creature driven by spirits not of this world. I'm an empiricist in many ways, but no number of such experiences teaches me anything about the nature of the life force that sustains the likes of Leonardo Mascagni."

I was left, by Sturgess, to draw my own conclusions regarding the nature of the murder, and of the disappearance of Derra. Leo was employed, I had no doubt, by a group known as the Society of Diana. I had no idea of the real nature of their business, though the name suggested something dark to me. It was obvious that their interest was in young women, and to that extent, I thought that some truth must lie in Leo's assertion that the Society provided some sort of education for their recruits. Undoubtedly, it all tied into what Detective Sturgess and I had uncovered at Middlemore – where beautiful young women were regularly filtered through some, as-of-yet- unidentified process.

Leo had sought out Sarah at the Society's bidding. I might be inclined to reserve judgment on how complicit the Society was on the final result of this union had the crime appeared to be one of passion, but from what I could guess, the night of the murder was no different than any other night when Leo might have relented and taken Sarah dancing. Indeed, it was likely that he would have done so – with it being New Year's Eve and Leo having yet another opportunity to be center stage. Even on such an occasion, however, it would not be unusual for Leo to tell Sarah that he was leaving without her. This time, he may well have told her that he had business that needed attending. Of course, she may have been suspicious, but his promise to meet her again in the appointed spot would have helped to chase the jealousy from her mind. With him leaving, there was no reason for her to stay. There would be no sign of quarrel, and their parting would have been on amicable terms should anyone be witness to these things. He returned, as promised, maybe a little sooner – perhaps securing a place of hiding until she was where he wanted her. He then killed her in cold blood. I would bet the farm on this scenario.

I am even more certain that the woman that he met later that night was Derra. It follows that she would have accompanied him to the airport, and flown with him towards their ultimate destination in Middlemore. This connection eliminates the coincidence of situations, and is appealing to me for that reason. But there are difficulties with such a conclusion. In the first place, it assumes that Derra was Leo's willing companion in these travels. But she certainly did not seem to be physically compelled to go with him from what I saw. And it is unlikely that she would not have found occasion to escape had she felt the need – especially with airport security being as tight as it is these days. There could, too, have been an element of blackmail to ensure her silence, but that seems a stretch considering her timing. I saw her walk straight from my home to the awaiting car. The driver of that car was, no doubt, Leonardo Mascagni.

Assuming an association between the two of them, Derra's attested character suggests an uneven one. At first blush, it might seem that Derra was yet another wayward scholarship recipient, and that she, too, had fallen victim to Leo's charms – but had been successfully argued into returning to the fold. But this does not quite fit with what I know about Derra. Her level of education was already much higher than that of the general populace – whether that had been accomplished formally or informally. Leo would have admired the cool confidence with which she deflected the advances of the male population. Though it is true that just such a quality would have fueled his ardor, there is every reason to believe that he was either rebuffed in his passes, or more likely, that he showed uncharacteristic restraint, and made no move on her. The explanation, that he had no interest in her, can be dismissed out of hand. Very few men would have no interest in such a woman. At worst, she intimidated Leo – but that would only have made him more determined. My guess, taking into account my assumption that she was not just another student, is that she had some rank with the Society of Diana, and that he was under orders to stand his distance. His business with her may well have been what he described as *looking after people's interests.*

The whole Derra assumption is still problematic. Her involvement with a society that, by all appearances, condoned murder does not gel with the person I knew. Admittedly, the person of Derra essentially does not exist at all apart from my recollections, and I am clearly infatuated with the thought of her. Strong infatuations can certainly distort perspectives, and create blind spots in one's direct line of vision. Yet I pride myself on being a level man – a man who could report objectively from the gates of hell. The image of Derra has been indelibly impressed upon my consciousness. There is witness to her, too, in the person of Father Luke. He contradicted nothing that I had to say about Derra. He, too, as I reflect upon it, is caught up in the magic and the mystery of woman. *Was that as a participant of this whole intrigue, or was it simply as an admirer?* Arguments could be made either way, but there are no facts to make either conclusion valid. Of course, Derra herself might well be a victim, living or dead, of this society. Her letter to me suggested as much. My inclination, if I am permitted one, is that this is so. My hope rests in the fact that she was not killed along with Sarah, but simply returned to the hub of activity. Her current absence from that scene, however, diminishes that hope somewhat – though it does not extinguish it altogether.

etective Sturgess's final interview with Leonardo Mascagni was conducted in a motel room that he had secured for the night. We talked about it some days later. Where Leo had gone during the break in the interview, Sturgess did not know. Maybe Leo had found some lunch. In any case, the nature of their conversation changed dramatically at that point, and Sturgess told me that he strongly suspected that Leo had been in conversation with someone from the Society of Diana. Sturgess had wondered, at first, if Leo would even bother to return, and believed that he did so only because he was under some sort of instruction from the Society.

"Leo's first words after the break were more or less a confession," Sturgess told me. "Leo described the Society of Diana as a fascinating organization, not usually interested in recruiting the assistance of men – adding that, under normal circumstances, a woman would be adequate for an assignment like Sarah. At this point, however, the mask fell from his face, and he put it to me bluntly: 'But what if Sarah had been less rational in her response, and had threatened to expose the Society of Diana – *a society that thrives on its secrecy?*'"

"I took the bait," Sturgess said, "and put it to him with equal bluntness. *Then you would kill her*, I asserted. My words were not a ploy. Leo had, for some purpose that was beyond me, just provided me with the motive for killing Sarah."

"Leo insisted that the Society is non-violent, and would find the death of anyone – particularly a young woman that they had taken under their wing – repulsive. It could have no part in such an act, and would support the execution of justice on the perpetrator of such a crime – that is, as much as it could without compromising its secret mission."

"I switched tacks, and asked Leo about Derra," Sturgess continued.

"My request triggered a response beyond my wildest expectations. Throughout my interview with Leo, especially in the afternoon, I had watched him squirm, but nothing compared to his state once I introduced Derra's name. Sweat seemed to gush out of every pore. His shirt soaked in a matter of seconds. His face went beet red, and his breathing came in rapid, shallow gasps. I was actually afraid that he was about to suffer some sort of stroke. I poured him some water, and he drank it as if his life depended on it. Maybe it did. After a few minutes, he composed himself, and I repeated the request."

"He insisted that he had never heard that name before. It was laughable, and had my business at hand been more laughable, I am sure that I would have succumbed to at least a chuckle. Instead, I just stared at him incredulously for several minutes. Finally, once I was satisfied with his degree of discomfort, I spoke again. I noted that he had reacted rather strongly to a name that he have never heard. But he held firm, and insisted that his reaction was due to a pre-existing condition."

"It was only once I had convinced him that I had a witness that saw him with Derra, did he relent. He admitted that he had watched her, and told me that she was not a student, but insisted that he knew nothing more about her – that he was there to protect her. When I told him that I knew he had accompanied her here, he looked at me anxiously. He was not sure how I had managed to add that piece to my puzzle. In the end, he confessed to that too, but was quick to turn my awareness of this connection against me. His colorful language returned. He told me that this interview had done me more harm than it had done him, that I had opened doors that I should never have opened, that I had made serious enemies. After he had caught his breath, he glared at me ominously, and spoke in measured terms *Do not take this as a threat from me – take it as a threat from those who remain unseen. You have done damage to yourself – not me, as you had intended!*"

"After his self-delusional comments, Leonardo Mascagni stormed out of the motel room and away from my questions. He never returned to either."

**6**

Detective Sturgess told me that Leonardo Mascagni's body had shown up the day after he conducted that last interview. A garrote had made quick work of him, I was told, but his contorted face showed some of the horror of his last moments. Many would call this justice, but I have never reconciled myself to the idea of death – even with its vilest of victims. Sturgess said that whether or not Leo had talked himself out of believing that this would happen to him, he could see it coming from the moment that Leo returned for the second part of our interview. As Sturgess described it, instructions that the Society of Diana gave Leo (which must have been something to the effect of implicating himself and deflecting away from them) were clearly a prelude to eliminating the trail that he had ultimately provided to the Society. If there were any doubt in his mind as to his fate, it would have been eliminated once the connection was drawn from him to Derra. It was clear that, whatever her role in the Society of Diana, it was distinct from the role of the students that the Society was recruiting. Leo had provided an insight into one aspect of the Society's business, but there were other aspects (towards which he might have hinted) that could not be allowed to go further than Leo.

There were, of course, no clues as to who murdered Leonardo Mascagni. Whereas a victim like Sarah had a social sphere from which certain clues might be gathered, Leo was, for all of his sexual encounters, a solitary man who interested no one socially. Apart from observing him on the dance floor, and on the sidelines in the process of making another conquest, no one would have taken notice of him – especially out of context in conversation with a stranger. Such conversations may not even have happened, and even if they did, they would not likely point to anybody in particular – with or without a witness. There is some small consolation for Detective Sturgess in knowing that the man who had so deceived and murdered Sarah had met a similar fate. The forces behind Leo, however, remain at large.

The research that I have completed to date, along with the mysterious gatherings that have taken place so regularly at the George over the last several decades, may provide some crucial leads with regard to the Society of Diana. The extent of the power that the Society wields, however, will dictate how far such investigations will take me. My concern is that, should I uncover too much information, the empty threats that the ill-fated Leo Mascagni spat at Detective might hold some water for me.

Given my circumstance, and given that Detective Sturgess has solved the crime of Sarah's murder to the satisfaction of his Seattle office (– no leeway was given for any conspiracy theories), apart from sharing his information with me as it pertains to my own search, Sturgess's work in Middlemore is over. But, although Middlemore is clearly a hub of activity for the Society of Diana, I doubt that its leaders remain too near for any length of time. I hope to observe, with some caution, the next influx of young women that arrives at the George. As for the workings of the Society itself, I really don't where to begin. Sturgess respectfully requests that I not share the details of my interview with Leo Mascagni with the police at Middlemore at this time. Their disinterest in the case, combined with his concerns that they might be involved in any conspiracy that might be afoot, begs their consideration on this count. In any case, I hope to remain in close contact with Detective Sturgess in sorting out the circumstance surrounding the death of Leonard Mascagni.

# FROM THE MEMOIRS OF DR. NOAH GILES: MARCH THROUGH APRIL

**M**y life in Middlemore, though markedly different to my life back in the Pacific Northwest, is still comprised of a quirky collection of routines which, it seems, I must incorporate to give my existence some necessary meaning. Initially, I did resist the urge to fall into such patterns. I tried to look at my long overdue visit to New England as a vacation of sorts – wherein I was free to live and act as was dictated by the moment. And, for some things, that seemed to work. My research, and many other routines into which I had fallen, began haphazardly, as I was exploring the region. Yet, once I had found my bearings, it was impossible for me to resist the urge to seek an orderly lifestyle, and thus I adopted one rather quickly.

I find that six o'clock is the optimum time for arising to a full day's work. I take my time in showering and grooming, finding this to be the only reasonable means of awaking fully with some degree of energy. I utilize the complimentary continental breakfast provided by the George – finding the croissants and black coffee sufficient to take me to the noon hour. And, rain or shine, I incorporate a daily walk from the inn to the center of town, and to my ports of research. The morning exercise puts a glow on my cheek, but more importantly, provides me with valuable time of meditation. On a more practical level, too, it allowed me to dispose of the rental car – which had become unnecessary within the dimensions of my little world. I seldom leave my corner of the library between eight o'clock, when it opens, and noon. A pleasant addition to the library routine, too, is the increased company of Jessica Burke. I soon discovered (and much to my delight) that the forbidding aspect of that lovely demeanor was, in fact, mostly a matter of self-preservation. The woman beneath that mask is even more beautiful than the woman portrayed by that mask. We started to take lunch together so that we could discuss the morning's research. It is valuable time – both for my work and for the pleasure of her company.

The morning is, by far, my most productive time. The regular routine of consuming lunches, I must confess, makes me rather drowsy in the afternoon. I return to the library to add some observations to my morning's research as garnered from Jessica. Then, I make my way to the back offices where an old overstuffed couch awaits me, holding me between its arms for the better part of an hour, before releasing me to continue my research once again. Usually, I take the time allotted to this second stage of my day's research to head over to the Historical Society. It is not as fertile a center of material as it had initially promised to be. After the initial deluge of information that I had gathered from my research in the Historical Society, practical results were painstakingly slow to uncover. Still, there are useful discoveries from time to time, and I never feel the need to remove the Historical Society from my routine. Besides, it is located almost next door to a delightful café, which serves the most exquisite British-style afternoon tea. It is a light meal but rich, and on top of my continental breakfast and regular lunch, it is more than sufficient to last me through the remainder of the day.

I am quite content to relax at the inn by the end of the day – usually settling in front of the television and falling asleep sometime after ten. It is a peaceful enough means of settling into reverie, but I sorely miss being joined in my repose by Bubastes. Of course, whenever I feel discouraged in that way, I reflect on how much more I miss Derra, and on the great need to find out what has happened to her since that solitary cryptic letter. I suppose that that thought crosses my mind at least once every evening, and it is always sufficient to inspire me to awake to another day's routine. I keep myself fresh, too, by incorporating different routines from Friday to Sunday than I followed Monday through Thursday. Friday begins much the same as the other weekdays, but at lunch, in Jessica's absence, I allow myself to shift into weekend mode by consuming two pints of a local brew with my meal. That marks the end of useful research for the week, but the beginning of a time wherein I can simply immerse myself in the magic of the town.

I do not use the term *magic* lightly. I would never have guessed that such a limited amount of land, tucked away in rural Massachusetts, could harbor magic to such a high degree. It may well be argued that I delude myself into such a vision as the result of my research, and the intoxicating effects of my Friday beer. I would suggest, however, that that is more of a launching point. As Middlemore begrudgingly surrenders more and more of its secrets, the options, following that last sip of draught, multiply. Sometimes I am led to familiar structures, like the chalet, or even the inn. Sometimes I am led along snowy trails, or into secluded woodland locales. Sometimes I find myself with groups of people (even sharing another pint), and sometimes I find myself remarkably alone – yet in communion with something eternal. The common denominator is the magic. It carries me through Friday night, and into my complex of Saturday and Sunday routines.

I visit the shops on Saturday. There is no need, in Middlemore, to spend much time in the grocery store, as I am not preparing my own food. The trinket shops, however, are of endless fascination. Mixed in with the usual tourist pieces are genuine artifacts of the region. I have purchased some of these, but most are beyond my means. Nonetheless, each tells a story – not necessarily directly related to my research (indeed, seldom so), but always touching on the town's rich history. There are books, too, dating as far back as the first settlement, that I bring back to the inn with me in scores – providing me with enough Saturday night reading to last me until the next century. Sunday morning, of course, is church. Despite my misgivings about Father Luke, under his direction there is a consistent aura of worship in the services that somehow transcends the failings of those of us huddled together in that quaint structure. The walk to and from worship continues to charm me, as does the Sunday brunch that is served regularly at the George. I always gorge myself (being naturally frugal and wanting my dollar to stretch as far as possible), and usually find myself indisposed for most of Sunday afternoon – especially when I succumb to the temptation of supplementing my meal with a glass on an excellent local Pinot Noir that the inn served.

Sunday evening, too, is a mellow time. I usually spend it immersed in conversations that run the gambit from religion to politics. If no one else is around, Tom Monroe is always ready to engage on some issue. Before he left, John Sturgess, too, preferred to come around at that time to talk about anything that would take his mind off of the case. And, on very special occasions, Jessica Burke graces me with her presence, and we would speak on topics that we would never broach during our lunchtime conversations. A new face has begun to visit me regularly on these occasions, since Detective Sturgess returned to Seattle, and at his instigation.

Mandy Endicott is a very pleasant distraction for me. She identifies with my loss, and shares my hope that my friend had not met the same fate as her friend. Our discussions are not so much about the business of my search as they are a time of reminiscence. It is not, for either of us, about the amount of time spent with our friends, but of the disproportionate impact of that time on our lives. Mandy's stories are decidedly sadder than mine. My times with Derra were all good, and apart from the aura of mystery around her (which, I confess, caused me some consternation from the moment that we met), the recollections fortify me. Mandy, however, often becomes wistful as she recalls her last times with Sarah, while Sarah was under the auspices of the late Leonardo Mascagni. The feeling that she should have been more sensitive to Mandy's pain in that relationship is, of course, intensified by Sarah's tragic end. Yet there is nothing but fondness in her words about Sarah. Mandy is anxious to learn about Derra. Derra has become for her, in a way, a second chance with Sarah. I think that, knowing how we both had developed an unnaturally close attachment to our friends in remarkably short order, Mandy lives vicariously through me in my search. And, in many ways, we are already alike. Both of us have been transplanted from the same town on the West Coast to the same town on the East Coast. We have both, temporarily, given up one lifestyle for another, solely out of an overdeveloped sense of loyalty to friends – one that is dead and another that is hopelessly lost. Mandy works in Fitchburg and has, like me, given meaning to her displaced situation by incorporating a series of routines. Fortunately, for me, one of those routines happens to be her regular Sunday evening visits with me at the George.

For weeks, I felt like I was spinning my wheels in my search for Derra, but by mid-March (to shift metaphors), the floodgates opened. Detective Sturgess' report on Leo Mascagni, while focused on a particularly distasteful subject matter, had helped me to draw the various strands of my research together. Although I had never seen Leo Mascagni clearly enough to make a positive identification, I am certain that the horrible little man was, in fact, the man that I saw with Derra on two occasions. Leo Mascagni seems to have admitted as much – at least, that he was the one that drove the car that took Derra out of my life. Although I am distressed to learn of such a dark connection, I am relieved, too, to know that Derra held some sway over him by virtue of her position – that he was subject to her, and not the other way around. Of course, the suggestion that Derra is a person of some rank in this Society of Diana, is of itself, rather disturbing. I contend, however, on the basis of my knowledge of Derra, and the tone of her letter to me, that her position in the Society is not the result of any choice that she has made, and that she is likely as much a victim in all of this as was poor Sarah.

I can shed little light on the Society of Diana, as it exists, beyond what I deduced from Detective Sturgess' narrative. The girls passing through the George at select times of the year are clearly recruits – or initiates. This is certainly a unique group of initiates, however, as my observations at the time of the March visit confirm. This is, in fact, the second group of young women that I have seen at the George. If there is, indeed, any overlap from the first group, I cannot tell. (But, then, how could anyone notice – with such an unrelenting onslaught of beauties?) In the first instance, I had been content simply to observe (worship?) from afar. In the light of my conversation with Detective Sturgess, however, the urge to slink in the shadows to try to uncover some of the details of the activities of tis second group is overwhelming. I have nonetheless restrained myself at his request, which came I contacted him about pending ceremonies. He pointed out to me that, should I choose to spy on the visitors, I would not only be subjecting myself to grave danger, but I would likely be unsuccessful – considering all of the safeguards that the Society has put in place. He assured me, too, that when the time was right, professionals (possibly even including himself) would investigate these activities with a degree of thoroughness that I would only make impossible by tipping off the Society at this stage. It is a very unsatisfying argument, yet one that I cannot refute.

I suspect that the Society took its present form in the latter half of the twentieth century, probably in the early sixties – when their regular visits to the George were first recorded. (It is conceivable that they met elsewhere prior to that time – though logistics would have been rather difficult to assign to such a theory.) In any case, whenever and wherever the modern group was formed, it adopted an earlier tradition, dating back to the first settlements in Middlemore, which it claims as its own. Considering the number of girls that have passed through the George over the years (even allowing the possibility of repeat stays), I have to acknowledge that the Society of Diana is an impressive organization. It is not the numbers alone that speak to this (– there have been countless societies that could boast such numbers). It is these numbers in conjunction with the veil of secrecy that the Society has been able to maintain. The case of Leo Mascagni would suggest that the Society is willing to go to great lengths to preserve this secrecy, but even so, there has to have been a remarkably organized system in place to enforce less drastic, though apparently equally efficient, means of maintaining silence.

For what purpose the girls were recruited, I cannot say. I have some ideas, based on my historical research. Any links between past and present procedures that I could suggest would be dubious at best. My natural assumption (isolated from the work that I have done) is that the Society is akin to a church. Christian history is rife with secret societies, and many continue to exist. Perhaps some of these societies have been able to maintain their secrecy to the same degree. (It is a circular argument, though, since while I had never heard of any particular societies like this, such a level of secrecy would automatically imply that I would have never heard of them.) The particular dates when the groups would arrive at the George, however, suggest that the Society of Diana claims to reach much further back for its heritage than the first settlements in Middlemore. The first identifiable set of dates December 21st, March 21st, June 21st, and September 21st, clearly relate to the Summer and Winter Solstices, and the Spring and Autumn Equinoxes. I deduced the second set of dates from the first set, since they fall at the traditional mid-point between solstice and equinox as marked by festivals on the pagan calendar. The festival of the maiden goddess, or the daughter of the mother goddess, took place between the Winter Solstice and the Spring Equinox from January 31st through February 2nd. The festival of the virgin goddess, falling between April 30th and May 2nd, was a celebration of sexuality – a tradition passed on to us as a celebration of the May Queen. The fire festival of the mother goddess fell at the midway point between the Summer Solstice and the Autumn Equinox (July 31st through to August 2nd), and the autumn Feast of the Dead, falling at the midway point between the Autumn Equinox and the Winter Solstice (from October 31st through November 2nd) is familiar to us in Halloween traditions that we have adopted. Yet, having said this much, the specific implications are not readily apparent to me.

Although I am concerned that Derra likely held rank in the Society of Diana, it is not the Society's hierarchy that concerns me. If the upper echelons are (as it seems from Detective Sturgess' account) guilty of crimes that include murder, then that is for the likes of Detective Sturgess to solve. Derra, I am sure, is outside of all of that. Her role, I believe, could be better compared to that of the British monarchy: Parliament, under the leadership of the Prime Minister, holds the power, but the Queen, holds higher rank – even though her power is purely ceremonial. I do not believe that Derra sits as high as in this society as a queen might sit, but I am nonetheless convinced that she functions separately from them – perhaps like part of a priestly class. As such, then, it is the day-to-day (or season to season) functions of this society that concern me. I want to understand what motivates the initiates, and what purpose they serve once they were welcomed into the fold. Only then can I begin to guess what role Derra might play.

But there are pieces missing. I strain my thought processes terribly trying to understand what I have not yet uncovered. It is made harder by my personal circumstance. I miss my home and my garden. I miss my cat. So often, in my futile struggle to coordinate my research with the reality that has removed Derra from my world, I just want to go home and forget about the whole business. But, as much as I love my home and my garden, and my dear Bubastes, I realize that my true existence was an empty shell before Derra entered my world, and that I have to find out *something* – because I owe her that much. Yet, as I continue to be bombarded with information that opens countless doors of discovery, it grows much worse. It is like a jigsaw puzzle, but all the pieces are jet black, and I don't know how many pieces are missing, and the puzzle seems to extend endlessly. I do not know what piece to link to another. Even if my guesses are right, I cannot guess the significance of what I had forged. It feels like it would have been much better to give up in despair of ever making headway than to forge on in the false hope of doing so. I can offer no suggestions about the present day Society of Diana. I waver in my conviction that I will ever be able to do so.

I t is of the earlier traditions in the region of Middlemore that I can speak with some small degree of authority. A useful ally in my more productive research has been Jessica Burke. My research into the history of the Nipmuc Indians began with Jessica's suggestion at a lunch session that we had with Detective Sturgess. I confess, as the original inhabitants of the region around Middlemore, the Nipmuc Indians are a fascinating study. It was, however, at the conclusion of the first stage of their history that their story ties into the mysterious events that have marked Middlemore from the onset.

A true historian of the region would note that the land grant was first issued for Middlemore concurrent with the so-called *King Philip's War* (1675-6). This was a war between the colonists (who were hungry for land), and the native people throughout significant sections of New England (under the leadership of Metacom – also known as Philip). One result of this bloody war was the virtual extinction of the Nipmuc tribe. Those Nipmuc who had remained neutral were sent to English confinement camps. Once Philip was killed, retaliation resulted in the death of many of the Nipmuc who had survived the battles. Most of the remaining Nipmuc natives were dispersed. Some joined with the St. Francois Indians in the north, as allies with the French. Others scattered to areas in Pennsylvania, Ohio and New Jersey. Those who remained in New England, if not confined to reservations, were organized by the Puritans into *praying towns*.

The praying towns were an interesting phenomenon of seventeenth century New England – and not irrelevant to the study at hand. In these towns, natives were essentially transformed into "Red" Puritans, renouncing their own culture and adopting a Puritan lifestyle. Although the start of King Philip's War marked the demise of such towns, it is from such post war settlements that certain Nipmuc Indians came to Middlemore. In protest to the Puritan lifestyle (that had only been adopted as a life-saving measure), they joined with those from the group set free from the Salem Witch Trials who (likewise having no love for the Puritan lifestyle) had also made their way to Middlemore at the end of the seventeenth century. Both groups of Puritan renegades, though revolting against that culture, were nonetheless deeply indoctrinated in the Puritan teachings. That particular variety of fanaticism, along with the pagan leanings of both groups, blended into a potent, and somewhat dangerous, admixture.

The pagan preference was for fertility religions that the refugees from Salem brought with them. They were serious about their beliefs, and may well have brought practices from Salem that had inspired some of the original charges of witchcraft. The Native American religion brought a natural element that gave the spirituality an immediacy that it did not likely have in Salem. Spirituality was a much more fluid thing for the Nipmuc, and that was a valuable asset considering their change of circumstance. For them, there was no separation between the sacred and the ordinary. The fertility leanings of their partners from Salem fit well with the native concepts of human sexuality as a mirror of the masculine and feminine forces at work throughout nature. Such practice as the Nipmuc brought with them, too, reinforced the spiritual energy. The vision quest, for instance, was similar to the initiation ceremonies of the fertility cults. Indeed, the very emphasis on rituals, and the institution of a feast at the conclusion of each ritual, was a common element of all involved in this cultural rebellion. In the end, the emphases on spirituality and fertility and vision were at the core of this drive to shed the shackles of the Puritan world. And the energy that it harnessed was not merely an energy garnered from enmity, but from an understanding of its enemy that had been handed to them all on a silver platter.

The study of Puritans, I am sure, supplements the research that I have done, but is to an extent disproportionate to the needs it would serve. That is to say that I feel that there are only a few areas in which the Puritans impacted the cult at Middlemore, and that most of those were more negative influences. The very drive to reform the high church rituals of the Anglican Church of the seventeenth century made New England Puritanism a rather dry and colorless form of faith in comparison. Despite the high view of Scripture, and the spiritual possibilities that are always opened by such a view, the effect on many the Nipmuc, who were simply forced to accept these teachings, might well seem contrary to the rich spirituality with which they were raised in their native setting. Those who had been born into the strict culture strayed for want of excitement – to whatever degree this natural rebellion dictated. Yet that is not to dismiss altogether the spiritual power of the teachings that all in such a culture would have received by osmosis, if by no other means. The tendency of the cult in Middlemore (whether or not like the alleged witches at Salem I did not know) was not towards darker things, but rather towards a richer communion with the forces around them. It was a youth movement, however, and the central focus in their escape from repression, naturally enough, was on sexuality. Yet it was not a matter of blind abandonment. All had been subject to the Puritan emphasis on education. And although scholarship was dismissed in principle, in practice they could not wander far from the restraints of academic discipline. Their religion was not, and could not be, formed in a vacuum. It was based on elements common to Christianity, native religion, and known elements that worked contrary to both. If there was devil worship (and I was certain that there was not), it was because Christianity had taught them about the devil. If there were attempts to command nature in malevolent ways (a possibility under certain circumstances), it was because native religion had taught them what was undesirable in the world around them. No doubt, too, that the Puritans had filled their minds with the heresies of the ages, and that the logic of some of these heresies just happened to be conducive to some of their needs.

As far as I can tell, this tradition carried into modern times. It is difficult to gather a sense of its size – though clearly it fluctuated over the centuries. Having learned its lesson from the Salem Witch Trials, the group managed to keep its practice secret – though records of the ceremonies can be found. It is not surprising, however, that it is so easily assimilated by the Society of Diana – which seems to have the advantage of both ancient tradition and modern execution (in every sense of the word) on its side.

The ceremonies of the Middlemore cult (either no name was taken, or no name was revealed) had parallels throughout the history of fertility religions. Whether this was mostly instinctive or mostly learned, it was hard to tell. There were certainly elements of both. The gatherings were much like one might imagine any woodland gathering – or, at least, any such gathering as related to us through those in commune with nature. There would have been an aura of magic to the gatherings, with a requisite of both white and black spells as dictated by need. In assessing the cult on that basis, however, I am also aware that this group was originally formed because of a common bond of ill feelings against their society. This was not only carried over by those from Salem, but was intensified by the treatment that they had received at the hands of Salem authorities. The Nipmuc had even more complaints, having witnessed the decimation of their way of life. Yet they did not necessarily advocate a total break with their society. In much the same way that the Puritans abhorred the practices of the high church, yet preferred reform to separation, the Middlemore cult sought to infuse Christianity with spiritual and sensual dimensions that were sorely lacking in the culture around them.

The gatherings were comprised mainly of females, and although there must have been male members as well, little reference was made to the men. There was no indication that any significant number of women ever left the group, but new participants were sought out exclusively among the young women of the community. A priestess would have led these gatherings, and I suspected that there might have been a priest as well – or, at least, a consort. The position of priestess, however, while certainly an honor, was not much more than ceremonial. It was declared (by acclamation?) seasonally. Those girls marked both by having completed the initiation ceremonies, and by emitting an aura of sensuality, were eligible. But it was really the group dynamic that ruled. The focus of the ceremonies was always on the initiates. It was in the instruction of the initiates that spells were demonstrated, and that magic (to the degree that we can believe such tales) was performed. In this, the older adherents were much more powerful than the priestess of choice. The young initiates, the priestess, and her contemporaries, however, took center stage to the older, wiser members largely on the basis of their youth and their appeal. This was essentially a fertility cult – complete with worship of nature, and in particular, the fertile female body. Although the Nipmuc influence on this was significant, Nipmuc participation was short-lived. The Nipmuc tribe members (as with many tribes subsequent to King Philip's War) were not welcome members of white society. Whereas the fair skinned participants could blend with the town while it was awake, the Nipmuc initiates remained refugees until they ultimately died out. (There are interesting stories about their daylight activities, but I found no relevance in these tales to my own research.)

Having learned this much, it was strange for me to discover that there was any Christian dynamic to this group. On the one hand, it looked more like a coven than anything else – naked female bodies, magic ceremonies, and orgy-like feasts. There was a primitive sensuality to it all that was quite alien to any forms of Christianity that I have ever encountered – let alone that of Puritanism, or of the High Church Anglicanism that Puritanism sought to reform. It was only, however, as I looked beneath the symbolism that I discovered the link, and I must say, it enlightened my perspective on both Christianity and the cult of Middlemore.

In the first place, I believe that one must form a picture of the Puritanism of Salem, and of the alleged witchcraft that it sought to purge from amongst its settlement. To my mind, at least, there was an identification between the persecutors and the persecuted. Both conjured images of something terrifying though, admittedly, in different forms. That is to say, that it would be difficult to choose between the evil of a woodland gathering of the witches (as depicted by the prosecutors), and the evil in a courtroom that had gone wild with accusation. It was a repressed society, and repression is always released in one form or another. With a number of the accused witches, it was released in sensual ceremonies. With the judges, the release was more of an implosion, boiling over in the courtroom accusations. No matter how much malevolence was presumed to have been enacted by the witches, the judges cost that society much more in human lives. What was the common link between these apparent opposites? I believe it was, at the most basic level, sensuality. Christianity, on the whole, takes a realistic approach to the issue – celebrating and encouraging sensuality on the one hand, and providing warnings against deviations and excesses on the other. The Puritans demonized sensuality, and by so doing, opened the doors to demonic spirits in a society which, despite its emphasis on biblical learning and discipline, was a spiritual vacuum. The so-called witches, on the other hand, glorified sensuality and likewise opened the doors to a demonic element.

What both groups sought was to come to terms with the world around them. In rebellion against High Church Anglicanism, the Puritans had chosen to dispense with the ceremonial in an attempt to reach more directly into the revealed word of God. Those accused of witchcraft, however, had reacted to this absence of ceremony by going to extremes in that area – in fact, bypassing the word of God. The Christian world, however, to understand the symbolism in both the revealed word and in the world at large, needs strong elements of both scholarship and ceremony. My own belief is that the liturgy of High Anglicanism could be a good route into both, but that the Puritans probably had a good case against the Church of England. Historically, the popular culture of Christian nations has been a much richer medium for the necessary symbolism of the Christian faith. The Middlemore group was much more in line with this stream of consciousness than was the culture around it. In my mind, the obvious negative elements in their ritual simply mirrored the more subtle, positive elements that they sought to inject into their society. That said, however, I am inclined to believe that the appeal that gave this group such longevity was more sensual than spiritual.

*5*

Jessica Burke's heritage, combined with an inescapable sensual appeal, should have made her an obvious candidate for the Society of Diana, if there were, indeed, an effort to tie that society to the rooted traditions of Middlemore. Yet any overtures that may have been made were certainly restrained enough not to be readily apparent to her, or to me, on the basis of what she has told me. My thought on this is that, despite the Society's high regard for female intelligence, there are certain areas where such a level of intelligence might be seen as a liability. It made me wonder whether Sarah had not merely rejected the Society's propositions, but was actually fleeing from them because she had learned too much. There seems to be an inherent contradiction in that theory, but I am not quite sure where.

Although Jessica had been well aware of the Middlemore traditions dating back to the end of the seventeenth century, she has said very little about it, even while we conduct our research together. She told me, once I had drawn my own conclusions on our findings, that she didn't want to prejudice my opinion with her own thoughts – on which she has been fixed for some time. As might be expected, we share a common perspective in many areas. Our differences, however, are productive for both of us. Jessica, coming at things from a more secular perspective, finds my link between the group's rebellion to Puritanism and the Puritan rebellion to High Church Anglicanism to be quite a revelation. As far as she is concerned, it had been a loosely organized pagan rebellion against an oppressive society. Adding a Christian element to it all seems to tie it all nicely together for her. As for me, I was surprised to learn how sinister Jessica (a Nipmuc descendant) feels that the Nipmuc influence on the group had been, and indeed, by her estimation, continues to be long after the native element had been extinguished from the cult.

"You must remember the extent of the oppression that the Nipmuc, in particular, had suffered at the hands of Puritan society," she explained. "From the beginning, the white man's only objective was to rip them from the land. That was not just a matter of displacement. Our religion, our entire culture, was tied to the land. We were slaughtered wholesale, and those of us who survived were forced to adopt the Puritan beliefs with no room to preserve our own. On our own, there was little we could do about it. In conjunction with the white dissenters, however, we stood a chance.

"In one way, it must have been particularly distasteful for those who had escaped the praying towns to join forces with white people of any description. The whole focus of their hatred would have been on those who had stolen their land and decimated their numbers. On the other hand, if one group of white people could be used against another, it must have been seen as an opportunity beyond their wildest dreams. The Puritans were the common enemy, and so long as the Nipmuc brought something to the table, I can hardly think that the color of their skin would have been an issue for the Salem group."

"So, what exactly did the Nipmuc bring to the table?" I asked.

"Curses, mostly – plagues and famine and storms."

"So you don't buy my idea that theory that they just wanted to reform Puritan thinking?"

"Not for the Nipmuc," Jessica asserted. "But I like your suggestion that that was an underlying aspect of the Salem group. I think the Nipmuc may well have gone along with them in order to serve its purpose. But I think that this particular group of Nipmuc was unforgiving – not only of the white man's physical oppression, but of the white man's spiritual oppression."

"Do you think that malevolent pagans and misguided Christians could co-exist in one group?" I asked.

"I haven't thought much on it," Jessica shrugged. "Remember, while you thought that the group was entirely composed of misguided Christians, I thought it was composed entirely of malevolent pagans. The answer must lie somewhere in the middle. So, why not a mix? It answers a lot of questions."

"Yes, and raises a lot more."

"But it also explains to me why Nipmuc influence was felt after the

Nipmuc participants died out," Jessica countered. "There must have been some sort of rift – not enough have cast out the original members, but enough to maintain a wariness about adding any more. Remember, too, that for all of our research on the origins of this cult, the reason for their existence, once the Puritan influence was no longer a factor, is a mystery. If this group of misguided Christians essentially disbanded when there was nothing left to reform, what motivated the remaining few to keep the cult alive into modern times?"

"The Nipmuc?" I asked, not quite sure where she was headed.

Jessica laughed – amused, I presume, by my confusion. It broke the tension that was building as a result of this onslaught of seemingly random thoughts. It also had the added bonus, for me, of returning to my focus to the young woman who was speaking. She rarely gave way to such a broad smile, but on the occasions that she did, it was absolutely breathtaking. The mesmerizing effect that this had on me worked to her advantage. I stopped rebelling against her hypotheses, and started to listen as she opened new doors to this magical history.

"Well, as I see it," she began, "some of those Christians were a little more than misguided. They were probably seduced by the powers that they had awoken and were reluctant to give up their practice – even in the absence of a cause. The decline of Puritanism hardly affected the renegade Nipmuc. They had no home or point of identity. White men remained the common enemy. A small, organized group of white men (white *women* especially) that still wanted to fly in the face of white society would have been a better alliance than none."

"Yes, I see, but then what would prevent the two groups from reuniting?"

"That idea probably occurred to the white element, seeing as how the original bone of contention, Christian reform versus paganism, was no longer a factor," Jessica explained. "But these Nipmuc had had their fill of white people. They returned to their own native practices, with a heightened emphasis on the magical elements, and simply acted as consultants for the remnant of the Middlemore group as it suited their purposes."

"I'm amazed that you could have deduced so much so quickly as a result of our discussion," I offered.

"That *would* be something," Jessica replied, briefly flashing that elusive smile. "But these are not new ideas. I've been at this research a lot longer than you, and while your conclusions gave me some new perspectives, the core of my thoughts on the matter remains unchanged – especially once the Christian element of the group was removed. But it makes sense that the Christian influence, as you presented it, was not entirely removed. It adds to my argument of why the Nipmuc rebels would have rejected any sort of alliance with the group."

"And, perhaps why the group, even under its current patronage, might reject trying to add such a likely prospect as you to their number," I added.

"Perhaps," Jessica conceded. "But I see another factor there."

I waited silently for this new revelation. It came in the form of a name: *Mrs. MacDonald.*

*6*

The first hints of a New England spring revived my spirits which, to say the least, have fluctuated considerably since my arrival in Middlemore. I have escaped the endless season of rain in the Pacific Northwest (pleasantly interrupted, I must admit, by the Christmas snows) to land in a much brighter atmosphere, much more conducive to my daily walks. Yet I had grown in the opinion that this region would always remain cold enough to require the dawning of several layers of clothing – even when the blood pumps briskly when I am fresh from my walks. The momentary influx of warm weather, however, blown in by some congenial breeze, is a pleasant shock to the system. The town is suddenly alive with the rhythmic dripping of snow and of ice unable to survive the rays of a newly energized sun. And though the landscape maintains its white blanket, the inhabitants have shed their jackets, and the overly-enthused have even bared their arms and lower legs to *Sol Invictus*.

Where the ground is bare, the crocus (*krokos*) can be seen peeking out – testing the climate in anticipation of its full-scale assault on the countryside. Magically, many of the deciduous trees are suddenly speckled in spring buds. As enchanting as the winter season has been, under the influence of this climatic spell I begin to long for the new season. In a younger, more vibrant, man, I am sure that this condition would take the form of what is commonly known as *spring fever*, but I consider myself immune to such folly, and am simply trying to enjoy the sensation of this unnamed state to which I have succumbed. I was inspired, too, by the company of Jessica Burke. She wore white low-slung pants, and a matched top, which left a fair segment of midriff exposed. Her dark skin was perfectly accentuated by this combination as her straight black hair rested comfortably on her bare shoulders.

The introduction of Mrs. MacDonald's name into the conversation seemed rather anomalous. The woman had passed away long before I had ever heard of Middlemore, yet the impression (gathered in brief snippets from Jessica) was firmly fixed upon my mind. Mrs. MacDonald had lost Mr. MacDonald while she was still but a bride, and had struggled to educate herself and establish herself as a respected member of the community. As is often the case of one who endures so much hardship, and who lives a solitary life, Mrs. MacDonald grew old before her time – or, at least, no one could really quite remember her not being old. Her quiet life as the town librarian might well have passed unnoticed had it not been for the arrival of Jessica. Middlemore was small enough, and petty enough, to look for scandal where none existed, and the idea of an elderly single lady bringing a Native American baby into her household undoubtedly set tongues wagging. As a result, Mrs. MacDonald and Jessica developed a fierce attachment to each other – to the exclusion of all others. Mrs. MacDonald was always equipped with a friendly smile as she greeted patrons in the library, but she never reached socially beyond the boundaries of her work. As such, she was pretty much left alone. Such a congenial defense did not work for Jessica – who was already very attractive by in her early adolescence. The warning pouts (that I have described elsewhere) were apparently perfected at a young age.

The story of intrigue that Jessica had presented to me, of the Nipmuc and the members of the Middlemore group remaining at odds over the issue of Christianity, yet collaborating in their magic against a world that both rejected, held more appeal for me as an explanation of the exclusion of Jessica from the Society of Diana than the protection of one little old lady. Nonetheless, Jessica was adamant that her stepmother had been the main line of defense. Although a quiet woman, Mrs. MacDonald was a remarkably learned and wise woman – according to Jessica. The regular influx of such distinctive groups of young women as the Society filtered through town, did not escape many eyes, she reasoned. Her stepmother would be on this like no one else – and would likely go unnoticed in the process.

"Did she ever talk to you about the Society?" I asked Jessica.

"Not *per se*," she mused, "but she did make *allusions*."

"Like?"

"Well, she talked to me about continuing on with the library. She told me that I was smart and that this really was the place for me – not to be duped by any offers of scholarships. That seemed strange to me at the time. But it clearly seems to be one of the Society's recruiting tactics."

"Were you ever offered a scholarship?" I asked.

Jessica just shook her head. She was deep in thought and clearly didn't want to be disturbed. I decided to bide my time and wait for any pertinent recollections that might surface. It was, in a sense, like she was trying to channel her adopted mother. There had been a deep bond between them, and Jessica had shifted from a reasoning mode to a sensing mode, and was searching for a way to explain the latter. I, always being in favor of stretching the horizons of our reality, was hoping that she could somehow prove what she only felt. But I was skeptical. I had no doubt about the elevated communion between the two while Mrs. MacDonald lived, but I had no faith that it extended beyond the grave. Jessica was a remarkably perceptive young woman. If Mrs. MacDonald had relayed some cryptic message for her, then I was confident that Jessica would have deciphered it soon after it was delivered. I expressed as much to her.

"I guess that's probably true," she conceded, "but, in light of all that we have uncovered in the last little while – both old history and new events – I was hoping that something might just fall into place. I've been in a sort of prayer to my mother that she might show me what I am missing."

"But does it matter whether she actually protected you from the Society or whether the Society simply wanted no part of you – other than for personal reasons?" I asked.

"If she did protect me, then she knew something that we don't know," Jessica asserted. "I don't doubt that she protected me. The questions for me are how did she protect me, what did she know, and why didn't she tell me."

There was determination in her eyes. Although we dropped the discussion of Mrs. MacDonald, I had no doubt that she would reappear before our investigations were complete. The questions that Jessica posed would keep her busy, and I knew that she would find answers if, indeed, there were answers to be found. For my part, however, I took the low road. I did not believe that the late librarian would speak to Jessica from the afterlife, and I felt that any leads that Jessica might uncover would essentially be superfluous. Nonetheless, as always, I am prepared to be pleasantly surprised.

Although my stories about Father Luke intrigued her, Jessica Burke refused to set foot in a Christian church. It was, she said, out of respect for her ancestors, who had suffered so brutally at Christian hands. She had no personal animosity towards modern day Christians, she told me. Mrs. MacDonald, a nominal church member, had instilled Christian values in her, and Jessica has no problem living and interacting in a Christian climate – my company included. She simply draws the line at formal Christian worship, citing it as a particular sore spot for her people. Mandy Endicott, on the other hand, actually made the effort join me at church one Sunday, and that sparked off a series of reactions that promised to be of some assistance as we attempted to unravel the mystery of the Society of Diana.

I had spoken to Mandy about my Sunday routine, but I never expected to see her in the lobby of the George, at the appointed hour, waiting to accompany me to church. My time of meditation was greatly enhanced as she walked silently at my side. The warm spells are more frequent now, and the soothing touches of spring are lingering in the air. I felt energized (if not twenty years younger) as I mixed stolen glances at her youthful profile with a broader, more consuming, focus on the awakening landscape. Some moments seem just perfect. This was one of them. It did not take my mind completely off of Derra, but when I did think of her, it pushed those perfect moments that I was sharing with Mandy to the forefront. It was this moment in time, however, in wordless prayer, with both Mandy and God at my side, that I would have extended endlessly were it in my power. Such moments, I believe, are evidence of both the shattered image of God in our lives and of the grace that holds it together. We so often despair of Truth and Goodness, yet I think that we can sometimes taste just a little of such things amidst the chaos of this world. That should be the missionary goal of our Christian advocates.

Father Luke was, as always, at the door of the church to greet me. I almost think that he waited for me there – though to what purpose I cannot say. His manner with me was always of the fawning sort. If I happened to try to slip by him as he was greeting another parishioner, he would interrupt his conversation to grab my hand, or to lean forward and smile, and wave briefly if I had moved beyond his reach. Were he so careful with all that passed his way, I would probably not have noticed. Certainly, he had a good game face for everyone that came to worship under his direction. But he only ever seemed to make the extra effort to ingratiate himself when there was something to be gained. The wealthiest and most prominent parishioners were easily spotted by the interest that Father Luke showed in them. I fit into none of the classes that should reasonably have garnered his attention. Nonetheless, I could neither come nor leave without subjecting myself to the excessive good graces of this curious man.

Arriving at the church in the company of Mandy clearly heightened the degree to which I gained Father Luke's attention. He flattered her shamelessly once I had made the introductions – though he was also careful to include me in his praises. He made a special point of asking us to speak with him after the service. And, again, as the procession marched down the aisle to open the service, he smiled and nodded at us as if we were visiting dignitaries. The service itself was, as always, a model of worship. It perplexed me that this bizarre man could perform his function so flawlessly week after week. He only had superficial interest in most of the congregation as far as I could tell, and that interest did not extend much deeper to those of us that had his attention. Although he had run a barrage of questions past Mandy when he met her upon her arrival, I could detect no real interest in the answers that she was providing – though his smile remained fixed. At best, he was an awkward man to engage in conversation, but his gestures never conveyed that fact to those who watched at a distance.

Father Luke's meeting with us after the service was, as I had feared, to secure us to dine with him. This had been his tactic when Detective Sturgess had accompanied me to worship – although what Father Luke stood to gain, either with the detective, or with Mandy, I could not tell. I was almost tempted to refuse the lunch invitation on behalf of both Mandy and myself. My two previous meals with Father Luke had been curious events serving only to create an even more confused image of the rector in my mind. I doubted that a third meal would serve to convince me that either the public or shared private persona of Father Luke was the genuine article, and I strongly suspected it would simply add to my perplexity. Mandy, however, accepted before I had the opportunity to rescue us from the quandary that I was mulling. My stomach growled in protest – not so much in dissatisfaction of the anticipated fare, but rather in despair of the lost opportunity to share the George's Sunday brunch with my lovely guest. I had been eagerly awaiting the feast since I first saw her that day. Of course, I should have known that we would be diverted. In fact, there could not have been much doubt in my mind about where we would be dining once Father Luke requested our little post-service meeting. Still, it was not until Mandy confirmed our presence that the reality hit me.

There were answers, I was sure, to be found at the heart of Father Luke. The problem, however, from my perspective, was how to find his heart. The man is a walking contradiction. He can orchestrate a worship service like a maestro, yet he seems to have no soul – or, at least, not one of any substance. He is fluent in the social graces, yet his disinterest in human nature borders on the sociopathic. His smile seldom leaveshis face, yet he is not a man who would strike a person as being particularly happy. The conflict, perhaps not rare in the human race, is all the more striking because of his profession. He might have been a good fit working as one of the businessmen to whom he was constantly ingratiating himself, but it seems almost a mockery to have him designated as their spiritual leader. I, for one, am not suited to any effort to expose the man. Besides, even if I had a solid complaint, I know how the Episcopal system works. So long as the rector has secured a compliant vestry, he is secure from assaults both below him and above him. It is a good idea for a good rector. I am not so certain, however, that the system is a good idea for those rectors inclined to indiscretions. In any case, I am sure that *Father Luke* thinks that the invulnerability of his position is a good idea.

Father Luke walked us to the rectory, and ushered us to the table at which I had twice dined. The sexton was there this time, and was soon busy ferrying back and forth from the kitchen to the dining table. I had seen the sexton at church services, though I had never actually met him. He was a strange looking little fellow, though nothing about him seemed disagreeable or incompliant. He probably did not quite measure five and a half feet. His dark hair was tightly curled. He wore eyeglasses that were obviously equipped with very powerful lenses, bulging his eyes out of proportion. He had a game leg that he was forced to drag a little, and that action had distinctively twisted his body over the years. (I am guessing that he was a man of around fifty years.) His subservient reactions to Father Luke's sharp commands, though pathetic at one level, were rather comical to behold. I could not help but thinking (and Mandy concurred with this image in later discussion) of Dr. Frankenstein in the company of his faithful servant Igor. Mercifully, there was no thunder at work outside, or I might have lost it altogether. Even so, had I known that Mandy was thinking the same thing, I am certain that I would have dug myself a serious hole.

Not surprisingly, the first thing that Igor brought to us (Father Luke had not deemed an introduction necessary, so I had mentally dubbed the sexton with this epithet) was the wine. I almost wanted to warn Mandy about it, but decided that it was probably best to let Father Luke orchestrate the visit around his own agenda – since I had none. I am not altogether certain that he did not drug our portions. I am unfamiliar with drugging effects, but the wine quickly produced a sensation that I suspected was not unlike the opium or laudanum sensation that is described so frequently in nineteenth century English novels. Indeed, my mind transformed the dining room into an opium den of sorts. The air itself seemed smoky, though there was nothing in place that should have caused this effect. It was, however, decidedly dim – especially considering the brightness of the day that existed beyond the walls of the rectory.

Although I was familiar with the effect of the wine from my previous visits, this was the first time that I had shared the experience in the presence of a beautiful young woman. There was a definite difference. An aura of sensuality encompassed the room. Although I had not been blind to appeal of Mandy, until now I had admired her from a more aesthetic perspective. That is, I found her pleasing to the eye, and I enjoyed her company – not solely because of her looks, but because of the way her inner beauty was so neatly complemented by what was on the outside. I had no irrepressible yearnings for her, nor did I waste time with fruitless fantasies about her. To my shame, I must admit that that was all altered during my session with her in the rectory. As we sat in silence, sipping steadily at the potion that we had been served, nothing of her lively personality came to mind as I surveyed her. What I saw was woman in her most raw form, stripped of all the nobler qualities and adorned in all the raiment of seduction. Indeed, the phrase *dripping with honey* that the Old Testament used to describe the seductress, echoed through my head as I watched her. Every look on her face, every curve of her body, every accentuated feature seemed designed to assault my senses – and was accomplishing its mission rather successfully. As much as I tried to fight against what I was feeling, I confess that I was too comfortable with my baser instincts to chase them away altogether. As such, I settled into the sensual euphoria in which I found myself, though I did my best to regulate the sensations, and to meter them throughout our visit – much more evenly than my urges were dictating.

The thought then occurred to me that, if I was receiving such a lopsided impression of Mandy on this occasion, though she was not normally a difficult person to read, how much more difficult would it be to form a balanced opinion of Father Luke – who was impossible to decipher under any circumstance? His character then, whether good or evil, had to be a non-issue for me. The only matter of importance was to determine how much he knew about Derra. I already suspected that he knew more than he was saying. It struck me that, in my last mealtime conversation with Father Luke, though I had been in the company of Detective Sturgess, the detective had not yet uncovered the name of the society with which Sarah had been affiliated, and with which, I feared, Derra had some unfortunate connection. I was a little afraid to introduce the name of that society into the conversation, but I nonetheless decided to look for an opportunity to do so. Meanwhile, the meal progressed most congenially.

The presence of Mandy at the dining table, as well as intoxicating my own senses, seemed to be having an effect on Father Luke. When Igor brought a fresh bottle of wine to the table, after having made the journey several times, and emptying one bottle (two?), Father Luke subtly signaled to him to leave the new vessel with us so as to leave us to our conversation. The rector seemed particularly intent on keeping Mandy's cup at its maximum level, and she, like Detective Sturgess and myself before her, sipped away unconsciously at the potent grog. Father Luke, it must be said, consumed his fair share as well. His attention was clearly fixed on Mandy. I could not tell whether or not she was aware of it, but she did nothing to discourage him. We were all in good spirits, though the sensations were certainly more basic than the loftier ambiance of my morning walk. Father Luke's laugh disguised any leering devil that was lurking within him. And it was, I must admit, contagious. He still showed little interest in her answers to his questions – though, I suspect, like me, he was enthralled simply by the way that she responded. It was, to me, as if he was trying to win her over to something. There were no overt signs that he was trying to seduce her. He was more like a politician trying to sway her vote. And, like a politician, there was little of substance in what he was saying, though he was trying to say it in a way that appeared profound.

"Are you familiar with the Society of Diana?" I asked him – throwing a bucket of cold ice over what had become a rather cozy gathering.

Father Luke's face, I thought, visibly paled. The broad smile disappeared, and his jaw set in what looked like a parental expression of disapproval. He quickly composed himself, however, and the smile returned as he answered my question with one of his own.

"Is that one of the names that you dug up in your…witch hunt?"

"Actually, no," I replied. "It's a contemporary organization. Detective Sturgess was actually my source on that one."

"I hear he's left," Father Luke observed. "I guess that this *contemporary organization* offered little to hold his attention."

"Well, he *had* solved the murder," I noted, "and the Society was something that he could investigate from a distance."

"A conspiracy?" asked Father Luke.

"Perhaps," I said in my best non-committal tone. "So, you have never heard of them?"

"Not specifically, that I can recall," the rector said, countering with a pensive tone. "But, of course, the name Diana is not rare in connection with the kind of cults that we find out this way. I suppose that it would not be unusual to uncover some sort of cult connection to a random murder. But I don't think that it would bear much investigation."

"Why not?" I asked.

"Well, if the name of some society blurted out by the killer is all that you have to go on, then I suspect that it is all that you find out. The associations with these groups is often rather fluid. My guess is that the killer was only casually acquainted with such a cult, or that he had simply heard their name somewhere – maybe even made it up."

"But it looks like this particular cult permanently silenced this particular killer."

"Interesting," Father Luke mused, trying to end the conversation on that note.

In retrospect, I would have employed a little discretion at this point. I had already said too much in my effort to probe the rector's mind. I could, perhaps, excuse some of recklessness to the drugged condition in which the wine had placed me. But my reasoning processes were still functioning, and no one was forcing me to ask what I asked. So I pushed once more, beyond what I should have said, opening others and even myself to forces that I should have kept bottled.

"There's good reason to believe that Derra is affiliated with the Society of Diana."

Father Luke was silent for a second, and then suddenly burst into long, boisterous laugh. Then the words flared from his mouth.

"Derra, you say? Derra, a witch? She was, indeed, a bewitching young lady – but so is our young friend here. I warned you that chasing old wives' tales was a fruitless occupation. And it puzzles me, I must say, that you, her friend, would be the one to make this association. Perhaps your time here should draw to a close."

This chastising diatribe marked the end of our lunchtime visit. The good-natured banter that had preceded it was clearly at an end. Whatever purposes Father Luke had up his sleeve by focusing on Mandy were now thwarted. None of us saw any reason to prolong the discomfort.

At the door, Father Luke was clearly trying to force a smile – without much success. This burst of anger, I suspected, was the first genuine insight into the true character of the man. For him, it was a tactical mistake. For me, it was an undeserved victory.

Mandy and I had walked most of the distance from the rectory to the inn before we could speak. Finally, the unclouded air, and the stimulating rays of the sun, broke up the dark reverie of our minds by which we had been consumed.

"I feel like I should be smoking a cigarette right now," Mandy said, at last. "What just happened? Or, should I be saying *was it good for you?*"

I laughed a little at the post-coital references – though neither of us found the situation from which we had just escaped very amusing. We shared a sense of inexplicable guilt, but we nonetheless felt all the lighter for being free of the rector and the sticky bonds of his spider web.

"It wasn't really good at all," I replied, "and I think I made it a little worse."

"You got us out of there," she consoled. "It was like it was going to last forever, and I couldn't move to save my life."

"What are your impressions of the man?" I asked.

"Man?" she asked. "Is that what he is? I was pretty certain that we were trapped in there with some mythological beast. I noticed that he took human form, but I thought that that was an illusion. At first, I thought that he was an angel – though a rather dark one. But the wine seemed to open other options to me. He was there, in some non-human form, casting a spell over me such that, despite his horrific appearance, I would have let myself be swept away with him to his bedchamber. You rescued me when you broke the spell. There, is that poetic enough? I think that the creative effects of the wine are still lingering."

"Poetry is perhaps the only device that might describe what happened in there," I noted, adding, "– though I usually think of poetry as more of beautiful thing."

"Poetry is an *expressive* thing," she corrected. "What were your impressions?"

"It was definitely surreal," I admitted, "though I didn't quite suffer the same hallucinations. Still, my senses were assaulted. There was something forbidden taking place, but I must confess that it was very alluring at the same time. I may have broken the spell with my rash questions, but I am not sure that that was the wisest route to take. I could see that he was fascinated by you – physically, at least – but I could gain no sense of where he wanted to take that."

"And I am in your debt for *not* finding out," she countered. "From the second that I entered the rectory, I was totally confused. It wasn't only my senses. It was the whole persona of Father Luke. I know that you had mentioned your confusion before I met him – but this was leagues beyond what I had understood. The worship service was, as you had suggested, perfect. I thought that he would be easy to read because of it, but even talking to him afterwards, I was confused. There was a shallowness about him – though I thought he must be hiding something. Once the wine hit, I was lost. I think that I only saw him as he is once you asked those last questions."

"I'll agree with that much," I said, still not really comforted about my *faux pas*.

We analyzed the event as much as we could, taking some extra time by sitting together on a bench outside of the George. I was glad about that move. Seated sweetly beside me, Mandy brought back the pleasant springtime mood with which my day had begun. Even though we talked about our session with Father Luke, it seemed like an ancient memory, or even a dark dream, that we were releasing from our systems in a cathartic exercise. I was sorry that I had exposed Mandy to it at all, but she seemed none the worse for her experience. When we had spent our last breath on the topic, I retired to my room for desperately needed nap. Mandy was agreeable to this separation as she had some practical matters that needed attending in town. We agreed to meet at the George for dinner, and to follow our dinner with the usual evening conversation – keeping free of the topic of Father Luke and his bizarre hosting habits.

Dinner was a refreshing contrast to our lunch. The smiles and laughter, this time, were genuine, and the wine served to make us lightheaded rather than groggy. Although we escaped falling into conversation about Father Luke, he remained in the background of our thoughts as we shared remembrances about Sarah and Derra, and posed a few theories about conspiracies that might be common to both. I don't think that anything productive came from this talk in terms of solving the mystery surrounding Derra, but it was a good time of bonding. Mandy would be a friend for life. If I never find Derra again (though that possibility is not allowed a foothold in my thoughts), Mandy will fill part of the void. That is a comfort, though one that I trust I will not need to explore. Derra remains fixed with me – a vision that hovers over my every moment. She is so real to me that I am convinced she could be captured by a photograph taken of me in any of the various situations in which I have found myself since beginning my search. At the rectory, I believe that she would be seen as a white glow resting just above my shoulder. In the pleasant times that I share with Mandy, when Mandy awakens the spring that is trying so hard to burst upon the scene, I believe that the features of Derra's face must be clearly discernable as an aura resting around and behind me. I turn, sometimes, to catch her expression. On occasion, I am convinced that I do. It is always the same: her eyes are slightly closed, her mouth is open in a warm, inviting smile. I wait for that serious look of hers when I know that something profound will escape her lips. But the vision is always too quick, and the promised words have not yet found their appointed time.

*9*

Jessica and Mandy fill segments of my time rather pleasantly in the absence of Detective Sturgess. I am, however, missing a male perspective on my work, and Tom Monroe is a poor substitute. Still, he is better than nothing. There is, no doubt, a mystery about the man. But it is a rather shallow mystery (if mysteries can be so described), quite unlike the deep layers of mystery that surround Derra. Tom is a practical man. He is always willing to be of assistance, but not until he is certain that his support will not cost him anything of value. And, Tom has a lot to lose. His inn virtually runs itself. Eight times a year, he can count on a significant influx of guests, and he is well paid for the accommodation. More than that, the nature of these guests provides the platform for what Tom is convinced is the perfect social life: meaningless dates with beautiful women whom he will never see again.

It can't be said that Tom Monroe lives day-to-day, but he certainly lives year-to-year. As the proprietor of a prosperous inn, year-to-year is a good thing. He keeps one step ahead of needed repairs; the food supply is always at optimum level; and the cash flow seldom takes dips. As a human being, however, year-to-year is rather shortsighted. There are no goals or personal ambitions for Tom outside of the year's coming events. Although he may have taken over the George as a contemporary of the girls in whom he so delighted, he grows older, and they remain the same age. It is, admittedly, a good age into which to lock women in perpetuity, but Tom's connection with the women has grown increasingly awkward. It is rather hard to imagine him keeping up the same lifestyle as he edges towards his sixties and beyond. Maybe that's what he wants. It just seems rather unviable. The Peter Pan syndrome, that everyone speaks of in reference to Tom, probably works all right so long as he can maintain the illusion of youth. But it is something that is starting to grow a little ugly around the edges. He may well have felt under attack from the probing questions that Detective Sturgess and I posed – which threatened to collapse, prematurely, the already shaky kingdom in which Tom has enthroned himself. Nonetheless, Tom has a conscience, and he does not want to sanction something that might be destructive towards human lives.

"Since the detective has solved his murder, do you still need the information about the addresses of the groups that are booking here?" he asked me out of the blue one evening.

"It might be very useful in helping me find my friend," I replied, doing my level best to quell any potentially false hopes. "Have you got something?"

"Well, there's nothing specific, mind you," he began explaining. "As you know, mostly the ones paying didn't leave any information – no addresses, no numbers. But, of course, they had to pay. These days, it's usually with credit cards, but back in the early years, I figured that they must have used checks, and that maybe I could find a cancelled one or something. It's interesting. There has not been one personal or corporate check – at least that I can find – in over forty years of visits. A lot of the payments were made in cash, and when the bills became too big for that, it seems that they used to draw up cashier's checks or money orders – though that seems like a lot more work to arrange than just to write a personal check. My father would have had no trouble accepting checks from such good customers."

"Did you find out anything else?" I asked, sinking a little inside. "Were there names, or anything that you could give me from the credit cards?"

"Not really any names," Tom said, almost as if he had designed this conversation to crush me. "Detective Sturgess made a list of some of the names from the register, but said that they were pretty much useless to him. He said that they could be false, and that there was no way to find out even that much about them without trying to match them to the credit slips – but I wouldn't give him those. He said it didn't really matter, because he couldn't legally start investigating them without some sort of a warrant."

"Then you've nothing to offer?" I asked, totally deflated.

"Well, there's one thing that caught my eye, and that I think I could offer without compromising my guests," he said. "There's an interesting connection between some of those bank drafts and some of those credit slips."

I managed to muster a little interest in what he was saying despite having given up hope that he was going to say anything of any use to me.

"While some of the bank drafts were set up through local banks, a number of them came from a *Barclay's Bank* – which, as far as I know, isn't anything from these parts. The name stands out, because I have noticed that a lot of the credit payments since I have been here have been on a Barclaycard. It just sounded strange. It worked all right. I think that they told me it was a bank in Europe somewhere. Like I said, not much – but, if I can help you without compromising anyone, I'm glad to do it."

I appreciated his sincerity on the matter, but really felt that there was more that he could do in the way of assistance if he wasn't so concerned about his own situation. Still, it was a useful bit of information. It suggests to me that, perhaps, this Society of Diana might have a base of operations somewhere in England. It is an angle that I had not considered at any point in my research, and I am wondering how much of an oversight this might have been on my part. I've strained my mind for any British connection, but I can't come up with much. Of course, the whole Puritan settlement was originally British, but then there was the War of Independence (or Revolutionary War– depending on one's perspective) between that time and this. More relevant, I think, is the religious aspect. There is that whole cycle of rebellion that seemed to start and finish with High Church Anglicanism. Of course, that's not how the Middlemore cult *looked* at the end of it all, but there is, in my mind at least, something of Anglicanism at the heart of that movement (as blasphemous as I am sure that would sound to the guardians of that faith). Other than that, it does strike me that the only person who seems to know anything about the Society of Diana (other than the late Leo Mascagni) is an Episcopalian priest. What that signifies, I have no idea. It is just interesting in light of this British connection.

As I slept that night, the tiny bit of information that Tom Monroe had provided grew large enough to initiate a shift in my thinking. Nothing, prior to this, in all of my research, or in all of the details of Detective Sturgess' research, as passed on to me, has so much as hinted at a location for the Society of Diana, and consequently, Derra. Until now, there has been this vague idea that we were at the center of things, and that Derra, and anybody else we needed to find, would not be far away. Suddenly, however, I feel as sure as sure could be that Derra is hidden away somewhere in England. Exactly where, I cannot say, but I believe that, with a little tweaking of my own research, and a little high tech assistance from Detective Sturgess, we can probably narrow the search considerably. I have resolved to make that contact forthwith, and I begin now to nudge my investigations into international waters.

**10**

Although I am willing to concede that my excitement may have been disproportionate to the meager information that I had gathered from Tom Monroe, I had nonetheless expected to hear from Detective Sturgess within hours of leaving my messages for him. When I had not heard after a couple of days, I decided to try again – reasoning that either the detective found my assumptions to be ridiculous, or that he had taken a much-needed break. I preferred to think the latter, but feared the former. I knew, however, that his work in Middlemore had been deemed a fortunate break by the department, and I thought it more likely that he had deemed my call unworthy of a quick response. So it was with some trepidation that I phoned his department – using the central number this time as opposed to the direct line that Sturgess had provided.

After a long pause, the operator transferred my call, but the voice at the other end was not what I was expecting.

"Detective Graham Kennedy speaking. How may I help you?"

I had assumed some error on the part of the flustered operator, so I offered my apologies and asked to be redirected to Detective John Sturgess.

"May I ask what this is concerning?" the voice continued from the other end.

I was a little irritated by his manner. I *could*, after all, have called Detective Sturgess directly if I had wanted – as I had already attempted to do. I considered hanging up and doing just that once again. I was in no mood to identify myself with a murder case that the department considered closed. I wondered whether I might be putting Sturgess into some sort of trouble by introducing one of his colleagues to issues that I believed were still alive. I began to excuse myself from the conversation.

"Would you mind providing me with your name, sir?" Kennedy asked.

It seemed rather odd, but I couldn't see the harm in it. I hadn't committed any crime, and should my direct call not reach its mark, it might serve as another reminder to Detective Sturgess that I was seeking his help. So I offered my name and prepared to disconnect.

"I was starting to wonder if it was you," Kennedy said in a softer voice. "I've been planning to connect with you, Dr. Giles, and possibly even meet you in person."

"I'm sorry," I said, quite bewildered, "but I think that you must have a different person in mind. I'm not familiar with your name, and actually I am calling from the East Coast – so I don't think it is too likely that we will be meeting soon. I have, however, spent some considerable time with Detective Sturgess so…if you could just connect me… he'll know what this is all about."

"I worked with John, here, in the early phases of the murder case that he went to investigate in Middlemore – from where you are calling, I presume. I thought that he was a little crazy taking it out there at the time. Everybody did. He came back a bit of hero, though. He solved the murder as far as we were concerned. But he was more obsessed with the case than ever, and people just got back into the habit of thinking he was nuts. I worked with him, though, and he was about as far away from crazy as you could get. He talked to me about his work in Middlemore – and your work. It was pretty strange as he described it. What I mean to say is that I bought into his conspiracy theory. I even transferred to the Seattle force because of him, moved everything out here, and I want to be of help."

"I'm glad to hear that, Detective Kennedy, and I am looking forward to meeting you," I said. "I'm sure that Detective Sturgess is quite relieved to have someone from the department on his side. And, I would like to discuss this further, but…if I could please talk to Detective Sturgess, I have some things to share with him."

There was a long pause, and in the ominous silence that dragged on unnaturally, more was spoken than in the simple phrase with which it was punctuated.

"Detective Sturgess is dead."

Now it was I who initiated the silence. There were a thousand questions rushing through my mind, but all were tainted with a deep sadness. Kennedy sensed this, I think – whether through professional training or personal instinct I am not sure. Finally, I blurted out the one question that kept pushing to the forefront.

"How did it happen?"

"The circumstances are a bit murky," Kennedy explained. "His car ran off of the road and caught fire."

"An accident then?" I exclaimed, relieved for a second until I remembered Kennedy's word. "But you said *murky*?"

"It was an isolated stretch, but the road was straight and wide. There was no alcohol in his blood, but it was suggested that he fell asleep. It was late at night. What bothers me, though, is that this is about the only stretch of that road where it would have been dangerous to go off of the side. Even at that, it seemed a bit of a freak that the car would catch fire. There were some marks on the car, too, like maybe it had been bumped, but nobody could swear that they weren't there before."

"How is the department treating it?" I asked.

"There's really no evidence to suggest other than an accident, and even if there was, it would be pretty much impossible to track anyone down."

"But you don't think it's an accident?"

"I'm like John that way," Kennedy observed. "I don't believe in coincidences. I'm not trying to get you all riled. Apart from the emotional aspects, it doesn't make a difference one way or the other to your work out there whether it was planned or accidental. But I think that you guys were onto something, and I'd like to help."

"I think that Derra is probably somewhere in England right now," I said, reverting back to my original purpose in calling.

"Ah, that's interesting," Kennedy mused. "What has you thinking that?"

"There's a cult there – the Society of Diana," I said. "That's why I wanted to talk with Detective Sturgess. I figured that he might have some high tech way of investigating things over there – that is, if he didn't think that I was just grasping at straws."

"John had the utmost confidence in your instincts," Kennedy soothed. "And I think his work would probably support what you are saying. Do you have anything else?"

"Noooo…," I drawled, searching my brain frantically for anything that might give the detective a head start.

"What about areas of England – north, south?"

A thought flashed through my mind.

"Keep it south," I instructed, "particularly Somerset and Kent."

"I think that might fit too," Kennedy acknowledged. "But why those spots?"

"It's the Christian link," I explained. "Canterbury is the seat of Anglicanism, and Glastonbury is the site of the first Christian settlements. Both places could be factors in contributing to the Christian elements of the Society of Diana – positively or negatively."

"Any other places?" Kennedy asked.

"Oh, probably hundreds," I said, "but let's begin with the most obvious."

In the excitement of obtaining Detective Kennedy's assistance in tracking down the Society, I had momentarily forgotten the tragic news that he had relayed to me. I felt a little guilty as the reality once again assaulted me.

"I've got something that I would like to send along to you," Kennedy said, picking up on my sinking mood. "I've only just got my hands on it, so I can't tell you many of the details, but let's just say that John Sturgess was pretty productive in his last days."

"What is it?" I asked, growing excited again despite myself.

"He seems to have recovered quite a little bit of information on this Society of Diana, and he brought in some expert help in assembling it. I think he was planning to send it to you."

My spirits again rose, despite myself.

"Expert help?"

"Someone, or maybe a few, from Washington State University, I think – though I'm not sure which campus. Whoever helped stayed anonymous. That's probably a good thing. As I said, I've only just browsed – mostly looking for names and addresses (which don't seem to be there). The summaries aren't too long, but there is a pile of papers attached to just about every point that's made. A lot of it is just meaningless rigmarole to me, but I've got a feeling that it might be a small goldmine for you."

On that note, apart from telling him where I lived and how he could contact me by email, we concluded our discussion. I was, of course, (despite the promising news of Detective Sturgess' work) rather depressed when

I hung up the telephone. If his death was, indeed, attributable to the Society, as I feared it was, that put the death count of which I was aware at three – certainly an indication that there were several more of which I was unaware. And, of course, the employment of Leo Mascagni as a "hit man" suggests high numbers. And with current theories in place, there appears to be others to take his place. My fears for Derra have increased with this news. Although I believe that she is, by nature, a valued asset of the Society, she is in a dangerous business – and who can guess what wind would have to blow to put her life in jeopardy? It is an unsettling thought. I slept little that night, and what sleep I did have was plagued with the most horrifying of dreams.

I try to work through my grief by adhering to the tight rigor of ritual that I use to dictate my daily activities. Detective Kennedy has been so kind as to e-mail me some news articles about the death and funeral of my friend Detective Sturgess. Kennedy apologized for not notifying me at the time, and assured me that he had had plans to bring me the news personally as soon as he can free himself of department business. He knew that I am staying at the George, but was not quite certain how to reach me there – or even that he should, given the widespread nature of the conspiracy that seemed afoot. Nonetheless, the package containing the information about the Society of Diana should, he promised, arrive within a day or two. Sturgess had not preserved it electronically anywhere, as far as he could tell, so there was a lot of photocopying and organizing to do just to have it ready for me. The narrative itself, he said, was easy to follow, but there were supporting documents related to various sections of the narrative that I would probably find easier to follow if they were inserted in the correct sections. He had spent the better part of the night pulling this all together as he had, at last, begun to focus on the details of what Sturgess had recorded. As a result of this, and of my suggestion of where to conduct his search, he offered the town of Glastonbury as the logical first focus of the search. He asked, however, that I confirm this once I had had a chance to look at the papers. So, though I walk my way through my daily routines, I remain very agitated in anticipation of the papers that are scheduled to arrive.

I was disappointed to return to the George late Thursday afternoon to find that nothing had been delivered to me. It was, I knew, on the early side of when I should be expecting something, but I had hoped that I would not have to enter my Friday (which is less structured than my other weekdays) with only my usual rituals in place. As a result, I took the unusual step of remaining at the inn that morning in order to be present the moment that any delivery should arrive. Initially, it looked like I had made a big mistake. I am a creature that does not fare well with unstructured time under the best of circumstances. Idling my hours away in the state of mind into which I had fallen was probably the worst thing that I could have done. Nothing was helped when the morning mail arrived without anything directed to me. By noon, I had resolved to walk myself to the library if, for nothing else, just to occupy myself – and hopefully relieve the anxiety that had consumed me. I was at the main entrance of the George, on my way out, when I saw the courier van pull into the driveway. It made sense to delay my departure until Tom had sorted through the deliveries, so I waited with him by the front desk.

"Expecting something?" he asked.

*Duh-huh* was my instinctive response, but I simply replied in the affirmative.

"There you go," he said seconds later, immediately after signing for the delivery.

I'm sure my eyes were glowing as I held the hoped for package in my hands. I thought of just taking straight to my room, but I preferred the idea of making an occasion of it. So I continued with my plan of walking into town. It was a soothing exercise, as I knew it would be, and I arrived in a rather pleasant state of mind – despite the traumas of the preceding days. Spring was in full bloom. My mood was, in fact, too euphoric to waste in a dark corner of the library. Besides, knowing that Jessica was taking the day off removed the only real appeal that the library could offer on such a day. So, with freshly settled stomach, I made my way to my usual Friday lunch spot, ordered myself a steak sandwich and a beer, and proceeded to bolster my already risen spirits. Once my plate was cleared, I ordered a second beer and opened the large envelope that Detective Kennedy had sent me. To be honest, I am not sure how many beers followed that second one. I just kept them coming. I was totally enthralled by the documents before me. Although I had high expectations, by consulting an expert (experts?) in the field of religious studies, Detective Sturgess far surpassed even that for which I had hoped. It was a document that brought me light years closer to unraveling the mystery surrounding my missing friend.

# DERRA'S REFLECTIONS RECORDED AT AN UNDETERMINED DATE (ABRIDGED)

**M**y first memories are of my grandfather in England. I lived with him in a small bungalow in Buckinghamshire. Although I was still quite young when I left, and it does not exist anymore, I still remember it as my first home, and all of the details are firmly fixed in my mind. Numerous daytrips with my grandfather come to mind, but I can only remember one occasion when our travels extended beyond one day. We left by train, one Friday, for Glastonbury in Somerset. It was quite exciting for me. It was a magical place. Grandfather had filled my head with tales of knights and faeries, and when we were there, he showed me a magical well and a magical tree. Although he was focused on historical details, this was quite unlike my grandfather's other instruction, and much more like the stories he told me at night. Reality and fantasy fused for the first time in my life, and I felt a thrill for living that I had never felt before. We stayed over on Saturday night as well, but remained only long enough on the Sunday to attend church service. It was a little dull for me after the previous day's adventure, but took new meaning as my grandfather carefully unpacked the sermon's message for me as we traveled home, and drew connections to the wonderful things that we had seen the day before.

I was not yet six when I was flown to America. The legalities that allowed me to be transported from my homeland across an ocean, and to the far side of an unfamiliar continent, were not an issue for me at such a tender age. The couple that provided me with the room that owned such a spectacular view of the Oregon coast, was not, in any way, related to me. They were not unkind to me, but I was treated like an oddity. In contrast to the type of education that my grandfather had started to provide for me, there was no interest on the part of my foster parents in preserving my childhood. The sole objective was to cram my young mind as fully as possible with knowledge absent of the magic. It was not an unhappy time – I had little time to be unhappy – but it was not a particularly happy time either. I was lonely. My break with my foster parents came when I was eighteen. I was sent to Seattle, allegedly to apprentice at a research institute. I had never had a job, nor even the routine of daily schooling, so the oddities of my situation were not readily apparent. The nature of the business, for instance, could not easily be deducted from the activity. On the one hand, though research was clearly ongoing, the topics for research were seemingly random. I was assigned work in the areas in which my education had prepared me. The object, however, was not to take my studies into new realms (as might be expected were this a typical academic institute), but to reduce them to their simplest forms – as if I were preparing articles for an encyclopedia.

Druid history has long been of particular interest to me. I discovered that my training, as strange as it may sound (particularly as expressed by a devout High Anglican!), is as a Druid priestess. Modern Druids would not recognize me. I must confess, too, that the whole idea sounds cultic to the extreme – if not rather pretentious. But, in keeping with the first century definition of a Druid, with the emphasis being on education and knowledge, I am pretty much in line with the basics. It is suggested that women only ascend to the priestly role only when a religion is in decline. I think, more accurately, that it is a sign of a religion in transition.

At first glance, it might be assumed that my grandfather knew precisely what he was doing in training me as he did – right down to taking me to Glastonbury as a very young girl. The oversight, easily made in light of exotic nature of a lot of my training, is that I was first and foremost raised as a High Church Anglican. Even my role as a Druidic priestess is subservient to that. Whatever my grandfather thought that he was doing, he would not have acted in any way that was contrary to the national faith. It is important to understand the place of magic in my grandfather's mind, untainted as it was by the realities that I have faced. The Christian mind does not, or *should* not, reject the everyday magical elements of this life that we encounter in legends, fairy tales and fantasies. In its basest form, such literature merely encapsulates something of our spiritual nature. Tales of faeries and witches have more obvious undertones, yet the more innocuous creatures often have their own cultic origins as well.

My case is not the norm. Unknowing, I was born into this cult and have been treated accordingly. My baptism, as an infant, into the Anglican Church was, in fact, my baptism into this cult. My Anglican beliefs have not been challenged. My Druid knowledge has been embraced. But the rich faith that my grandfather knew has been transformed to something ugly – just as fine wine, marvelously intoxicating in reasonable doses, can become a terror when consumed without limitations. There was a tradition of Diana, dating centuries back in New England. It survived, though barely, well into the twentieth century. Infused, however, with Glastonbury tradition, it has become something terrifying in its pagan aspects, and powerful in its Christian tradition. The spirituality that is unleashed, even through those with good hearts, is an ugly spirituality because it is filtered through the fallen human soul. It is into this world that I have been placed.

Once I had left my foster home, a "guardian angel" was assigned to me. The term is not something that I would have chosen to describe the creature that shadowed me. If there were anything of the angel about him, it was most certainly that of fallen angel with all the dark implications that such a nature implies. I was unaware of him at first, but hints of his presence surfaced early – though he was certainly skilled at making himself invisible. In the days when I was only vaguely conscious of his unseen presence, a certain terror possessed me. I cannot say that the terror abated altogether when he made himself known, and described the nature of his assignment.

Leonardo Mascagni was a horrible little creature. In the confusion of traditions in which I have become entwined, he was more like a goblin than anything human. I was never comfortable in his presence. His leering eyes undressed me as he spoke. I suspect that only orders from higher up protected me from his assaults, yet though he was aware of my status, I was still concerned about the strength of the bonds that restrained him. I found it best to deal with him as if he were indeed a goblin, and that he was subject to my power under the Druidic hierarchy. I scolded him as I would a naughty child when he spoke insolently to me. Nonetheless, I had no recourse when he relayed orders to me that he had been given from the leaders. Still, it galled me to see him successful in anything that had to do with me.

As a rule, Leo kept to the background as far as I was concerned – surfacing only to bring me information. The information was usually in the form of instructions – *orders* – from the leaders. Sometimes, however, there were cautions. Although I am granted relative freedom in choosing my activities and associations, there are certain dangers in becoming too involved in anything outside of my religious functions. Most of these warnings, I ignore. I know that my freedom comes to an end when I am in danger – though the preference is to allow me to steer clear of such dangers on my own (as perceived with the aid of the warnings). If the warnings are, instead, directed on behalf of someone else, then I must take notice. In any case, the messenger is usually worse than the message. I always knew when Leo was near, and that was bad enough, but when he uncloaked himself, I felt a sickness that reflected the agony of my tortured soul.

For fear that the veils of mystery that have encumbered my life should blot out altogether the goodness that life can hold, I must conclude by stating that I have not been altogether unhappy. My brief time with my grandfather, though ending much too soon, was happy beyond description. Indeed, the light of those years subjected the subsequent years to unreasonable scrutiny. My foster parents, though sorely lacking my grandfather's heart, were dutiful, and in given situations, were even generous in their care for me. Although a want of love created a deep cavity in my soul, I wanted for little else – save companionship. And that which my heart was missing then has been more than compensated in the brief companionships of more recent times. Indeed, my years at the institute, and my subsequent flight into freedom, gave me a fuller appreciation, not only of human relations, but also of the worldly things with which God has blessed us. If my formative years were somewhat thin in happiness, I have since glutted on happiness despite the cloud that shadows me.

Perhaps the more desperate phase of my life that has just begun will also transform before it consumes me. The smallest ray of hope is, I know, much more powerful than the darkest forces that this world can muster. In this, too, my faith has sustained me. The Church, though always corrupted at the hands of humankind, though certainly manipulated by the cult with which I now contend, has, at its core, something eternal. From time to time, I stumble across that fact, or someone points me to it, and I bask in the light. But, just as quickly, it seems, that light is almost extinguished once again. I have been trained in religious matters like few others. And, if I am helpless to untangle the parasite that has worked its way around the message of hope, I despair of the chances of those who hack blindly at the thick vines that are choking the enchanted palace in which so many are imprisoned

EXCERPTS OF NOTES ON THE SOCIETY
OF DIANA AS RETRIEVED BY THE LATE
DETECTIVE JOHN STURGESS (COMPILED
AND ASSESSED WITH EXPERT ASSISTANCE)

The Society of Diana (TSD) represents the threefold tradition that has existed since creation. Christianity, though represented in its fullness in the person of Jesus, has existed eternally. Christian practice, however, in its focus on the person, has tended to ignore both the true feminine and the true spiritual aspects of the faith. Although it is impossible to separate these aspects from the true person of the Christ, they are best represented in two separate traditions: the Druid nature-tradition, and the Goddess tradition or the tradition of Diana (from which TSD takes its name).

The Druid nature-tradition has ancient roots, and many branches extending through the first century of the millennium of our Lord. The true spirituality of this tradition is evident in its magical potions and spells, learned through years of intensive training in the ways of Wisdom (Sophia). The Druid caste is a priestly caste. The true Druids (not resembling those who claim the name in modern practice) are sages who wander the earth providing spiritual guidance to true believers. They are those whom the Bible describes as "angels amongst us." Their faith anticipated, and was complementary to, the Christian faith that arrived on the British Isles in the generation contemporary with that of the Lord himself. They walked openly in society until persecution from many sectors (including the Church itself) forced them underground. The tradition nonetheless survived and continues to channel their spiritual Wisdom into the true faith.

The tradition of Diana, too, extends to the outer reaches of history. Diana, representing the inherent contradiction in the feminine, weaves her heritage from Eve in the Garden of Eden. Diana is the tempted and the temptress. Diana is the virgin maid and the sacred whore. Diana represents light and darkness. She is manifest in the black magic of Hecate, and in the eternal purity of the Holy Mother. Her influence, too, reached out in many directions in the first century of the millennium of our Lord. Worship of Diana, known as the Goddess Religion, anticipated and was complementary to Christianity in the British Isles in the first century, and mixed with the Druid traditions that were likewise in place. Its history, too, was interrupted by the Church, which deemed their celebration of the feminine as heretical, labeling it as witchcraft and making it anathema to the Church. Modern day practice of the Goddess Religion has distorted the ancient tradition by dissociating it from the original Christian practice (although many of the modern faith seek to align their beliefs with certain Christian traditions). True adherents of the Goddess Religion, however, were forced underground (like their contemporaries, the Druids), but did not disappear from history. Rallying under the sacred name of Diana, the women of the Goddess Religion have maintained their alliance to the true Christian faith. There is a resurgence of that faith in modern times, and many women, free to celebrate their femininity, have received the message of Christ in its fullness and not just the message as stripped of many of its spiritual and feminine dimensions.

Christianity, just as the other parts of the threefold tradition, has undergone many changes in its manifestation. Although successful at promoting its eternal nature through its pre-Jesus history, the full message of its true adherents in the first century has often disappeared, though the true faith has managed to survive even within the established Church. The nationalization of the faith always signified its downfall, and the British Isles were no exception. The simple message of faith, that the first generation of Christian disciples brought to, and mixed with, the Druids and the adherents of the Goddess Religion in Somerset, was buried once Christianity was sanctioned in the region. The Catholic Church repressed the spiritual and the feminine in favor of the practical, masculine values of the medieval world. The Reformation, sparked by a mixture of spiritual and practical concerns, revived the faith of England through the establishment of a Church independent of Rome. Nonetheless, as history teaches us, in the establishment of a National Church, the true faith is soon smothered. This remains so through to modern times. The true traditions of the Church of England, however, captured in the liturgy of Cranmer and others, allowed the true adherents to function within boundaries set at Canterbury. Nonetheless, their practice remains sterile when not infused by the remaining parts of the threefold tradition.

*Editing note*: This section seems to be an attempt to establish the Society on the basis of historical religious tradition. Although the history of religions may bear out the arguments to some degree, a subtle rewriting of history has taken place. The highly interpretative nature of this historical section is evident in the excessive use of the word "true" in defense of TSD tradition. The so-called "documentary evidence" (attached) is rather random in nature and would not likely withstand academic scrutiny. Nonetheless, several examples could be cited of dubious material holding mass sway over the opinion of the general populace. People are generally ready to believe anything – so long as it feeds into their preconceptions. Other sections of TSD manifesto bear this out.

**S**pirituality has become a meaningless catchword in unenlightened Christian tradition. There is no agreement on how it is manifest. One extreme professes that it is evident in good works, while the other extreme professes that it is evident in the raising of arms and vocalization of glossolalia. While such acts may offer some degree of self-satisfaction to the participants, neither provides any evidence of true spirituality as distinct from practical or emotional elements of everyday life.

True spirituality is evident in acts that extend beyond our normal empirical expectations. Such acts would include, though not be limited to, spells that demonstrate power over individuals and over nature, extraordinary acts such as levitation, flying and shape shifting, and potions for physical and emotional health. True spirituality, as well, allows Christians to see the world from the Divine Perspective, unfettered by empirical bonds. Remnants of such visions exist, to a limited degree, in the folklore and myths that society at large has collected. Access to true spirituality, however, comes from Wisdom (Sophia) and Wisdom is acquired through years of intensive training in the priestly caste (Druids). The true Christians experience true spirituality as it is shared with them through the Druid caste. Such spirituality may be of a temporary nature, or may offer lifelong insights into the spiritual nature of human existence. Although only few are born into the Wisdom of the Druids, all true Christians have access to that Wisdom, and may acquire the gifts that are appropriate to their personal needs.

The greatest gift, accessible to all true Christians to varying degrees, is the vision of the world from the Divine Perspective. In this, not only the threefold tradition becomes evident, but also the rich input of other traditions – both spiritual and historical. The broad spectrum of spiritual existence (shut tight by the Catholic Church and opened briefly by the Church of England) has been preserved through the Druid caste (though that caste bordered on extinction prior to the break with Catholicism), and has been expounded in worldwide folklore traditions. Religious traditions, too, have attempted to preserve these elements in their doctrine or practice, but the admixture of false doctrine and practice has generally contaminated the message. Seen in the light of ancient tradition, however, the message can sometimes be rescued and provide insight into the nature of true Christianity. There is, in fact, widespread evidence of true spirituality, preserved, not only the broader philosophies and Wisdom of folklore, myths and a variety of religious beliefs, but in the incantations, spells and alchemic potions that have been preserved throughout the ages.

*Editing note*: Spirituality here might be better defined as magic. The extent to which these magic tricks are actually in place is impossible to determine. The idea that they *might* be in place would hold widespread appeal for the adherents – particularly in as much as the adherents are allowed to pick and choose their tricks from a "spiritual" smorgasbord. There is no suggestion here of spirituality as simple commune with God unless, of course, such commune results in the ability to perform one of these magic tricks. The so-called "Divine Perspective" appears to be nothing more than the simple broadening of one's horizons through a psychological examination of our religious and historical roots. The religious perspective offered borders on phenomenology, and has its appeal by virtue of its vagueness. The documentation here [attached], though rather extensive, is particularly weak – containing little more than a hodgepodge of ancient allegedly magical scripts, collections of myths and folklore, and scattered documents from both Eastern and Western religious and cultural tradition that offer points of overlap with the TSD perspective.

The feminine is a notoriously overlooked aspect of Christian tradition. True Christianity, however, embraces the feminine equally with the masculine. The historical imbalance, necessitates a heavy emphasis on the feminine in modern times. Christian tradition begins with the feminine in the person of Mary the Mother of Jesus. Reverence for Mary as the Virgin Mother begins early and has been sustained, though perverted, in the Catholic Church. The paradox in her title points the divine nature of her role. As the vessel in which our Lord was formed, she is inseparable from him. Her divine nature is further defined in those women who have foreshadowed her and who have reflected her glory.

Mary Magdalene mirrors the role of the Virgin Mary. Mary Magdalene is also physically linked to our Lord, but as the consort. Whereas the paradox of Mary the Mother of Jesus is between her virginity and her motherhood, the paradox of Mary Magdalene is between her holy nature and her whoredom. This tradition, alive in the early stages of the faith, has been officially buried by the Church throughout the centuries. It has, nonetheless, surfaced at various points in history, notably in the subtle Renaissance rebellion against the Catholic Church. The Reformation, however, though a positive influence in many aspects, quickly quelled the resurgence of the Magdalene tradition. The misogyny of Western Tradition was too deeply seated to make allowances on this account. A long history of dismissing spiritual women as witches, or "Dianas," and a society without the infrastructure for supporting the rights of women not born to privilege, worked against the reinstatement of Magdalene to the prominence that she deserved.

The roles of the Virgin Mary and of Mary Magdalene, though deliberately outlined in true Christian tradition, were essentially symbolic.

They pointed to the positive and negative aspects of the feminine as represented in the Christ. A more encompassing representation, however, is found in the person of Diana. The name, *Diana*, first found prominence in Roman tradition. The woman depicted by this name was the feminine ideal. As the huntress, she was supple, agile and elusive. She was the temptress, yet she was the perpetual virgin. Parallel depictions of her as the Greek Artemis highlight her fertility and her motherhood. These were not isolated images. Fertility cults reaching back to the Garden of Eden have always worshipped these images. Eve herself, as a prototype of the feminine, offers all of these qualities in their fullness. Such fullness recurs in the Diana of the Goddess Religion at the time of the earliest Christian tradition in the British Isles. The true Christians of that time found no conflict with their faith and with the worship of Diana. Indeed, Diana worship was blended with Christianity until it was deemed heretical by the Catholic Church and was ultimately pushed out the faith altogether as Christianity gained state recognition.

It is impossible to determine the extent of the persecution suffered by those women who sought to preserve the feminine aspects of true Christianity. There is much documentation regarding those who have been tormented as witches. Such systematic harassment began early in the British Isles, and was resurrected in America against those who sought to return to the fullness of the Christian message. Although such witch-hunts have been utilized to serve a variety of purposes, the most damaging purpose has been to repress the feminine element of the divine. Though more subtle methods are used in modern society, the purpose is the same and prejudice against women who express their spirituality through their own femininity is rampant.

True femininity expresses itself in ways that are often similar to the self-expression of true spirituality. There are spells that demonstrate power over individuals and over nature, extraordinary acts such as levitation, flying and shape shifting, and potions for physical and emotional health. As mothers and consorts, however, there is a strong sensual side to women that is indispensable in the true expression of the Christian faith. This is the greatest void in the current practice of the Christian Church. As a result, it is not sufficient merely to guide the adherents of the faith in the way of Wisdom. Wisdom itself must be seen in the person of Sophia and the person of Sophia must in turn be seen as the Divine Diana. Although wise and spiritual, the most dominant feature of Diana is her sensuality. This sensuality is expressed in both her role as the virgin temptress and as the fertile mother. The role of the true Christian woman is modeled in the person of Diana, and because this role has been systematically erased from the Christian Church, this is the single most important role in true Christianity. Even the role of the Druid priestess, while spiritually superior, can be preserved by relatively few women. The role of Diana can only be preserved by a revival that encompasses many.

*Editing note*: There is no shortage, in these days, of advocates for the feminine element in Christian faith and practice. Enticing apocryphal tales have existed, almost since the advent of Christianity, that focus on the Virgin Mary or on Mary Magdalene. The former, in fact, has essentially gained divine status in the Catholic Church, where she is perceived as the perpetual virgin as opposed to simply the virgin mother of Protestant tradition. Mary Magdalene has not taken such prominence in any Christian tradition, although, early on, those uncomfortable with either the Scriptural silence about Jesus' sexuality or the simple fact of his maleness, have introduced Mary Magdalene as a consort to satisfy what they feel is a glaring omission. She, too, under the weight of such a perspective, has essentially gained divine status. The irony of all this is that the arguments are initiated by those who give the biblical account little creditability, but is based on material that is decidedly less reliable than the biblical accounts. The documentation here [attached] is familiar to many, and has already been shown not to withstand scholarly scrutiny. More interesting is the documentation regarding the Diana tradition [attached] that purports to trace that tradition to Eve. There is decidedly some cultural, historical and religious enlightenment to be gained from that material, though the interpretation from TSD is too subjective and prejudicial to hold any value outside of that society's immediate purposes.

True Christianity embraces the truly spiritual and the truly feminine, but historically, the Church has failed at embracing either of these. The last full manifestation of true Christianity was the threefold tradition that appeared in southwestern England in the first century of the Christian era. Once the Christian Church garnered sanction, from Rome and from the state, true Christianity was virtually wiped from the face of the earth. Partial revivals have occurred from time to time, but usually as a result of a rebellion against the Church authority of the time. The separation of the Church of England from the Roman Church allowed for a number of elements of true Christianity to return to the Church, and many of these have been preserved in the Anglican liturgy. The door was only open briefly, however, and the state-sanctioned Church soon resorted to many of the bad habits inherited from the Roman Church. Aspects of true Christianity that remained, however, were rejected by Puritan movements that sought to strip such vestiges from the Anglican Church and establish a Church in America, well separated from Rome, but equally distinct from true Christianity. Rebellion against this austere religion was natural enough and took the form, not only of a return to Anglicanism, but as a true revival injected with both spiritual and feminine elements.

While the Episcopal Church (as the Anglican tradition is labeled in America) is guardian to some of the secrets of true Christianity, it is a repository to be utilized only under caution, and its message is best relayed to true Christians through the mediation of the Druid priestesses and priests. Historically, the Christian message was best served when it was interpreted only from the pulpit by those qualified to relay the message. Although noble in its intent, the distribution of the Bible to the masses has been the single most corrupting influence on the Christian message.

A message robbed of its exclusivity is a message robbed of its power. Fortunately, elements of the true Christian message have remained hidden from public eyes throughout the centuries. The great risk of the Church of England, in the beginning, was in representing these elements too vividly in its liturgy. Fortunately, however, the admixture of some of the more acceptable Catholic declarations has helped to disguise these elements. New elements are uncovered as the time is ripe, and remain hidden in the sacred libraries of the Archbishop's Church.

The re-establishment of the true Church in America is part of the natural evolution. It was carried as a seed with the Puritans. At birth, however, the Puritans recognized it as a bastard child, spawned by the Church against which they had rebelled. Like their Catholic fathers before them, many Puritans denounced their child with terms such as "witchcraft," but others realized the hypocrisy in their condemnation. In association with strong native traditions, the true faith flourished anew, in contrast to the watered-down traditions that remained on British soil. Although the movement remained small in the first centuries, it was revived by new discoveries. These discoveries, from the cradle of civilization, were passed along to the cradle of the true Christian faith under the auspices of the Church of England. Activities of TSD have rescued these documents from the vaults in which they have been stored, and have initiated a revival of the true faith in America of unprecedented proportions. It is at this point in history, with the migrations complete and the final secrets of the true Church falling into the appointed hands, that we see the culmination of God's plan and his desire to incorporate us in the revitalization of human existence.

*Editing note*: Although it seems essential for TSD to preserve its links to Christianity, these links are tenuous at best. The focus of what it calls "true Christianity," though dating to the first century, is in southwestern England as opposed to Jerusalem, Rome or places in between. Although this is argued on the basis of the presence of Druidism and Goddess Religion at the same locale, the choice is, nonetheless, arbitrary since Christianity, at its nascent stages, would not logically have needed outside traditions to supplement its message. It would be better argued that such balances had become necessary later, when the original message had suffered some corruption. The links to the Anglican Church, and to America, are equally arbitrary. In many ways, TSD attachment to the Church of England makes less sense than an attachment to a non-conformist church that does not have state sanction. The liturgy, however, appears to be an essential element of TSD worship, and misgivings with Roman Catholicism severely limits their options. The national attachment, too, has certain advantages, as a large dose of British Israelism seems to be at the heart of their Christianity. In that sense, the further migration of the true faith to America (safe from the Beast that is Rome) is not totally unexpected. Mormonism, in fact, sometimes traces its routes through a similar path. Yet the American tradition to which TSD attaches itself [see attached documentation] seems more a matter of convenience (as in ceremonies akin to witchcraft – which have roots in both Christian tradition and fertility traditions), than of any distinctive historical link. The documents recovered from Asia Minor (?) through the Church of England might explain some of the motivation behind TSD.

TSD expresses Christian culture in its fullest and richest form. Feminine spirituality is the highest expression of this culture. The name "Diana" is symbolic of realizing this level of enlightenment. Unlike the Druid priestess, who has a distinctive calling and must live separate from the world in the continued pursuit of Wisdom, the Diana is called to remain in the world and to blend with its conventions – though clearly having knowledge that extends beyond normal human boundaries. The Diana, as well as pursuing the spiritual in her worship and celebrating the feminine in her ritual, adapts to a career to which she is uniquely suited, and in which she can best serve true Christianity. Traditionally, such occupations have been in the arts. Sciences are also of undeniable value, but only when pursued in combination with the metaphysical. Conventional medicines, for example, are accepted for their limited functions. Better, however, is the development of potions to treat both body and mind as passed on to us through ancient formulae preserved by the Druids.

Literature provides a rich source of enlightenment on true Christian culture, but read selectively, it distorts the vision. Just as Christian history cannot be understood solely on the basis of Church-sanctioned material, secular history must be understood both through the accumulation of empirical facts and mythological or folklore elements of a given society. Such elements, although often repressed and rewritten by the Church, still point to the deeper truths of human history and insight. The most universal, yet the most understated myth, is the Diana-myth. The full impact of its influence is not apparent because of the many forms that she takes. Such forms include, but are certainly not limited to, the Virgin Mother, Mary Magdalene, Divine Huntress, Moon Maiden, Sacred Whore, Great Mother, Crone, Hecate, Morgana and the May Queen. In addition to mythical literature, there is a wealth of ceremony and symbolic folklore representing Diana. Diana is the most irrepressible link between ancient fertility cults and Druidic custom. As representative, too, of the Christian Marys, Diana completes the circle of femininity, spirituality, and Christian tradition.

The richness of human culture has been scattered across the nations. TSD, in this time of revival, assembles the fragments within the individual, and the individuals collectively redefine Christian culture. This redefinition is not a recreation. It is a compression which, through its richness, advances civilization along its divinely appointed path. The secrets, gathered and dispersed by the Druid priestesses, are stored within each Diana as best suits her personal gifts. Conventional education and training is revitalized as it is redefined by the secrets that are shared. Expressions of this redefinition are apparent the ritual, the artistic, the scientific and the metaphysical qualities of the Diana. This Wisdom is not shared outside of TSD as such a diffusion would corrupt the efficacy of these gifts. Within TSD, however, this Wisdom is the life force that remakes the world in the image intended in the establishment of true Christian faith.

*Editing note*: Culture, as defined by TSD, is distinctly marked by the feminine, not only by the introduction of such phrases as "the Diana," but through subtly limiting the Druid priestly role in the gathering of secrets to the "priestess." This section demonstrates the appeal of this cult to their qualified prospects. The prospects, it is apparent, are women (in their early twenties) who are in the prime of both their physical appeal and their sensual urges. While it is true that women much older than this can also be in their prime, the younger women are more suitable because they are at a stage in their lives where they can more easily be molded by their studies, yet may already come equipped with some degree of independent thinking. Most cults would prefer their prospects not to be marked by this latter quality since brainwashing is a major part of their program. TSD, however, promotes its own program with a remarkable degree of confidence. Aware of how readily the general public will take up any new cause (even those with only the thinnest veneer of scholarship) that allows them to incorporate secular predispositions into established faith, TSD has more than enough material at hand to make their prospects believe that they are being shown the road to enlightenment. Such a plan, though not foolproof, must certainly have a high success rate. In short, as the supporting documents show [attached], TSD offers young, beautiful, sensuous women a celebration of, not only those qualities, but of the deeper cultural and magical elements to which we are all drawn, but to which very few find any direction outside of TSD.

# VII

THE MAY CEREMONY AS WITNESSED
AND RECORDED BY DETECTIVE GRAHAM
KENNEDY, WRITTEN AT A LATER DATE

ery shortly after I had sent the package of the late Detective Sturgess'
findings to Noah Giles, I received an urgent telephone call from Dr.
Giles requesting my immediate presence in Middlemore. At the best of
times, the department was not receptive to sudden requests for leave, as
unplanned absences tended to leave any number of active cases unattended.
The idea of my heading out to the same remote locale where Detective
Sturgess had spent so much time simply aggravated those in a position to
grant my request. Although Detective Sturgess had been lauded for solving
the case that had drawn him to Middlemore, his preoccupation with that
case, until the time of his death, had been a source of some embarrassment
for the department. It was clearly hoped that the case had finally died with
him, and no one was happy to see me don the late detective's mantel.

I suppose that, in taking up John Sturgess' cause, I surprised myself
as much as anyone else. I liked John as a person, but I was not an advocate
of his detecting methods. Part of my hesitation was the degree to which
he would immerse himself in a case. His preference was to enter into the
minds of those involved in the crime – whether it be the victim or the
killer. Although there was a certain value in such an approach, there was
also a certain risk. With John, the risk was not (as it may well have been
with others using this method) with misrepresenting the thoughts of those
with whom he attempted to commune. It was more a matter of suffering
ill effects in his own mind as a result of channeling these unfortunate
people. I was surprised that his career had extended so long without a major
breakdown as a result of the stress that he placed on himself. Obviously,
he had ways of dealing with this stress which, if I had such skills, might
have made me more sympathetic to his methods. As it is, however, I am
from the school of detecting which emphasizes the accumulation of clues,

and the use of the power of deduction in uncovering the path to which these clues point. John would suggest that there was a little too much of Sherlock Holmes in me for my own good. I, in turn, would point out how much more valuable it was in the courts to have a clear trail of evidence pointing the criminal as opposed to a gut instinct – however, strong that instinct might be.

I must confess that, in pursuing Detective John Sturgess' case, I was following gut rather than reason. I might still have been reluctant to head that route had not the physical evidence that John had assembled fallen into my hands. The evidence, admittedly, pointed to no crime – but it did demonstrate the existence of a cult that John had hitherto been unable to confirm. On top of that, the timely call from Dr. Giles, in search of Detective Sturgess, convinced me that the cause was a righteous one, and that there might yet be some answers at hand. Dr. Giles, as described to me by John, sounded like the perfect point of reference in this case. The volume of research that he had produced (as reported by John) appealed to my practical tendencies. Yet, by all accounts, the man was driven by the same sort of gut instincts that had served John Sturgess. It was an encounter that I did not wish to postpone. So, I fought hard for my leave. The time I was granted was very brief, though sufficient for my purposes. My first purpose was to meet Dr. Giles before he left the country. My second purpose (as fixed by Dr. Giles) was to witness the proceedings of an expected influx of young women, scheduled to be completed by the second of May.

Dr. Noah Giles was much as I had expected he would be. He was a likeable man, somewhat reserved, but with knowing glint in his eyes. His story of his friend Derra was much as John Sturgess described it, though Dr. Giles' subtle passion for his friend was deeper than I had supposed. In a strange way, it reminded me of John's own passion for the young Sarah, whom we had only known as deceased. John's passion for a dead woman had rather unsettled me at first. I was glad that there had been no evidence that Dr. Giles' woman had attained such a state. He was certainly convinced that there was every chance of finding her alive. In fact, it was that hope that was drawing him out of the country. He believed that she was currently living in Glastonbury, in the county of Somerset, and as a result of this conviction, he was very anxious to learn whether or not

I had made any progress in my investigations concerning possible TSD activity in this county. For my part, I was eager to see how the massive documentation that I had sent him had molded his own extensive research into new theories.

The restaurant at which we met was pleasantly situation in the town center, and allowed us to dine outside in the warm spring air. Dr. Giles was clearly no stranger to this establishment and had no need to peruse the menu. There was no reaction from the waiter when I chose the club sandwich, but I noticed that he leaned forward expectantly when he asked me what I would like to drink. Dr. Giles, too, froze momentarily in his relaxed reverie. On a tip gathered unconsciously from the late John Sturgess, I asked for a pint of their local brew. Both the waiter and Dr. Giles immediately exhibited subtle signs of relief. A brief nod from Dr. Giles confirmed that he would have the same, and from that moment on, I knew that he would be a willing confidant in all matters related to the search for his friend. I gloated a little, inwardly, over how effective my detecting skills were in even such a mundane situation a luncheon meeting.

I had decided against staying at the George while in Middlemore, despite the initial urging of Dr. Giles. I had no dispute with his contention that the inn matched the perfect example of quaint New England hospitality that he had always harbored in his mind, but I wanted to keep myself hidden from the expected crowd. This created a minor commuting problem, but I was not overly worried about that. I did, however, want to arrange a meeting with the proprietor of the inn, Tom Monroe, whose role in all of this I found rather confusing. It was best, however, to leave this meeting until after the girls were gone – just in case he might feel it in his best interest to warn them about me. My best starting point would be the chalet. I had no hopes of being privy to any of the meetings there, but I figured that I could easily follow them from there, undetected, to the location of their secret ceremony – which Dr. Giles was convinced would take place on the Eve of May, April 30, and possibly begin even earlier.

Dr. Giles explained to me that May Day was an ancient Druidic holiday known also as Beltaine, the day of Bel, the god of the sun. The Eve of May was traditionally a time of feasting and celebrating the end of winter as marked by the return of the sun and of fertility. As well, historically, it was a celebration not unlike Halloween, when revelers, disguised in animal masks, were led by Diana to the hunt. In the more agrarian societies Diana became the Queen of the May. The Queen of the May was chosen among the maidens of the village to rule the crops until harvest. The original Celtic practice of Beltaine was a three-day celebration, initiated when the Druid priests lit fires on the top of hills that naked revelers bounded through to receive healing and protection. The Eve of May celebrations, however (as Dr. Giles described them), were even more relevant. At that time, young men and women remained in the forest, until the first sunrise of May, making flower garlands to decorate the village. Puritans outlawed this custom in 1644, however, because of the high percentage of young women who returned home pregnant from the night's escapades.

I was amazed at the degree to which the ancient customs tied into the beliefs of TSD, and expressed as much to Dr. Giles. He simply smiled, signaled the waiter to bring a pitcher of ale that we had already enjoyed in individual pints, and said: *You don't know the half of it.*

had envied John Sturgess' ability to tune out of a case for a moment in time, and simply enjoy being alive. Undoubtedly, it was this gift that had saved him from the breakdowns that should have been inevitable with most of his cases. I, on the other hand, tend to be rather more agitated while on the job – though I seldom take a case home with me or carry it past its conclusion. Whether part of me interpreted the trip to Middlemore as a vacation, or whether the beer had struck me a little more forcefully than I had anticipated, I slipped into Dr. Giles' mellow reverie as I sat at that little restaurant under the soothing rays of the springtime sun.

It was still serious business for both of us. Once our session was over, we would both head into the unknown. Dr. Giles was set to fly from Boston to London, and from there he would travel to the magical site where he hoped the answers to his questions might lie. My journey would not involve such distances, but it would take me just as far in terms of entering a magical realm where I hoped that I could find answers to *my* questions. Our brief time together, though, had bonded us in our quests, and as such, was a time to be treasured, and not wasted as merely a fact gathering session. This was clear to me – despite how contrary such revelations were to my usual practice. The long pauses in Dr. Giles' dialogue were not the awkward silences of a man fumbling for a means of expressing his thoughts. His eyes showed deep reflection, but there was always the hint of a smile on his lips. I guessed that there were memories of Derra filling his mind, and that while he had come to terms with her absence, there was new hope in finding her at the brink of his new adventure. My work, too, would supplement his own, and when he spoke, he was careful to explain all of the elements that might factor into what I hoped to witness.

Dr. Giles continued his instruction by describing the mythical features that underscored the May celebration. On the Eve of May, he told me, it was believed that witches flew to the hilltops on their brooms, and danced all night around the bonfires. Other mythological creatures, too, roamed freely – such as ghosts and faeries. The Queen of the Faeries, according to the story that he related, rides out on a snow-white horse looking for mortals to lure to the Land of the Faeries for seven years. If you sit beneath the willow tree on this night, you may hear the bells of her horse. If you heed this warning and hide your face, she will pass you by. If you look at her, however, you may be chosen. In the celebration of love that marks this time of fertility, another manifestation of this myth, the Goddess, comes to call you out of yourself, never to return to the world that you once knew. The May Queen, dressed in white, represents this Goddess in her maiden state.

The tales came to life as they fell from Dr. Giles' lips. It was very much as if I had come under some spell. My senses, a little numbed (it is true) by the brew which we continually sipped, feasted on his words as if he were describing events that were a natural, albeit magical, part of our everyday lives. Stories of witches and faeries and ghosts, anathema to my keenly developed sense of reason, made sense in the context of Dr. Giles' narrative. What amazed me was how exactly the tradition of the May celebration fit into what I knew, by this time, of TSD. Dr. Giles assured me that the several other annual celebrations fit equally well, but that there was no point in adding to the confusion by introducing one of them before its time. They were, in essence, different aspects of the same thing, he said. TSD, he believed, was so successful in its appeal because it did not waiver too far from culture and practice that had been cultivated, in many aspects, since the beginning of history. Derra, he suggested, was a good example. While she had an undoubted distaste for at least part of what transpired with TSD, she had been unwittingly trained as a Druid priestess, and the dimensions that she had been able to explore unhindered all spoke to the secret Wisdom that she had acquired. The only ones who recognized that Wisdom belonged to TSD.

The most surprising thing that developed from listening to Dr. Giles was an unwelcome sympathy for TSD. I had been motivated to pick up on John Sturgess' case because I believed that he had uncovered a conspiracy of cold-blooded killers. I did not waiver in that conviction, but certainly found it hard to reconcile with any feelings of compassion for the case at hand. It was a constant battle for me to continue treating facts as facts, and to distance myself from Sturgess' more instinctive style of detecting. In the end, I compromised – a little. So long as I could keep the facts in front of me, I figured that having some understanding of TSD thinking might help me in determining motive. After all, a degree of sympathy for the killers did not necessarily handicap the case. More than once, I had brought a strong case to court against a battered wife who had found the only foolproof means of ending the abuse. At that point, I left justice, whether earthly or divine, in hands other than mine.

**S**everal hours had passed before Dr. Giles had finished sharing the fruits of his research with me. I'm sure that he could have spent several more on peripheral issues, but I believe that he made his selections wisely. In the time that was allotted to me, it was not my business to gather all the threads that John Sturgess had unraveled in his time in Middlemore. It would certainly have seemed madness, from my department's perspective, to see yet another detective go down that path. Like Dr. Giles, then, I had been selective in my choices. The prospect of witnessing the May ceremony, especially as related by Dr. Giles, held an abundance of opportunities for me – all of which would be past in very short order. And time was the one thing that I knew I could not overspend on this visit.

In short, I was content. My mission had certainly been justified by the details with which I had been provided. There was a pleasant numbness in my thought processes – aided, no doubt, by an extended session of sipping fine draught beer. I cannot say for certain whether the one pitcher that had been brought to the table replenished itself through some divine intervention, or whether Dr. Giles had simply signaled for refills once, maybe twice, without my detection. Both explanations strike me as miraculous. Although I had been totally immersed in Dr. Giles' narrative, I find it impossible to believe that I had missed any of the obvious occurrences taking place around me. Yet, it must have been so. I had never felt so mellow in my entire life. Existence had never extended to such dimensions for me, and yet, here I was on the inside track of something very important, with the most exciting events yet to take place. I suspected that Dr. Giles felt much the same

I only wished that I had had more to offer Dr. Giles in our time together. Although his research on Somerset had been more of an afterthought following the volume of research he had conducted concerning the Middlemore traditions, it still dwarfed any information that I could provide to supplement it. In truth, I could really not see that what I had to offer would be of any significant value to Dr. Giles on his planned expedition. Of course, I did not touch on the historical and religious details concerning which Dr. Giles' expertise was so profound. As usual, I had concentrated on gathering facts. It was, however, a sparse harvest, given the considerable restraints of time and distance. Before I had met Dr. Giles, and been exposed to the detailed exposition of his work, I had been rather proud of the tidbits of information that I had unearthed for him. With my mind swirling from his narrative, however, I was embarrassed to offer the handful of addresses and telephone numbers that I had found in exchange.

Dr. Giles, I am happy to say, was not disappointed with my offering. I had apologized profusely, and had been careful to emphasize that I had, for the most part, been guessing, and that there was no guarantee that I had provided anything of value. Dr. Giles simply dismissed by misgivings with a wave of his hand. It was information, he said, that he could not have accessed by any means. Without it, he added, there was really no starting point. Although he had equipped himself with the most comprehensive details of the Somerset religions, without my information, he would be once again forced to start from scratch with only vague hopes of falling onto to some useful trail. If only one of the addresses or numbers that I had given him related, even indirectly, to TSD, then I would have taken him light years ahead in terms of accomplishing his mission. Put in those terms, I felt much better about what I had done. I was confirmed, too, in the value that I place on approaching a case with the deductive method. If a handful of minor clues can weigh so comparably to such detailed research, initiated by the strongest instincts, then there was certainly no need for me to adjust my techniques.

It was with a degree of sadness that Dr. Giles and I parted after our prolonged lunch. Although neither of us had both known John Sturgess for very long, his passion for his final case had spilled over to both of us. Dr. Giles, of course, had his own motivations. Together, these two men confronted me with a powerful force to which I willingly succumbed. I was sad that John could not have been with us as the colorful presentation of the May celebration unfurled. I was sad, too, that Dr. Giles would be thousands of miles away by the time I would be ready to describe the events that I planned to witness. I wondered, too, if our paths would ever cross again. Practically speaking, I suspected that they might – with both of us living in the Seattle area. But the gut instinct, that both Dr. Giles and John Sturgess had managed to plant inside of me, told me that, if we met again, it would not be in the world to which we had grown accustomed. Indeed, we were both already starting to grow unaccustomed to that world. Yet, as Dr. Noah Giles walked away from the restaurant, and from my sight, towards his final evening at the George, I felt a glow of inspiration, knowing that, shortly, we would both be stepping into worlds where few had ventured to tread.

Normally, my first order of business would have been to check in with the local police. John Sturgess had cautioned against contacting them, however, in that they might have a role in some the mysterious activities that took place in Middlemore. Given more time, that was an avenue that I might like to have explored. With the May celebration at hand, however, it made no sense to stir up controversy that might affect the proceedings. It was decidedly best that I remained obscure, moving only when the time was right.

I might, in all modesty, declare myself a bit of an expert at going unnoticed. Whereas, your John Sturgess type might as well have had the word "cop" tattooed on his forehead, it was not so obvious with me. In the first place, while of average height, I am rather thin. John Sturgess filled a room with his presence. I am usually asked what time I arrived – several minutes after the fact. My face is not particularly noteworthy. It's a little pointy, perhaps, in keeping with the rest of my physique, but there is nothing particularly unique about it. My eyes peer through the narrowest of slits, and it is doubtful that anyone could tell you their color after a first meeting. I never wear anything that would draw attention to me, and I seldom attract comments. I like it that way. I think of my body as an office from which I can safely observe the world around me. I doubt very much that the waiter who catered to Dr. Giles and myself for so long on one day would have recognized me had I reappeared at one of his tables the next.

I was aware of the location of the George, but it was not necessary for me to go inside. All indications were that the young women would leave for their chosen site directly from the chalet. That was to my advantage. The chalet was a very public place that remained opened year round. It would have been particularly conducive to my needs in the heart of the ski season, but I was not overly handicapped by the decreased crowds. I simply took my steps cautiously, and let the unimpressive nature of my physical self take care of the rest. In no time at all, I had inspected the entire premises, and attracted no more attention than a wandering spirit. It was a remarkably satisfying experience. Interrogation, though I used it regularly, was never my favorite means of gathering information. Because of my unobtrusive presence, I had to compensate when asking questions by pushing myself right into people's faces – like a yapping dog. I much preferred the leisurely conversations (like the one with Dr. Giles), or the simple stealth operations (like the one at the chalet). Among other things, I discovered where the girls would be located during the daytime hours of the Eve of May. The seminar rooms were booked solid until the late afternoon. I figured that these meetings, covering the final preparations for the ceremonies that would take place that evening, would provide me with an excellent point of departure. I would arrive well in advance, though, so that nothing would be left to chance.

I also spent some time scouting the countryside. The whole setting was rather picturesque. The town of Middlemore did not extend more than a few blocks, yet the tight packing of the tourist shops, and the liberal smattering of pubs and restaurants, made it seem much larger than it was. Both the chalet and the George were a reasonable walk away in different directions, but they were far enough from town, and from each other that most people used their cars, or a taxi, to reach each point of the perfect triangle that they would have formed on a map. The hills, of course, rested in the direction of the chalet. They were high enough to catch their share of snow, but were certainly not near what I was used to in the height of the Coastal Range that separated Seattle from the rest of the state. The rest of the landscape was a wonderful mixture of forest and scenic fields, crisscrossed by well-worn paths and quaint makeshift wooden fences. I had determined that, since the May celebration was going to take place outdoors, I should familiarize myself with the natural boundaries as opposed to the man-made ones. The forest had any number of points of entry leading to any number of hilltops, most of which would remain relatively secluded – depending on how far the revelers chose to traverse. If the celebration were to take place away from that small triangle of civilization, the options multiplied exponentially. The bus that brought them to Middlemore provided those options.

I returned to the chalet in the late afternoon, but the bus had just left the parking lot. I briefly considered following it, in case the celebrations were to begin before the Eve of May, but fortunately decided against it. It was not likely that the conference rooms had been booked for the next day simply to throw me off of their trail – since they didn't even know that I was on it! My guess was that they were all headed back to the George for a good meal, and a good night's sleep, before beginning the marathon of events that lay before them. There was an outside chance that they might spot me following them, and that would have scuttled my hopes of following them undetected on the Eve of May. So, instead, I took my dinner at one of the many restaurants in town, and left Middlemore for my motel by way of the George where, in passing, I noticed that the bus was resting comfortably for the night. I, too, decided to relax, and to conclude my preliminary investigations – despite all of the options that I had left unexplored. It brought to mind a recurring nightmare I had had about trying to prepare for a French exam after ignoring the course all semester. It did not surprise me that, despite the long hours that I spent in the motel bed that night, at least part of that sleep had been disturbed once more by that same dream.

## 5

had settled myself several yards outside of the chalet in the mid-afternoon of the Eve of May. From my location, chosen carefully in advance, I had a full view of the entrance as well as the bus that the girls had used to ferry themselves back and forth to the George. Although both John Sturgess and Dr. Giles had provided me with some description of the groups that came to Middlemore for these ceremonies, I was in no way prepared for the vision that met my eye as I reached the chalet that evening. A seemingly endless stream of the most beautiful young women that I had ever seem flowed single file out into the approaching night. They were beautifully and colorfully dressed, almost as if they were headed to a prom or some such formal event. The style of their dresses, however, was neither formal nor modern. Although long and flowing, the dresses were much more akin to the illustrations that I remember in some of the old nursery rhyme books that I had been read as a child. This impression was greatly enhanced by the long old-fashioned aprons that all of them were wearing. I was not witnessing a beauty pageant, but a parade of milkmaids and ladies of the court. In dream-like sequence, they lilted across the parking lot like an animated daisy chain blown softly to and fro by the yet warm spring breeze.

I slipped into an unshakeable trance as I fixed my eyes on this unearthly sight. It was well after the fact before I noticed that the magical train had slipped past the waiting bus and proceeded directly onto an adjacent path. It struck me at the time how foolish I had been not to have anticipated this – instead assuming that they would take advantage of transportation to keep their locations secret. A few older women hovered, however, flitting back and forth like hummingbirds, watching the path ahead and the path behind for unwanted spectators. Although they were hooded and garbed in long dark cloaks, I had assumed that they were all older women on the basis of the features I caught of one of them in the fading twilight. She was not, by any means, ancient or unattractive, but by comparison, she might have seemed that way. My guess was that she had participated in such a ceremony as a young woman – maybe twenty years ago – and that she was now fully entrenched in whatever rituals were in place. I had to admire the efficiency of it all. With no disrespect, I realized that poor John Sturgess could not have stumbled his way in pursuit of this crowd without being detected. I thought it rather providential that I had been called upon to complete his good work at this precarious stage of events.

Providence, too, was at work in preventing me from committing a blunder of colossal proportions once the girls and their guardians had disappeared onto the trail. I had already left my vehicle, and was about to move in their direction, when I was halted by the headlights of a minivan entering the chalet parking lot. At first, I cursed my bad luck over what I felt might be an insurmountable loss of time in having to wait for clear passage to the path. I thought, perhaps, that there might be confederates aboard the bus, set there specifically to prevent such spies as myself. I was totally unprepared, however, to witness an entire vanload of confederates – not set there to protect, but to participate in the ceremonies at hand. Again, I was astounded at my uncharacteristic lack of perception. *The May ceremony was a ceremony of young love, and it takes two to make love.* And, specifically in ceremonies focused on fertility, one might expect the presence of both genders – despite TSD's emphasis on the female role. The good Dr. Giles had either assumed that I would make this connection, or had also suffered a glaring oversight. But now was not the time for such speculations.

The men in the group, seven of them in all, compared favorably to the women in both age and health. They seemed less concerned with being followed into the woods than the women had been, and they chased down the path at a fair clip. In a way, this made my task less daunting. I had no doubt that I could follow this lot undetected, whereas with the girls, I had been somewhat concerned about the stealth of their keepers. I was, however, kept continually out of breath in my pursuit of the young men. Still, it worked well. Another positive effect of being interrupted by the boys was being snapped out of the trance that the girls had conjured simply by their overwhelming presence. I didn't know whether or not, in the process, the boys had had any contact with the girls prior to this night, but if not, I wondered how they might react to their first vision – knowing that there would be some level of interaction with these enchantresses. In fact, even if they were already familiar with their consorts, the level of anticipation must have been at fever pitch for them at this point.

The journey to the hilltop was long and rather arduous. Again, I thought how much better suited I was to this task than my late friend. My conditioning was of great benefit to me in surviving the trek. Still, I realized that I was not in the same league as the boys ahead of me – nor likely the girls whom they followed. The older women, I guessed were probably fine, too, likely having gone this route many times before, and having thus trained for the journey for any number of years. Nonetheless, I reached the hilltop in one piece and undetected – as I always assumed that I would. The completion of that first task, however, had been more trying than I had anticipated. All in all, though my run to my point of observation had been successful, I was disappointed with myself on several counts. I had not anticipated that the route to this hilltop reached directly to the chalet. I had not anticipated that there would be a contingent of males joining the young women. And, I had not anticipated that, in following a well-conditioned group in the prime of life, I might be pushing my endurance to its outer limits.

**6**

When all had arrived at the chosen site, a man (a priest I would assume) opened the ceremony in prayer. Apart from striking me as a little strange, this scene drove home another personal failing. *From where had this white-haired gentleman appeared?* His robe matched those of the older women who had watched over the group, and I wondered if he might have come from amongst them – since I had not been able to observe more than one of them definitively. I quickly dismissed that idea, however, since my senses had not detected any masculine qualities in the way that any of them had moved in and out of that exquisite line of associates. Besides, the priest was too old to have kept pace with a group that I could barely track. Logically, he had preceded them, and had prepared and lit the fire around which they had all gathered.

I found the priest's presence rather unsettling. In the first place, it reflected poorly on my detecting skills that he had proceeded to the site totally undetected and unanticipated. There was every possibility, then (had he possessed even a portion of the gifts of perception with which I have been endowed), that he might have detected me snooping around. Hopefully, either he did not have my heightened sense of detection, or else his mind was too preoccupied on the matters had hand to make use of such gifts. There was, of course, a chance that our paths had not crossed. There was something unsettling, too, about the presence of a solitary older man in what was to be, I was reasonably certain, a celebration of sexuality. Beyond that, the idea of cloaking this whole ceremony in Christian attire did not sit right with me.

The priest's prayer was long, though it seemed well rehearsed. Although I was, by no means, an expert on religious jargon (even as it relates to the Christian faith), most of what was said, during the initial segments of the prayer, sounded distinctly Christian. I have attended the services of a variety of Christian denominations, ranging from Baptist to Catholic, and I must say that words of the prayer struck me as much closer to the latter. I cannot speak with regard to the precepts of the Catholic faith (of which I know nothing), but rather more to the format. It is my understanding, too, that of all the Protestant denominations, Anglicanism, and other orthodox Churches, can lean more the Catholic way than the Baptist way. Of course, Dr. Giles had given me a heads up on this, and I was inclined to think that what I was hearing was some form of Anglicanism or Episcopalian prayer. About three quarters of the way through the prayer, however, the tone shifted with the introduction of the Virgin Mary to the center of worship (and I knew that this was more of a Catholic focus than an Anglican one). I had barely adjusted to this, however, before the focus shifted again, this time to Mary Magdalene (for whom I had never encountered prayer or worship in any Christian context). Then, predictably, there were words to the May Queen, the Virgin Goddess of sexual love. At this point, the young men and women seemed to have worked themselves into an ecstatic state (not unlike the expression of "tongues" that I have witnessed in some charismatic churches).

What followed the prayer was nothing short of chaos. The young people scattered in every direction, running and squealing their ways into the thoroughly blackened forest. The long skirt of a strikingly beautiful young woman brushed my face as she passed by. I was saved detection not so much by the darkness (as her face was perfectly clear to me) as by her preoccupation with the celebration at hand. The vision of her face at that moment, however, is firmly fixed upon my mind. It haunts me even to think of it now, and I hesitate to assume how much I might have subconsciously added. She appeared to me exactly as I had remembered an illustration from one of the nursery rhymes of my childhood – probably, one of the many rhymes about Maying that I have only since discovered were on that topic. (I tried subsequently to discover that illustration, but I am afraid that it, and the book that contained it, have gone the way of the countless baseball cards that would have secured my retirement by now.) So, I am not totally certain whether it is her face, the illustration's face, or some hybrid, that I see so constantly. There was a timeless sweetness about her, yet there was a hint of mischief in those rosebud lips, and in the sidelong glance that she was casting at the youth around her. I suppose that all made her the perfect celebrant for the activities at hand.

As I stand at a distance now from by far the most bizarre undercover work in which I have ever engaged, I marvel at my own incompetence. In countless cases preceding this investigation, I have worked my art to perfection. I have few regrets over the manner in which I have conducted myself, and I cannot recall more than a handful of instances where I might have changed my procedures. My performance at the May celebration, however, was a complete debacle. Not only was I guilty of the several miscalculations that I have already recorded, but I committed the most grievous sin of all. *I fell asleep!* Even on the most tedious stakeout imaginable, the thought of sleep was never a possibility for me. Yet, armed with research that cost my fellow detective his life, bolstered by the scholarly input of Dr. Giles, and thrust into a beehive of the most fascinating behavior imaginable, I managed to catch forty winks! It is true that the young people were well out of sight before I succumbed, but the activity around the bonfire was just beginning. Many of the "older" women cast off their robes, revealing naked bodies that had fared remarkably well against the ravages of time. (I am assuming their ages on the basis of timelines that were revealed on their faces in the glow of the flames.) Back and forth they leapt through the flames in what seemed to me a remarkable display of endurance. How long this feat continued, and what part the solitary priest played in the procedures, I cannot say. I could not have witnessed this scene for more than a few minutes before I unwittingly closed my eyes for the night. I would like to think that I slept in response to some spell that had been cast. I suppose an argument could be made for that. I, however, do not believe in such things, and will therefore, not be the one to present the evidence for such a case.

I awoke, as dawn was breaking, with the sounds of joyful singing in my ears. Queued by the sun's first rays, the young people were making their way back to the site of the now defunct bonfire, with scores of wildflowers overflowing from their knotted aprons. The random gathering soon formed into an orderly (though still mirthful) procession behind a few of the young men who were carrying the prized pine tree – which had been freshly cut and trimmed for the May Day ceremony. Already decked in woodland ornamentation, multicolored ribbons were secured to the narrow end of the Maypole as it arrived in what had been the site of the bonfire. As two young men secured the Maypole in the designated spot, the young women arranged their flowers in colorful patterns that encircled the point of worship. When all was set, the young revelers disappeared into the surrounding bushes, emerging within minutes disguised in an assortment of human and animal masks – which clearly had been previously transported to the site and hidden in the night (again undetected by me!), no doubt, by the solitary priest. Hats and trinkets that appeared to be of native origin had also been found, and covered the young people to varying degrees. Hand in hand they circled the pole. The priest, I saw, stood next to the pole, still in his robe, yet the robe had become almost obscured by garlands of flowers.

It occurred to me that my place of hiding had either been particularly fortuitous, or that I had already been discovered (possibly in my sleep), and that my presence had been deemed insignificant enough to ignore at this time. Of course, what would they have done with me (short of human sacrifice!) had they deemed me to be a threat to the proceedings? My guess was that, if they had indeed spotted me, they would save any actions until the conclusion of the ceremonies. At that point, I could be reported to whatever authority might take action, and they could find the best means of dealing with my intrusion. I shuddered to think of it as I recalled John Sturgess' untimely death. I had the sickly sensation that, despite still silently watching the proceedings from the shadows of my chosen cover, I had switched roles in the night and become the watched rather than the watcher. I was certain that, despite their precautions, they always anticipated the presence of unwanted spies, and came to these sites prepared for that eventuality. Considering the multitude of ceremonies, I was sure that I was not the first to have wandered into their sacred zone. As much as I wanted to believe in the efficacy of my hiding spot, I could not assume that I had remained shielded from the protective eyes of those who were guarding the area. In any case, I had no option but to see what would unfold in the daylight festivity.

Shortly after the circle around the pole had gathered steam, two of the celebrants emerged from the woods. She, also decked in bright garlands, was not hidden by any mask. Neither was the boy obscured by disguise, and he carried with him a brightly decorated staff. They danced their way through the flowers towards the loop of frenzied partiers. The circle parted to let the couple enter to approach the priest, and it closed tightly behind them. Even from my own ignorance, I knew that this couple was the King and Queen of May, and that a wedding ceremony was to take place under the sanction of this priest, and before the many witnesses (myself included) at hand. The dazzling gala continued for some hours, however, before the priest's voice called the celebration to order. An atmosphere of solemnity overtook the proceedings. Again, through a well-rehearsed yet unfamiliar prayer, Christian elements were infused into this seemingly pagan celebration. Only in reference to this beauteous May Queen did the clandestine references creep into the Christian liturgy. The picture of purity, yet virtually brimming with sexuality, the May Queen stood joyfully at the altar as her husband-to-be watched in expectant wonder. Upon completion of the ceremony, chaos again broke forth, though this time confined to the immediate vicinity of the venerated pole. Masks were lifted or discarded to consume the food and drink that had also been transported (again unbeknownst to me!) to the celebration site.

I had wondered, as a child, when I had first heard of Puritan rule in England, why the Puritans had had such disdain for the colorful and joyful Maypole celebrations. I wondered no longer. Though there was, indeed, something warm and inviting about what I was witnessing on this obscure New England hilltop, it was not hard to tell how such a celebration would clash with the austere Puritan doctrine. Although the raucous sensuality that I witnessed did not proceed past passionate kisses and tantalizing dances, who knows what took place under the cover of the nighttime forest while I lay fast asleep? Although history told me that the Maypoles returned to England with King Charles II, I was also aware that they had been permanently removed as a noteworthy fixture of American society by the strong influence of the Puritans that had brought the first English settlements to New England. Nonetheless, I felt that, in chopping down this emblem of fertility, American culture had somehow been castrated, and that, in this harmless vigil to the most ancient of traditions, was an attempt to heal the wounds of the past. Such a noble cause could not justify the vigilante actions that had taken the lives of such innocent souls as John Sturgess and the young woman whose death had so occupied his thoughts. Yet no such thoughts entered my mind – which was, itself, too full of the nostalgic merriment that surrounded me.

The celebrations continued into the twilight hour with no further noteworthy events taking place. The party essentially withered away as the young people dispersed singly or in couples while the elders remained to gather the discarded masks and empty cups. Before nightfall, all had been efficiently cleared, and but for the flowers and the charred remains of the bonfire, there was no trace of any extraordinary event remaining at the site. I waited until it was dark to take my leave – in case any stragglers should spot me. I am a man with a strong constitution, but I must confess that I have never been so terrified as I was when I made my way down that dark woodland trail. Every rustle in the bushes, every bird or animal that stirred, brought images of goblins and faeries – long since buried with my childhood – to the forefront of my mind. It seems silly as I reflect on it now, but I feared being whisked away to some apocryphal realm as I dodged from tree to tree. If there were any magic in the air during the celebrations, it had all gathered in my thoughts as I made my fearful way to the safety of my waiting car. Even the parking lot that I traversed in those final steps, though vacant, seemed to host such spirits as I would never have imagined, in one last portentous dance. I doubt that a less empirical mind than mine would have survived this journey.

# Addendum

As a postscript to the details that I have recorded regarding the May celebration in Middlemore (for posterity and for Dr. Giles' examination), I must say that I have never been so happy to be in Seattle. Time did not allow me to follow up on the aftermath of what I witnessed – and I am most relieved that it did not. Once I had reached my car, I could not shake the feeling that I was being followed. This, of course, was impossible. One of the many skills that I have perfected in keeping with my exceptional ability to remain undetected (the Middlemore fiasco aside) is an expertise in following vehicles without being spotted. Conversely, no one can follow me without being detected, because I know all of the tricks. I was *not* followed – but that was an issue of little consequence. An amateur detective could have traced me to my motel easily enough simply by recording the license number of my rented car.

My state of mind was no more stable during my trip back to Seattle, ahead of schedule, the next morning. When the plane encountered turbulence in mid-flight, I was absolutely certain that it had been sabotaged in some exorbitant scheme to eliminate me with no regard to collateral damage. Even the taxi ride home from the airport had ominous overtones for me. Fortunately, however, in the security of my own apartment, the acute anxiety started to subside. My nervous condition, however, had exacted a physical toll on my body and mind, and I remain on sick leave two weeks after that fateful night. The time has been fruitful, however, for perfecting my account of the May celebration, and for contemplating any recommendations that I might make to Dr. Giles at this time – as the only current recipient of this report. Our brief telephone call, just last night, helped to dissolve any remaining anxieties regarding TSD issues, as I had also suffered somewhat on his account, wondering if it had taken a similar toll on him. He assured me that he was well, and we could exchange reports upon his imminent return.

When we spoke, I offered Dr. Giles a warning of the need to take caution, and I suggested that he return directly to the West Coast rather than stopping at Middlemore. He assured me that he had already planned to do so, and was quite looking forward to returning to his home and his cat! I further suggested that he might like to limit any contact with me, as I was quite certain that I was a marked man, and that he may well be endangering himself if he should be spotted with me. Dr. Giles brushed this suggestion aside, however, insisting that TSD was most definitely aware of his existence, and that, if anyone would be placing anyone in danger, he would be placing me in danger by contact. I was not so certain of his reasoning on this point, but I assured him that I was not worried for myself should he choose to spend some time with me upon his return.

My usual procedure in summarizing any investigation is to let the facts speak for themselves. When all is said and done, however, what facts have I submitted in this case? I traveled from one coast to the other, and did no more than witness a group, comprised mainly of youth, celebrate May Day in what I gather (on the basis of the input from Dr. Giles' laborious research) was a very traditional ceremony. Nothing that I uncovered took me any further in discovering any possible culprits in the untimely death of Detective John Sturgess. Indeed, the collective facts suggest that there was no calculated plot in play. On the basis of factual evidence, I would have to say that, not only have I done nothing to further the case, but I have actually done more *to set the case back*! The facts have spoken strongly with regard to religious and historical traditions that are being kept alive, but such information demonstrates no sinister links to any secret society – even though the name of an active secret society has been revealed (no thanks to me!).

While I would concede that TSD, as defined in the research of Detective Sturgess and Dr. Giles, may well have a predilection towards protecting their secrets by nefarious means, there is no evidence of a conspiracy behind the death of the young woman, Sarah – whose circumstances so preoccupied the late Detective John Sturgess. All hard evidence points to a single perpetrator, by the name of Leo Mascagni. John Sturgess' intuitive report provides no hard facts to suggest that the secret society, known as the Society of Diana, had any role in either Sarah's death or Leo's subsequent death. It is only mildly coincidental that Leo died around the time of being interrogated. His sort continually consorts with a very unsavory lot, and for all we know, he could easily have been killed over nothing more than a petty debt. The case was only kept alive by John's obsession with it. And, as I have been careful to point out, John's style of detecting was seriously at odds with my own. He had the ability to channel into the thought processes of both victim and attacker, and had met with some success in so doing. I believe that my focus on the facts has consistently provided more airtight court cases – though I wish that Middlemore had offered a better argument for my methods.

It is, perhaps, as a result of the roller coaster of emotions that I have endured since the Eve of May, that I have set aside my tried *modus operandi* (for this case only!), and submit my final conclusions on the basis of more intuitive observations. The passion for uncovering details of TSD exhibited by both John Sturgess and Dr. Giles speaks volumes for that society's involvement in operations that extend beyond those that are strictly religious in nature. Even the religious aspects of their operations call for scrutiny. TSD is, by my own experience and by the experiences that have been passed to me, a powerful organization fueled by powers that I would suggest border on the magical. Its religious practice appeals to all aspects of human nature, but its overriding need both to fuel and to protect its secrets has forced the Society to branch out into more clandestine operations. The recruitment of young women who are at their intellectual and sexual prime fits well into their purposes – at least in so far as Dr. Giles' research has currently defined them. Likewise, the elimination of undesirable elements (whether they be innocent victims like Sarah and John Sturgess, or guilty perpetrators like Leo Mascagni) is a predictable result of their preoccupation with protecting the sanctity of their faith. But nothing is proven.

As I observed the May ceremony, I fell under the Society's spell – figuratively, and, perhaps, literally as well. Childhood images of faerie stories and nursery rhymes filled my consciousness from sundown to sundown and have remained there as a warm refuge for me ever since. On the other side of things, I feel as if I have been violated in some way – that some sort of tracking device was implanted on me, and that, should I make just one misstep, someone will push a button to make me disappear. In my condition, John Sturgess would undoubtedly say that he felt haunted (as he indeed expressed regarding his own condition in his final days). I will not concede more than that I am suffering the remnants of a nervous condition regarding which I expect a full and complete recovery. Nonetheless, my nervous condition traces back directly to the Eve of May. The power of that impact reinforces my concern that the conspiratorial theories of John Sturgess (aided by Dr. Giles) were not misplaced.

# VIII

FROM THE MEMOIRS OF DR. NOAH GILES:
LATE APRIL THROUGH MID- MAY

left Middlemore for Glastonbury shortly after I met with Detective Graham Kennedy. Detective Kennedy seemed to absorb everything that I told him. This was no small accomplishment, as I poured out information from almost four months of rather intensive research. It was a good session, and I took my leave of the George and Middlemore confident that the right man would be taking notes on the woodland activities that I was convinced would begin on the Eve of May.

I had not allowed myself much time to catch the May celebrations in Glastonbury, but I knew that I would not be facing the difficulties that my counterpart in Middlemore would be facing – so there was little preparation necessary for my visit. While there is little acknowledgement of May Day in North America (outside of the sporadic labor issues), the tradition remains alive and well in Europe. Whereas Detective Kennedy would be forced underground to spy upon a clandestine ceremony at Middlemore, I knew that my celebrants in Glastonbury would be hidden in plain sight. There is a flurry of activities scheduled as far as I can gather from a distance, though none of them are likely targets for me. I noticed that "Rhiannon's Festival of the Lover at Beltane" was scheduled for the Eve of May at the Glastonbury Goddess Temple, but despite the coincidence of location names, I know that this festival is only indirectly related to what I am seeking.

Rhiannon of the Birds is the Virgin Goddess of sexual love. The seeming contradiction of this title is typical of the May celebrations. The Glastonbury tradition of Rhiannon tells of her riding her white horse in pursuit of Pwyll, King of the Summerland, near the Glastonbury Tor. When Pwyll finally asks her to stop for him, she does so and their love becomes symbolic of the season's festivities. Many other May legends touch on this story and it is not surprising that the Temple picked up on it. But the Temple itself, where the Goddess Religion as it is now practiced, is only historically related to TSD beliefs. TSD, of course, focuses more on the origins of the Goddess traditions in the early stages of the first millennium, and only in as much as those traditions intersect with Christian and Druid faith of that same period. The challenge that I face upon arriving in Glastonbury is the challenge of not becoming bogged down by the countless traditions and celebrations that are in play. It is necessary for me to sift through the maze of festivities to the heart of what the Society considers the true celebration of the occasion. So, while the preparation time is short, there is very little that I can do before the celebrations actually start to take place on the Eve of May.

It is with a great deal of sadness that I bid adieu to Middlemore. Although the mission that had brought me there still tugs at my heartstrings, the memories are good ones, and the routines will be sorely missed. Although I still have no definitive answers about Derra, the research had been productive, and I feel that my time has been well used. The George has offered me months of rather idyllic accommodation, and Tom Monroe has provided me with many hours of entertaining conversation in the process – despite his reluctance to give up too much information about his regular visitors. So long as I kept my distance from the church rectory, I must confess that the church services, conducted by Father Luke, were a continued source of spiritual enlightenment. I have spent parts of two seasons in the district, and I have been enchanted by the subtle natural changes that seemed to happen on a daily basis – whether the landscape was blanketed in snow or bursting forth with spring flowers. I would have liked that chance to spend the rest of the year there – to see the annual cycle through to its end – but it is not practical to do so, and now is as good a time as any to bring my stay to an end.

Mostly, I will miss Jessica Burke. I would never have guessed the deep, warm friendship that would develop between the two of us on the basis of that first impression. She seems too sensually beautiful, and too aloof, to give a person such as myself the time of day. Yet our friendship grew by leaps and bounds over the course of my research (that she so willingly aided) at the library over which she presided. It was a pleasure to see her each morning, and to know that she was there to share in whatever exciting results that that day's research might unearth. Our social times, too, were always highly animated and infused with the kind of spirit that I had always thought was reserved for those who were young and in love. We are committed to our own situations at either side of the continent, but I know that we will never lose touch. Still, it is a sad thing to think of the miles that will separate us, and of the infrequent occasions we will have to bridge that gap. Yet, it will happen – we both know that. Meanwhile, she will be my eyes and my ears in Middlemore. Middlemore is a topic of research for which I foresee no end.

The seemingly endless flight from Boston to London finally deposited me with British Rail, and the sharp edges of my jetlag were pleasantly blunted as I rode the tracks eastward in the comfort of my first class booth. The lush green countryside, speckled with stone cottages built in centuries past, is a vision that I had postponed for far too long. I have read enough about Britain, and have watched enough movies, that there should be nothing about the land that should catch me by surprise. Yet, when I see that pub sign, swaying in the wind as we slow for our first country stop, it is all I can do to restrain myself from hopping from the train and running through the front door to see what a British pub is really like inside when housed such a quaint structure in such a quaint town. I do realize that the twenty-first century has reached England, but from what I can see, strong evidence of past centuries still remain. If any questions remained as to why TSD had seen this land as the guardian of their ancient religious secrets, they were quashed by the experience of a visit to Castle Cary.

I knew very little about Castle Cary beyond that it was the closest train station to Glastonbury. The history of Castle Cary is much shorter than that of my nearby destination. Apparently, the first noteworthy event in Castle Cary was the erection of a Norman castle there around the end of the eleventh century, but the castle was destroyed half a century later. Anticipating my sense of exhaustion when I arrived, I had booked myself a room at a hotel, near the marketplace, only one mile from the train station. I could not resist choosing the particular hotel, as it is not only known as the George Hotel, but it dates back to the thirteenth century. Its location, as well, is particularly fortuitous, resting next to a path known as Paddock Drain. As it was still light when I arrived, I decided to take the physical exercise that I would need for a good night's sleep by ascending that path to the top of Lodge Hill, from where I was able to catch my first distant sight of Glastonbury Tor. The descending twilight obscured my view somewhat, but with the aid of a local resident, I pointed myself in the right direction and could make out the hazy outline of this much-heralded site. My sleep was, as hoped, full and deep. I arranged for a taxi to take me the ten miles to Glastonbury early the in the morning, but I regretted my haste once I viewed the Castle Cary, prior to my departure, with a leisurely morning walk. In close proximity to the George Hotel stands the Round House and Market House – both dating to eighteenth century. The area near Market Place, too, is filled with the quaint shops that made Castle Cary so enchanting. I saw, too, near the end of my walk, the Anglican Church, with its distinctive spire (apparently rebuilt in the nineteenth century), and it beckoned to me from a distance. But there was too much business at hand, and little time in which to manage it.

Nonetheless, a rush of excitement fills me as the taxi heads northwest along the winding road, and I caught my first close glimpse of the soft green hill known as the Glastonbury Tor. The stark tower at the top of the Tor (that had only been faintly visible in my twilight viewing) marked it for me – but that was not necessary. The Tor itself dominates the landscape, and emits its own aura of mystery in a manner that permeates the surrounding area. I know from my research that Glastonbury lies just to the west of the Tor. As I draw near, faint traces of the terraced pathway encircling the Tor become evident. The patterns of this pathway, starting from the bottom and spiraling to the top are said to be almost identical to the labyrinth found on ancient Cretan coins, and in Native American representations of Mother Earth. I waited breathlessly for the opportunity to explore the region. The town itself is no less enthralling than was the Tor that watches over it. In short order, I found the site of the famous Glastonbury Abbey – to which the annual pilgrimages of both the Anglican and the Catholic Churches lead. The actual Anglican and Catholic Churches of the town lie further west – but are not of pressing interest to me. More fascinating for me is the Chalice Well. (I have spent hours researching the traditions surrounding this famous site.) On the Eve of May, the women traditionally meet beside the Blood Spring of Chalice Well to welcome the Goddess of springtime. Opposite the Chalice Well is the White Spring – the alleged entrance to the underworld and the realm of the faeries. The highlight of my first quick tour, though, is the Holy Thorn of Glastonbury (*Crataegus mongyna biflora)* on Wearyall Hill. It is just in bloom, and will not bloom again until the Winter Solstice. Joseph of Arimathea reputedly brought the Holy Thorn to Glastonbury. It is significant too as a representation of the sacred marriage between the King and Goddess, and of the springtime fertility of the King's bride.

I suppose my sense of serendipity also has a hand in choosing another ancient hotel known as the George and Pilgrim. It dates to the fifteenth century, and offers many attractions to me (though at a considerable price). Still, it is equipped with full amenities as well as its famous Monk's Cell and Confessional. It would be a priority to visit for any tourist, but despite the wondrous adventure that my trip has already become, I know that I am there on business, and that my business begins that very day – being the Eve of May. The bustle in the small town increases as twilight nears. Still, my time is adequate to inspect the sites of interest, and even to make the trek up Glastonbury Tor. I sense that Detective Kennedy would likewise be spending his day gathering a sense of Middlemore in the regions that extend to the like named inn that stood there. Of course, he has five more hours of daylight left than remain for me. Still, our assignments, though pointed at a similar end, are not really of the same nature. His purpose is to infiltrate magical ceremonies and ancient rites. As for myself, though there certainly are any number of such activities (or counterfeit re-creations) taking place around me, it is not my business to learn from any one offering. I am seeking the corporate heads, and it is my hope that the occasion might draw them from the woodwork.

It might well be asked how I expect to encounter members of a highly secret organization (about which I still knew relatively little), in a foreign country, in a town brimming with revelers – many of whom are in such disguise as might represent those whom I seek. I do not have a good answer. My hopes, however, are not pinned solely on the hours of the May celebration. The celebration, nonetheless, is a good opportunity that I would have been foolish to ignore.

My first step is to gain familiarity with the sacred sites. I am convinced that the elite of TSD, though not necessarily planning to partake in any of the festivities, are still likely to pay homage to their holy sites on this holy occasion. I do not expect that I will recognize them amidst the throngs, unless, of course, I encounter Derra herself (which I deemed highly unlikely). But I will tuck the faces away in the back of my mind for future reference. What I hope, most of all, is to gain some sense of the unity of faith that originated at this site some two thousand years ago. I want to sense Christianity in its fullness, before the Goddess and the Druid had separated from it, taken the magic from it, and gone down their own uncharted paths. I know that this will not be easy. All of the separate elements of the faith will be there in the full conviction that they are celebrating the day as it was always meant to be celebrated. I, as a believer in High Church Anglicanism, would be guilty of the same – were I there to worship. But it is not my own belief system that is at issue here. I need to push that aside, and trust my senses.

The sights and sounds of Glastonbury are overwhelming. In some ways, exploring the town for the first time on the Eve of May is the best way to do it. The distinctive history of Glastonbury is on full display, and there is no better place on earth to find Western religion so tightly encapsulated. Yet I might wish to have experienced this place on some previous occasion – when the celebrations were not so prominent – just to have had something to compare to this first experience. It is necessary, as well, to take my own excitement into account. The trail of research that has led me here has turned this site into some imaginary realm – perhaps not unlike the Island of Avalon which, long ago, mixed history and fantasy in giving birth to tales about this very spot. There is a wonderful collection of mystical elements here, and I am not surprised that the many legends of the Holy Grail originate here and point to here. If there had been more time for me to prepare for my visit, I would certainly have done more research in that area.

I could record pages on the events that I witnessed on the Eve of May in Glastonbury (and, at some point, I may well do so), but little seems relevant to my mission. Certainly my historical perspectives are broadened. I also learned a remarkable amount about Druids and Goddesses as they exist in modern culture. But such information, though provoking some curiosity, is really not much more helpful than trying to define TSD solely on the basis of modern Christianity. Collectively, however, I must say that there is something truly magical about the events of that day – and even more so as day gives way to evening. I stayed up well into the night, half expecting to see the outline of witches on broomsticks against the bonfires that glowed in the darkness. I wondered if, on such a night as this, Derra had been whisked away to the faerie kingdom – reputedly in the hollow of that great hill that watched over the night. But then I remembered that, as a Druid priestess herself, she is already a part to the magical realm that is running rampant.

I lingered longer than was absolutely necessary, mostly in the hope that I would chance across Derra. Where pretty girls gathered, I inched closer, carefully examining the features, not merely to see if I could spot Derra among them, but to discover what could be learned from their expectant eyes. There are clusters of such girls liberally spread throughout the town – though not nearly in the proportions found in Middlemore. Their accents, to which I have not grown accustomed, add to their appeal, and perhaps make them appear even more beautiful than they actually are. I am much too enchanted to provide an objective perspective on that issue. I wondered if TSD drew from such groups, or whether these girls were already members, waiting for the dawn and the enactment of the sacred ceremonies. It is unlikely, however, here in the openness of the town, that a genuine ritual will be performed. Many of these girls will undoubtedly dance around the Maypole, but for them, it will just be for a lark. The deep significance of the fertile tree will be lost on most of them, and nothing more than an almost forgotten history lesson will come to the minds of the rest. The modern Druids and Goddesses might lay claim to a good part of that history, through legends and tales, but where were the few who will wrap the whole myth in the sacred garb of the Christian faith? If I spot them, I am unaware. Eventually, I give up on all of my searches and retire to the comfort of the George and Pilgrim. The ghosts of ages past are housed there as well, but they are friendly spirits that watch over my sleep, and gently wake me in anticipation of the morning festivities of the May celebration.

Perhaps the spirits had had their time in the dark hours preceding the daylight hours, but there is no evidence of any extraordinary events on the first day of May. I don't know that I am either disappointed or surprised by the nature of the festival that I encountered in Glastonbury. It was lively enough, and unique historical themes could be detected in many of the events, but in many ways, it was just another May Day commemoration – not unlike hundreds of others that were also falling into place across the nation. Certainly Glastonbury could boast a rather special status with regard to the May Day traditions, but that was blatantly true about Glastonbury with regard to most ancient traditions on any given day of the year. This rather unimposing village is one of the holiest spots on the face of the earth, and yet its fame is more of a curiosity than a point of common knowledge. And though God knows how many different religions and cults were milling about with their own distinctive take on the day, the sheer volume of these options seems to blend the celebrations into one rather ordinary mixture – like a promising recipe that has simply been overdone by the combination of too many ingredients.

My day was pleasant enough. There were children everywhere, oftentimes engaged in Maypole activities – totally oblivious to any significance in these pristine imitations of the fertile symbol. Various mystical events were scheduled, but many of these were just special versions of meetings that took place in town on a weekly basis. I did not waste time attending anything that I saw advertised. TSD strikes me as an organization that would only target a highly susceptible market, and would not tolerate much rejection from amongst its prospects. Any appeal to the public, therefore, I dismissed out of hand. I employed much the same strategy that I had employed the night before – visiting the holy spots again and again, looking for faces that might belong to those I sought. It seems a more futile exercise than it had been the first time. I saw few visages that would even qualify amidst the slew of youngsters that were gathered at each site. I safely assume that, if I had unwittingly encountered someone from TSD, it happened in the darkness of the Eve of May, not amidst the daylight frolicking of hyperglycemic schoolchildren.

The pretty girls are back. I recognize some who had caught my attention in the clusters that I had inspected a few hours previous, but there is nothing to draw my suspicions to them. A few male faces are familiar, too – the stern ones that seemed rather out of place in the festivities. But, again, there is nothing to link them to my search. I wonder, too, whether I am right in assuming that the inhumanity of their actions would be evident in aging lines or in hollow eyes. I have never known anyone who has applied violence in defense of a cause deemed worthy of such actions. It is difficult for me to conceive that any resultant beauty could obliterate the ugliness of destroying human life. And, from what I could tell, if one is guilty then they are all guilty. Derra, too, if she had resigned herself to the cause for which she had expressed such distaste, had her share of responsibility. The thought of that, however, runs contrary to the generally blissful mood in which I find myself – surrounded by revelers on such a happy occasion, and in such a sacred place.

The highlight of the day for me, however, has little to do with the events, or even the specific sites. It takes place once "the yardarm is up" (as my father used to say), and I land in a rather charming little pub for the one dining occasion for which the British have actually gained a positive reputation. I opt for the ploughman's lunch (more for its name than for any Epicurean reasons), which consists mostly of cheese. I suspect that the fame of the British pub lunches is as much a factor of the beverages served as any food item listed on the menu. In testing that theory, I am willing to concede that the beverages are as good a measure as anything else, and that the British likely have an edge on the competition on that count. It is a long break for me and a valuable one. My head has been too crammed for too long both in preparation for this visit, and in exploring the myriad of sites and events that are packed within the magical boundaries of Glastonbury. I need time to reflect. My senses are all ready to explode, and the mellowing effect of the town's finest bitter is the best medicine imaginable. When I finally emerge from the pub, my perspective is pleasantly altered. No longer does a kaleidoscope of contrasting traditions overwhelm me. Instead, there is a collection of ordinary people simply enjoying a rather wonderful day. This is the perspective that I need if I hope to accomplish my mission.

I cannot say that much was accomplished before twilight brought most of the special events to an end, but I had moved comfortably through the crowds that afternoon, and I had felt a part of the divine plan even as it unfolding on that holy ground. It was not, however, a mystical experience. It was something more real – a realization that, while we are all merely human, we are all truly spiritual. This is as true for the cynic who has merely stumbled across the curious rituals of the site as it is for the devout practitioner who is trying desperately to express a reverence for the occasion at hand. Thus it is necessary for me to detach myself, and to absorb the scene from the divine perspective, and to lose myself in the wonder of it all. The magic, after all, is not really indigenous to this locale; it is simply a product of human existence. Those who seek to disrupt this magic in the name of higher forces cannot be overcome on their own turf. They have to be met on the same plain on which we have all been distributed. If I can maintain my perspective, I will see them. Better still, they will see me.

The May celebration in Glastonbury was a magnificent experience that I will always remember, yet I was not sad to see it draw to an end. The subsequent week (at the exorbitant rates of the George and Pilgrim) was relatively uneventful. The town is, of course, an historical and religious goldmine, and there is no end to the hands on research available to supplement the work that I have done in Middlemore. Yet I can think of nothing substantive that was added to my understanding of either Glastonbury or TSD. I continue to walk the town, to explore the pubs, and to make myself as much a fixture there as is possible in a matter of days. A woman led the Anglican Church there, and the worship was satisfactory, but I miss the deep sense of meaning that Father Luke had somehow managed to conjure in Middlemore. I long, too, for the more traditional service back home in the familiar pew from which I had first spotted Derra. I am recognized in Glastonbury now, I know, but I am beginning to wonder if I will ever make any serious contacts. I have made several casual acquaintances, but there is no one in whom I can confide, and certainly no one who is likely to be of any use to me in my search for Derra.

Already, I have started to slip into some rather predictable routines. Starting on my first Monday there, I began my day with a long early morning walk. I picked out a few favorite routes during my extensive explorations at the time of the May celebrations, and now make use of them. After my walks, I return to my hotel for a rather extensive breakfast (complete with all of the delicious poisons of British cuisine) that is my first meal of only two that I take during the day – having neither the tooth for the elaborate cream teas, nor the stomach for the notorious evening meals. The pub lunches have grown on me, and I am careful not to wash them down with more than a pint of warm beer in the absence of any special event that might warrant more. The hours between meals are spent leisurely studying any one of the many sites that I inspected so hurriedly on the Eve of May, and to a lesser extent, on May Day. Tourists are evident, but the weekdays are much less hectic than was the weekend – especially the weekend that I had chosen.

My Thursday routine began with no more promise than the other weekdays. I was a little drowsy by the afternoon, but it was a good time to stroll through the shops, lingering in ones where I could strike up a conversation. The local architecture is fascinating, too, and I oftentimes find myself in charming corners of the town where a bench would support my weary bones, in an aesthetically pleasing spot, as I sorted through the web of intrigue woven throughout my head. I had just settled into such a spot (one that I had actually used the day before) when a man, distinctive only by his broad smile, approached that same bench and sat down beside me. It struck me as rather odd that, with other benches in the vicinity and with British reserve usually in play, he chose the social option. I figured he must have been a tourist – though nothing in his appearance suggested that to me. Apart from a greeting nod, I tried to ignore him. This was not out of any sort of snobbery. Indeed, any human contact was a valuable thing for me at this point. But I had learned already that the best way to gain the trust of an Englishman is to give him his space. Once the buffer zone is established, a common ground can be reached. When he spoke, however, I realized that my social etiquette had been unnecessary.

"Have you found our little town as interesting as you expected, Dr. Giles?"

A shiver ran up and down my spine. This man knew me. I knew him, too – though not by name. He was one of those whom I had sought. There was no relief, however, in the discovery – or, rather, in being discovered. His presentation blended perfectly with the town, but his accent was American. He never stopped smiling. I doubted that he was forty, but the contortions that his face underwent in the formation of a smile had forged deep lines, spreading from the outer edges of his eyes. I did not seen him approach, but I could tell that he was not too tall – maybe five and half feet. His hair was full and curly, and although he was not fat, there was a thickness about him that was particularly prominent in his face. The smile was by no means endearing. There was, I thought, a kind of sarcasm about it – like he either did not mean, nor care about, what he was saying. I chose not to answer his question. In any case, I was too frightened to speak.

"Come, I've got a car waiting," he said, standing and at the same time reaching to help me to my feet.

I let him help me. My knees were too weak to make the effort on my own. His touch (especially the mechanically friendly hand to the back of my shoulder) repulsed me, but I lacked the energy even to cower from him. Even if I had wanted to run, I would have been physically incapable. Yet, despite my fear, there was no desire to flee. One way or the other, I knew that this was the end of my long journey.

"We've known about you all along," he said as we drove the winding road out of town. "I think that you are much more naturally suited to research than cloak and dagger work. You would never have found us here, even if you had accidentally stumbled upon us – which, in fact, you did. Perception is everything. You seem to be quite perceptive in your research, but I think you are more of a book person than a people person. Don't get me wrong. People like you all right. But I'll bet you're a bit of a flop at a party, right?"

He rambled on like this throughout the drive – punctuating many of his remarks with a question, but never waiting for an answer. Not being familiar with British roads in general, and the roads around Glastonbury in particular, I had no idea where we were headed. The route seemed circular, but it was impossible to tell by the nature of the roads. The day was overcast, but on the basis of initial glimpses at the Tor, and with some direction from the sun, I guessed that we were headed northeast – towards Bath, or more serendipitously, towards the Salisbury plain and Stonehenge. We stopped what must have been well short of either destination, however, at some locale that I could never find again if my life depended on it. I seriously wondered if my life did depend upon it as we entered the front door of the stately home.

I was led down a hallway to a room that was clearly set up for business purposes. A long board table was lined with well-dressed men who all stood to greet me. It had the familiarity of many business meetings that I have attended – with the notable exception of me being the order of business. The ride had allowed me time to compose myself, so the prospect of standing before this high tech cult was not as unsettling as one might have guessed, and to be fair, they were doing everything within their power to make me feel comfortable. Still, I knew that the purpose of this meeting was not to determine what I could contribute to TSD. They knew everything that I knew, and much more than I would ever uncover. The purpose of this meeting was to determine whether or not I was a liability to their cause, and there was every likelihood that they had made up their minds on that issue before we even began. I knew that too much knowledge was a capital offence in their eyes, and that the odds were not in my favor. For some reason, however, I felt remarkably calm. I think that my initial fear upon being discovered had simply given way to a strange feeling of relief. I had reached the end of the road in this obsessive search, and there was something aberrantly peaceful about that.

**M**y meeting with the executive of the Society of Diana is a blur to me now. It was not, as I had expected, some sort of interrogation. If my mind had been clearer, I would probably have guessed that. They already knew all that they needed to know about me – except one thing. They needed to know how relentless I would remain in my search for Derra. I think that dawned upon me about three quarters of the way through the session. If it were clear to them that I would not relinquish my search, then I was a liability. Otherwise, I think that they considered me to be relatively harmless – despite what I had uncovered. Unfortunately, I did not see what direction they were taking until I had already convicted myself.

The whole procedure was conducted in a rather businesslike manner. It struck me as rather odd that it should be so, considering the whole magical element that made TSD so distinctive. I was not really prepared for the collection of courteous faces. I think, at this point, I would have been much more accepting of an evil eye glaring down at me, ready to turn me into a toad, or more realistically, someone taking me deep into the forest from whence I would never return. I would almost say that I was disappointed – were the circumstances less frightening. As it was, I was in a meeting that must have resembled a Mafia high council (although I have no experience of such things), where the brutal business at hand is being masked with a legitimate façade. My fear was only suppressed to the degree that my anger was felt. I did my best not to show either, however, and remained silent for much of the proceedings. When I spoke, I tried to choose my words carefully. They listened respectfully, though in retrospect, I see how skilled they were at manipulating me into saying more than I wanted to say. Still, I do not feel entirely to blame for the fate that they had chosen for me. Their minds had been made up before the meeting, and the final sentence was pretty much a formality.

When the hearings had concluded, they asked me to wait outside. I was not restrained or confined in any manner. They knew that I knew that escape was not an option. At any time, even since my first arrival in Middlemore, they could have plucked me from my situation and brought me forth to answer questions. I am not sure why they waited so long. In many ways, I wished that they hadn't. While I may not have been causing too much damage to their organization, I wondered what part I had played in bringing about the untimely demise of Detective Sturgess. I wondered, too, whether I had brought Detective Kennedy down that same fateful path. It would have been best if I had kept my research to myself. Jessica and Mandy might be in danger. Certainly Tom Monroe's cushy business arrangement was in jeopardy. As I reflected on all of these things, I think I was more depressed than nervous about their final word.

My wait was not long. I was called back into the meeting with the casual friendliness of someone being called back into the classroom after a vote for class president. Their faces were unchanged as they apologetically pronounced their verdict. I did not react. There was no surprise in anything that they had to say. In a way, I felt more sorry for them than I felt for myself. For all the richness of tradition and life experience that TSD has uncovered, the society itself is bankrupt of any real meaning. It is an ironic state of affairs, wherein this cult could give life so many layers of meaning, and appeal so easily to the cream of society, yet be totally bereft of any redeeming values. No moral argument can call upon the end to justify the means. The end may, indeed, call for drastic measures – yet such measures can never stand as part of a moral argument. All of its cultural impact and spiritual enlightenment counts for naught in the face a leadership that is willing to extinguish human life without a second thought. It is true that one could probably rise through many of the echelons of the organization without facing any serious moral dilemmas. But, once at the top, the shady business that preserves this organization cannot be dismissed – even in the face of overwhelming arguments for the good that TSD preserves.

I was told that I had less than twenty-four hours to live. My final hours, they said, would be as pleasant as any hours that I had passed in this life. They promised to comply with any requests that were within their power, and carefully noted that such requests included pretty much anything that would not comprise the Society. My death was to be quick and painless, and my body would be treated with respect. Although they appreciated that my pending passage into the next life would be a rather large distraction at this time, they encouraged me to take full advantage of what they had to offer in the short time that I had left. In a way, they said, I would be a martyr to the cause. There was nothing objectionable about me, and they believed that, if I were willing, I could become a valuable asset to TSD business. They were convinced, however, that I would never be able to commit fully to that business, and as such, had to be eliminated. There was a definite sadness about that, they said, and they thought it best, for all concerned, that my final hours should be as full as possible.

Most of us will never have an opportunity to find out how we would really respond if we were told that we had less than twenty-four hours left to live. I don't know that I would recommend that experience to anyone, but if I did, I would most certainly recommend that TSD cater that occasion. Twenty-four hours, of course, is not nearly long enough to do even a part of what needs to be done at the end of life. There are too many books, prayers, conversations, and reflections to cram into such a short span of time. There is not enough time to mourn those things that are already at a close, or to celebrate those things that have enriched one's earthly existence. The Society met its obligations, however, much better that I would ever have guessed. I was given free range of the beautiful grounds, and I was given full access to the most idyllic of rooms. That room was filled with books and music. It was furnished with a pool table, a gigantic television, and a full bar – equipped with a selection of Britain's finest beers *on tap*. And, not only was there a collection of the most beautiful young women imaginable placed at my disposal, but there was a rather endearing cat housed there to assist me in my meditations. (I am still not certain how they anticipated the extent my need for feline companionship.)

The women themselves bear some comment. I wondered, at first, whether or not (considering TSD's integral celebration of sexuality) they were placed there, in part, to service any carnal needs that I might feel needed fulfilling at the end of my life. As a terminal bachelor, I must confess that this was a valid consideration. Morally, however, I could not take full advantage of this situation. Of course, the Society would have known this. There was, on the other hand, a parallel emphasis on purity, especially as it related to the more elite members. The young ladies served a valuable purpose with regard to the integrity to the group, and it was, in a perverse sort of way, a great compliment to me that I was allowed to spend my final hours with them. They were not, as is often the case when looks are paramount, simply appealing ornamentation. The level of their intellect was quite astounding, and on several occasions throughout my stay in that room, I found myself slipping into deep conversation with a number of them. Such conversations brought to mind similar discussions with Derra, and I found myself so lost in the dialogue that I quite forgot my dire circumstance. These women were enchanting in every sense of the word. As I sipped slowly on the intoxicating brew, feasted my eyes on these stunning visions, and bantered about the issues closest to my heart, I knew that I stood on sacred ground: inhabited by myself and by representatives of the true bloodline of the Druid priestess. It was an astonishing time – even though it was designated as my final time.

The time of my death drew near. Apart from wondering if my search for Derra had had any negative rippling effects on those with whom I had shared my research, I came to that final hour with no regrets. Long, wasted years had been redeemed once I had met Derra, and a torrent of unexpected worlds had opened to me in the short time that I had known of her. TSD had delivered, with unexpected success, on their promise to make my last hours as pleasant as any hours that I had passed in this life, and I was prepared to meet the next life as best I could hope.

The nondescript little man, who had plucked me from my reverie on that park bench, was clearly assigned the duty of assisting me in my transition. He approached me, with hand extended, and smile in place, as if he were about to introduce me to some important colleagues. I suppose, in some strange sort of way, that was how he looked at it. For all of their enlightenment, there had to be some sort of illusion, into which they all bought, to allow for the violent means that were employed in the preservation of the Society. I wondered how any one of them would feel if suddenly deemed a liability by the other members. Would this oh-so-civilized parting of ways seem so inconsequential – just a matter of business? My mental preparations for this escorted walk down death row, and whatever allegedly painless solution was in place, was interrupted, however, by the most miraculous of visions.

I was not the only one totally stunned by the sudden appearance of Derra in the boardroom. Her presence was clearly unprecedented – as could be seen on the faces of each and every person in attendance. She appeared, not as the warm friend that I had come to love, but as someone aloof, and otherworldly. She struck me, I must say, as someone whom I had encountered in a faerie tale. She was not the beautiful young princess, however, so much as the wicked queen – whose more mature beauty had been supplement by an aura of power. Derra was, indeed, the dominant presence in the room. The men seemed to cower, and the words that spilled forth from her mouth certainly gave them reason.

Derra did not so much as glance at me as she spoke. Her words were harsh, and her voice had a shrillness to it that I would never have guessed. Although she spoke in my defense, her words were not kind. The gist of her argument was that I was a man of no consequence, and that if the decisive element in their verdict was my unrelenting search for her, then the point was now moot in that I had now found her. She would vouch for my future actions as they related to the Society, though she believed that it would have been unnecessary to do so had they not reached such a hasty decision. There was not one word of retort to her comments. Indeed, the men looked relieved that she was only making the solitary demand to spare my life. *I wondered what other demands were within her power.* There was no doubt in my mind, from the very onset of her monologue, that I would not die on this day. I was relieved, of course, but there was a myriad of other emotions at play. Derra had saved me, but what should have been a faerie tale ending to my long search had more marks of a nightmare than of the pleasant dream that it should have been. This Derra bore little resemblance to the object of my search. I could see nothing of the sweet giving young woman who had spent so many hours with me arguing the intricacies of life. This was a powerful being who, even in defense of me, showed nothing but contempt. Still hauntingly beautiful, her face now showed a hardness where those dark corners of mystery had once accentuated that glow. In what should have been, at many levels, a moment of triumph for me, I felt nothing but defeat.

Her exit was as sudden as her appearance. I think that all of us in that room could easily have been persuaded that we had encountered a vision of Derra rather than her actual flesh and blood presence. Either way, it really didn't matter. She had spoken. Her position in TSD was clearly more prominent than that of a Druid priestess. The Derra that I knew would have fit well in the charming group of priestesses with whom I had passed my presumed last hours. She was well beyond that now. Her words were not mere expressions of spiritual guidance, but of divine ordinance. There was no doubt in my mind that my life had been spared. I could have taken down one of the ornamental swords and hacked at the men in that room like so many trees… and my life would have been spared. As shocked as I had been by Derra's transformation, I was a picture of calmness next to that group to whom she had directed her words. In their minds, they had seen the face of God and the judgment had been… not so good.

My non-descript little friend was the first to act. He looked at me, recovered his smile, and placed his hand on my back. He escorted me out of the mansion as if I had been the most honored of guests (and, in a way, I suppose I had). He opened the car door for me, hopped into the driver's seat, and followed the winding roads back towards Glastonbury. He was not so chatty on the way back, but he continued to offer me smiles, and occasionally slapped my knee in a good-natured display of congratulations. When I finally caught sight of the Glastonbury Tor, I breathed the first relaxed breath that I had breathed in some time. Life suddenly became much easier for me. Not only did my would-be-executioner take me directly to the George and Pilgrim, but he escorted me to the front desk, paid my existing bill, and covered me for an additional week. He then shook my hand, patted my back one more time, and left me – smiling and waving until he was out of sight.

The day was still young, but I took myself straight to my luxurious room, and collapsed somewhere in the middle of the oversized bed. I slept straight through to the next morning, when the nearby ringing of church bells awakened me. I would like to say that I had been refreshed by that long sleep, but I had battled through the most vivid and disturbing dreams of my life all night long. I am sure that the details of those dreams would make interesting script, but it was all a blur by the time I had come to my senses. I only know that I had embarked on several fantastic adventures where elves, goblins, faeries, and witches – all blended into one indiscernible mess. I think, too, that I died in many of these adventures, but was revived from the dark abyss to take on the next task. Flashes of beautiful women, Derra among them, came to my mind's eye, but what role they played in my dreams I could not tell. The best I could do was to shower myself, pull on some clothes and drag myself to church without the benefit of the hotel's highly addictive breakfast. I felt ill, and the service was nothing special. Still, I had made the right decision, and I felt truly grounded for the first time since I had left my home.

**8**

My second week in Glastonbury was the most revitalizing week of my life. I had virtually come back from the dead, and I was determined to live the remainder of that new life to the fullest. I did not put myself under any pressure. I simply allowed myself to live. Life, I have discovered in the four months since I had left home, is not at all what I had always thought it to be. Success, pleasure and knowledge – all of the worthy (and not so worthy) goals for which we strive – have been redefined for me. The three-dimensional perspective that my eyes have always fed me is actually a distortion. There are other dimensions that I have suppressed – probably because I was afraid of what I would see – filling out the complete picture. Pain and suffering are as integral to the life process as the more pleasant sensations, and knowledge is no more the key to understanding than is daily experience. My revelation (if I can call it that) is that all things work together for good. If we can see that, to even the smallest extent, then every day is validated, and merits some moment of worship.

My week, too, was a time of mourning for Derra. She had died to me the night that she had left. The letter was simply a last gasp – a death rattle. I had been in denial until she appeared to me, and to the assembled group, on the day of my rebirth. That moment, in many ways, was more painful to me than facing the fate that had been decreed for me. Yet it, too, allowed me to pass from one life to the next. And, in that next life, I am able to come to terms with Derra's fate – the fate that I had known all along. I must have looked a fool, as I lingered in the pubs those first days, with tears mixed of joy and sadness streaking down my cheeks as I recalled my times with Derra. I did exceed my quota of pints, but not to the extent that it must have appeared as I huddled by myself in deep reflection. But it was all good, and by mid-week, I was able once again to restrict myself to the solitary pint that softened the edges, yet kept my senses intact.

The layers of sacred history, of which the site of Glastonbury is comprised, also gave way to a less foreboding scenario. Enchanting as that town remains to me, I no longer see it as hallowed ground – at least, no more so than any other ground on God's good earth. I spent my last week there as any other tourist might. I remained in awe of the history and legends, but I was equally in awe with the landscape, the quaint architecture, and the carefully positioned tourist traps – to which I succumbed as readily as any tourist who had ever stumbled across the town. I soaked in everything that I could, for I knew that, should I ever return to Britain (which I hoped I might), I would not revisit this spot. I might visit nearby Bath, or pay a quick visit to Stonehenge, but Glastonbury would not be on my itinerary. There is much too much to see in this world, just as there is much too much to read, and you can spend only so much time on one book – even if it might be the best one ever written.

My time in Glastonbury had almost expired before I realized that I had committed two major oversights. Not since I had left Middlemore had I communicated with either Lucy or Detective Kennedy. Communication with Lucy was simply a practical matter, as she knew nothing of my research or the nature of the trip that I had undertaken. Still, it was only reasonable that I let her know of my intended return so that she could make her arrangements, and that I be spared the ordeal of becoming an intruder in my own home. Detective Kennedy was another matter. Not only was he intricately aware of my situation, he had faced his own situation – which may well have subjected him to a similar degree of danger. I was sick at the thought of him having suffered the same fate as Detective Sturgess, and of my own selfish neglect of his condition. I was relieved to the point of exuberance upon hearing his voice (though he only spoke in monotone), and readily agreed to exchange documentation of the events that we had experienced upon my return. There was no longer any urgency about reading what Detective Kennedy had to say, but a morbid curiosity still lingered, and I was anxious to learn what had taken place.

The train ride back to Paddington Station whetted my appetite to return to Britain someday, but could not overcome the severe homesickness that I was suffering in anticipation of seeing the rain-soaked countryside of the

West Coast, and settling by a warming fire with my dear Bubastes curled in my lap. I wondered, though, as we drew near to London, how many eyes had gazed blankly onto those soggy rows of houses, day after day, with senses numbed by the rhythmic click that had resonated unbroken since the Industrial Revolution. The blackened skies hid the country's charm, and history seemed like just another word for old. Yet the tiredness of the land did not lessen its appeal for me. There was something so very basic about it. I knew that I need only peel back a layer or two from that sooty scene to uncover a lush green world that was home to more fascinating tales than any person could peruse over many lifetimes. And I had only muddled my way through one of them.

# DETAILS FROM JESSICA
# BURKE'S NOTES: MAY

Since the departure of my friend, Dr. Noah Giles, Middlemore has become very much like a ghost town to me – in every sense of the word. Not only does it feel deserted by the human element, but it feels as if it has been repopulated by unfamiliar spirits. In some ways, that is not a bad thing. My ancestors were certainly more at home with spirits than they were with white men. I'm afraid that I have always been a little like that – though I do count certain white men as my friends.

The little historical study, upon which Dr. Giles embarked, certainly turned out to be much more than either of us had expected. To be honest, I had initially thought that it might be a good idea to use Dr. Giles, with his mad obsession, to follow through on some research that I had begun, but had not been able to develop. It *was* a good idea – but maybe a little *too* good. I found out more about my people than I really wanted to know. Of course, as dear Mrs. MacDonald used to tell me: *Don't ask questions if you are not prepared to receive the answers.* I always thought that it was maybe one of her librarian in-jokes. I never expected that it would apply to anything that I would ever have to ask. When I asked *her* questions, she always provided the right amount of answer. When I asked Dr. Giles, however, his answers would overflow and touch on any number of topics – most of which Mrs. MacDonald would have deemed irrelevant. I think that is why Dr. Giles didn't trust Mrs. MacDonald, and why he dismissed my continued dialogue with her. His obsessions were certainly at odds with her philosophy that *everything in moderation* included moderation in knowledge.

The information about TSD certainly came as a shock to me. I'm sure that it fit into this broad landscape that Dr. Giles was painting, but it was overkill on what I had been spoon-fed by Mrs. MacDonald.

She never mentioned any society by name – or, for that matter, even suggested that there *was* a particular society. In retrospect, however, it is clear that she knew that TSD was active in Middlemore. Whatever collective wisdom that society might wield, I believe that they had met their match with Mrs. MacDonald. She would not only have been up to the challenges of protecting me from them, she would also have been able to convince them that their secrets were safe with her – and thus avoid the fate that seems to befall those who are deemed a threat to their practice. She promoted a solitary existence for me, and (though I am well aware of all of the psychological implications) she was successful in that purpose. Awareness of this has not changed me – though it has cleared up some of the confusion. Mrs. MacDonald was no man-hater, having been happily married herself, yet she clearly instilled a slight distaste for that gender within me. That is not to say that I have a preference for women, or that I am averse to male companionship, but as far as physical relationships are concerned, I have no interest in either gender. But I am particularly repulsed by males – who never seem to give up in their pursuits to that end. The way I feel, I realize, is precisely the way that Mrs. MacDonald wanted me to feel.

I never knew Mrs. MacDonald to be afraid of anything. I think that, if it were just her head to head with the grandmaster (or whoever's in charge of TSD calls his or herself), she would knock him or her down without flinching. Caution, I believe, was only employed for my benefit. She did not underrate my toughness, but she protected my vulnerabilities. She was not grooming me for spinsterhood, but for the fullness of womanhood, without the vulnerabilities. She was, in fact, running a counter-operation to TSD – though with a team of only one. Will I be more receptive to male advances, now that I know what she was doing and now that I am capable of defending myself? Perhaps – with therapy. For the moment, however, it is a non-issue. I have years to sort through that sort of thing, and I must confess to feeling rather content with my current lot in life. Right now, my priority is to unravel the mysteries of the pervasive influence that TSD has had in this part of the world – a pervasiveness that is made clear to me, not so much through the recent research into matters, as by the insights that my foster mother subtly relayed to me that that research awakened. Thanks to Mrs. MacDonald, I believe that my insights into the true nature of TSD are as insightful as those of any living non-member – Dr. Giles included. It was from this premise that I launched my own investigations, with the purpose of replacing their invading spirits with spirits more indigenous to this part of the world.

It struck me that, if Mrs. MacDonald knew about TSD, there may have been others who knew as well, and have survived to talk about it (– if, in fact, anyone would *ever* talk about it). This possible conspiracy had its likely suspects, and I decided to begin where it would be easiest for me to make some headway. It took about half of a second for me to decide to pay a visit to Tom Monroe at the George.

I knew Tom, casually, as a fixture around town, from my earliest memories. I became more familiar with him while Dr. Giles was resident at the George, and I read on his face pretty much all that there was to know about him in a matter of minutes. My visit with him was not so much to uncover new information, as it was to confirm what I already knew. The facts were clear. He has a severe weakness for pretty women, and is pretty much living out his life in terminal adolescence. He is not particularly intelligent, but is more aware of things around him than he is inclined to admit. He had inherited, at the George, an ideal lifestyle. Most of the work was done for him, but for the business to run smoothly, it required a much-needed discipline on his part. The steady flow of attractive female visitors has satisfied his fantasy life – if not occasionally his actual life. This, above all else, is essential to his healthy existence. TSD secrets were safe with him so long as the Society's continued patronage was at issue. Surprisingly, however, there is a strong conscience at work for (or against?) Tom. His solution of choice is to opt for ignorance over deception whenever that option is available to him.

Tom was in a state of deep depression when I came to visit. His spirits were somewhat lifted, I could tell, by the presence of a woman that appealed to him, but even in our conversation, his mood ebbed and flowed according to his focus. The cause for his distress was the recent cancellation of the group booking scheduled for June. Although, for the moment, the remainder of his bookings remained intact, the unprecedented cancellation of this forthcoming visit augured, for him, the beginning of the end. Knowing what I knew, I suspected that his instincts were accurate on this count. The dual threat, to the survival of his business and to his one solace in this life, was almost too much for him to bear. Short of offering my body as a sacrifice to his cause, there was nothing that I could do to comfort him. Pity did work against my better judgment, however, and I was more receptive to his irrepressibly flirtatious nature than made me comfortable. Still, a few minutes of discomfort on my part hardly compared to the miserable pit of despair into which I could see him helplessly spiraling.

Playing to his desperate state with my feminine charms made my fact gathering relatively easily – though I am ashamed to admit that I employed such means so insensitively. I justify my behavior by pointing out that, not only did I do him no harm, I actually did him a favor by temporarily alleviating his pain through the sort of company with which I provided him. It made no difference to him whether or not I was real or illusionary. And, for me, the bottom line was extracting information. His ultimate fate was not in my hands. Besides, it was not likely that TSD would resort to foul play in Tom's case. He was harmless enough. What counted for him was his lifestyle, and that would rapidly evaporate as the bookings dropped – domino style. You could see it all in his face. So it was. I stepped in not unlike the Nazi colonel who was handed a broken prisoner of war. I can't say that I am proud of myself. On the other hand, it was rather therapeutic in terms of cleansing myself of some of my distaste for this type of man.

As I suspected, Tom was aware of the most obvious things – like that the bookings were related and controlled by a secret cult. He figured that what went on beyond that was none of his business so long as he was well paid, and the women kept appearing. He was not going to jeopardize that by asking unwanted questions. He stumbled across some additional information several years back when he had slept with one of the girls who happened to have loose lips as well. She spoke to him about preparation for ceremonies of initiation. He could neither recall the exact time of year (spring, he thought), nor whether the girl herself claimed to be an initiate. What struck him, however, were her remarks about male castration (whether actual or symbolic he was not sure), and the frenzied party that would precede the act. He remembered this in particular because, he said, *the idea of frenzied party with all of those girls sounded so amazing, but it crashed right down to earth when she talked about dismemberment.* I'm not quite sure what to make of all this, but it was the only thing that he said that really added to the discussion. I'm rather dubious about a eunuch priesthood being in place (as such an initiation ritual would suggest), but the symbolism was certainly interesting.

To Tom's credit, though he never thought of himself as a potential victim, the one thing that caused him concern was that TSD appeared to be complicit in murder. The possibility had never crossed his mind until Detective Sturgess had arrived and talked about Sarah. He claimed that it was his intention to be of assistance to Detective Sturgess right up to the time of his departure, and I believe him. Tom was clearly shaken when I broke the news of the detective's death to him. Not wanting to upset him any further, I assured him that, by all accounts, the death was accidental (– and who's to argue with that?). He looked relieved – probably because the idea of his own vulnerability had finally crept into his mind. The remainder of my time was spent reassuring him of his own safety, and of the fact that there was nothing that he could have done to forestall any of the deaths in which TSD might have had a hand. I left promising him that I would come to see him again soon. I justified this particular lie as good medicine. After all, what did he have left if not the few scraps of hope that might be charitably tossed his way?

**M**rs. MacDonald, though universally acknowledged as a good Christian woman, never inflicted that burden on me. It must have seemed odd, in the eyes of many, that this upright parishioner should leave her heathen ward home from Sunday worship. I'm sure that there were even some who felt that my Native blood was beyond redemption. Well, perhaps there was some truth in this. My own prejudice against the white man does center mostly on the white man's religion. If an open mind to the tenets of the Christian faith is prerequisite to salvation, then I am surely damned. I chose to worship as my ancestors did, and for some reason, Mrs. MacDonald was not only amenable to my choice – she actively encouraged it.

Anyone who knows anything about me (and there are very few) would know what struggles I recently endured in forcing myself to attend the morning worship at the Episcopalian Church. Certainly, I felt eyes fixed upon me throughout the service – though none more firmly than those of Father Luke (as he insisted on being addressed). I knew that he would be aware of some of my hidden nature through my late foster mother. To what extent I have ever been discussed, I do not know. Apparently he knew enough to be surprised that I would ever venture to darken the doors of his quaint little edifice. I have nothing with which to compare it, but his little sermon seemed to be delivered with a degree of unease in my presence. Dr. Giles has often spoken of the unexpected power in Father Luke's words, and how they blend so potently with the entire liturgy. I saw nothing of this. I'm not sure whether it simply did not exist on this particular morning, or whether my perspective was so tainted as to blind me to the message. In any case, I endured. The pain was not eased by the attire that I had chosen. My best business dress was clearly still too short for the wandering eyes of most males in my vicinity. There was, perhaps, a subtle hypocrisy there – but I will not pass judgment on any particular issue since I was not paying particular attention to what was being preached.

I was warmly greeted by the men (with ritual handshakes and the occasional hug) after the service, but few women participated in this ceremony. The most ingratiating of them all, of course, was Father Luke – who, predictably, invited me to the rectory for lunch. This, of course, was the object of my visit. I had no doubt about the success of this mission. I knew that, if curiosity didn't work in my favor, male hormones would – unless he was one of those eunuch priests that Tom Monroe had planted in my mind with his talk of castration. I wondered, though, whether he might include someone else in the invitation to spare himself the raised eyebrows of those who might question the idea of a man in his position spending time alone with a young (and, in all modesty, *appealing*), unattached woman. Apparently, he was secure enough in his position not to feel the need for such safeguards, and I was his solitary guest. I was not at all frightened by the prospect of being alone with him. In fact, Dr. Giles' reports had made me very keen on the experience.

Father Luke very quickly dispelled the myth of the eunuch priest. His advances were subtle, as were my defenses, but it was very clear to me that, if he had ever taken a vow of chastity, it was not something that he would have considered binding under certain circumstances. I wondered that he had chosen to remain single – since I was aware that this was not a requirement of an Episcopalian priest. I suspected that it had something to do with his role with TSD. (I had no doubt that he was integral to their operation in Middlemore.) I anticipated finding the answer to this question, along with several others, as the afternoon progressed. He clearly likes cat-and-mouse games, and plays them well, but arrogance is his weakness. I suspected that he had never met anyone to whom he did not feel superior. It is a type of psychopathic behavior – though rather more subtle than the criminal type. I can't say I feel any more forgiving of him than I do of someone whose mental illness leads more directly to violence. If, then, in his mind, no one person or collection of persons is above him (including, I am pretty sure, even TSD), I like my chances. After all, I already knew how he operated. My biggest asset, however, is his own misogyny. He would never even think to be on his guard against a woman.

Father Luke saw my presence at the table as a pleasant opportunity to gather information from a woman (whom I have already noted was appealing to him) who had a series of interesting connections in Middlemore – from Mrs. MacDonald to Dr. Giles. I, on the other hand, saw him through the eyes of a sworn enemy. I had no tolerance for him as a man, as a Christian priest, or as a secret member of an aggressive cult. I knew what to expect as he emptied the contents of an opened bottle of red wine into my oversized goblet, but I had no fear of the effects. *Let him think that he has made me vulnerable*, I said silently to myself as I watched his eyes open widely in anticipation of the drugging effect that was forthcoming. Unlike those of my ancestors and contemporaries, who had easily been undone by alcohol, I have developed a practiced tolerance to its effects. It is not that my system was unaffected by its impact. It clearly was. But I have learned to harness my mental response to the physical consequences of pretty much anything. It is, after all, just an issue of mind over matter.

So I drank freely. I must confess that the intoxicating effects were extraordinarily pleasant – just as Dr. Giles had reported them to me. I wondered what sort of mixture, added to wine, would create this effect. I wondered, too, with an unwelcome sense of disgust, whether this potion might be Father Luke's means of seduction. In any case, short of making me unconscious, it would not make me receptive to any of his amorous schemes. Otherwise, our tense battle had transformed into a very comfortable parlay. The flag of truce that Father Luke saw me wave, however, was an illusion. Even as he spelled out the conditions of my surrender, my mind leapt forward – planning my next attack. Convinced that I was at his mercy, he leaned forward, allowing his questions to ooze out of those sugary lips. I answered in such a way as I knew would lead to him to a pervasive sense of self-satisfaction. Trapped, then, by his own smugness, I began my assault.

4

"**Y**our qualifications seem well beyond what is necessary for an Episcopalian priest," I observed casually.

"We're generally a learned lot," Father Luke answered coyly.

"So, you're average?" I asked, knowing how mediocrity would grate on him.

"I didn't say that," he said firmly. "I have special qualifications, but it has suited me to stay with this parish."

"Indefinitely?"

"Never say never," he said with a broad smile. "I may soon leave."

"Where your special qualifications will be put to use?" I asked lightly.

Father Luke moved his face close to mine. For a second, I thought that he was going to try to kiss me. I could feel the warmth of his breath, though, as he spoke to me in hushed tones – even though we were alone.

"I could put my special qualifications to use just about anywhere," he stated in a very serious tone. "Some situations are better than others. As you know, Middlemore has some unusual history. I can be a particular asset in such a community."

"Are you suggesting that your qualifications have an aspect of magic to them?" I asked in pretended awe.

(I was hoping that, by leaping ahead so far beyond what had been stated, his guard would be down and he would be unable to resist the urge to brag a little.)

"Magic is such a relative term," he said condescendingly. "We do not have to set the clock back that far to have many of our daily conveniences look like magic. But I see very little magic in our scientific advances. It is in the age-old secrets of communion with nature that real magic is found."

"And you have such skills?" I asked, almost choking on my sycophancy.

"As you would not imagine," he said smugly.

Mercifully, he leaned away from me. He crossed his arms, waiting expectantly for my adoration. It was a hard role for me. I could tolerate Tom Monroe's adolescent behavior because it was so harmless. I didn't like Tom much because of it, but I didn't really dislike him personally either – just his type. Father Luke was a different story. He was manipulative, and his manipulations were potentially dangerous. Had he ever killed or raped? Probably not – though that might depend on your definition of rape. He had seduced, and he had turned a blind eye towards injustice – of that I was sure. And there might have been some excuse for him if his manipulations were for what he saw as some greater cause. But there was no greater cause for Father Luke than Father Luke. The same manipulative magic that he spun in his worship service to woo the likes of Dr. Giles (who was by no means gullible, and was in fact rather perceptive), was the same magic that I knew he would spin in defiance of TSD. I had no love for either traditional Christianity or for the cultic spin that TSD put into practice, but I hated men who could not be trusted at any level. Father Luke was like a double agent – playing one side against the other for his own personal benefit. Still, I mustered the strength to offer him his desperately needed look of total devotion. If he had taken advantage of that moment, however, to make another move on me, I would have demythologized the role of the eunuch priest.

Firmly believing that he had me in his spell, however, Father Luke suspended any physical advances in favor promoting his cause in my mind. I could not have been more delighted with this choice. He began with a brief history lesson, building on what I had selectively told him of what I knew. His storytelling skills were undeniably well honed. (No wonder he was so effective in his church – even though he could not have believed half of what he was saying!) Indeed, his art was well beyond storytelling, and bordered, perhaps, on conjuring. Vivid scenes flashed before my eyes, and more than once, I feared that I would lose the control with which I prided myself, and actually fall recklessly into such a spell as he had already deemed I had fallen. It was tough to keep my balance, but it was certainly worth my effort. Worlds were opened to me about which I had only ever read. The secret world of Middlemore was unfurled for me. From a spiritual vantage, it was not much different than my native instincts had told me. Corporeally, however, the players were surprising – though I can imagine Dr. Giles reading what follows and exclaiming: *Of course! Of course!*

*5*

"I am a Druid priest," Father Luke declared.

In any other situation, such a declaration coming from an Episcopalian rector, adorned with the vestments of his trade, might sound a little strange. Nothing could have sounded more natural, however, in the truly magical atmosphere that Father Luke's stories and drugs had woven in that room. He explained to me, with great care, the difference between what he meant by that statement, and what most modern day Druids would mean by that statement. In essence, he claimed direct lineage to the practices of Druidry that were in place in Britain before the Christianity was in place – such practices that were deemed magic, even at the time, but that had more to do with wisdom and an intuitive understand of natural resources. He condescendingly observed that some of "my people" had a similar commune with nature, but that it remained relatively untapped until "his people" arrived on the scene.

By and large, it seems, his parishioners were unaware of his moonlighting activities. Occasionally, members of TSD's hierarchy, who were committed to the cause of Anglicanism, attended his church – but their presence was always temporary. Long term residents who were affiliates of that society (such as the management at the chalet) did not participate in worship with him, but did maintain social contact, and were available to him as needed. The police force was a longstanding arm of TSD, utilizing their legal authority to keep intruders at bay, and to ensure smooth operations while recruits were in town. The power invested in them by TSD had created a bit of a monster, seriously corrupting an easily corruptible core of officers, but TSD discipline had brought them relatively under control. I was spared a description of the nature of this discipline, but my imagination could not be totally repressed on this count. The police force as a whole, however, harbored no ill feelings towards these taskmasters, and the relationship seemed to flourish.

A few other inhabitants of my town (the postmaster, for instance) played more minor roles in the business of TSD that are not worth recounting. The impression, overall, was that TSD influence was pervasive, but that we were not talking about some science fiction scenario where the town had been taken over by aliens. There seems to be different levels of influence. Father Luke was clearly at the top of the food chain (or so he would have me believe), but the lower levels may not even have known who was calling the shots. It was rather like what I've heard about the 1960's and CIA influence. To read about it, you would almost think that everyone in the country was linked to the CIA in one way or the other. The truth, I suspect, was somewhat less extreme. The CIA, while likely keeping scores of recruits available for any given situation, kept a considerably lower portion of the population in active duty. The others were just insurance. TSD seems to have picked up on the efficiency of this system, and (so long as the purposes were less grandiose than invading Cuba!) used it to maintain security without compromising secrecy.

The situation in Middlemore, Father Luke noted, was now in a state of flux. After a long association with TSD, Middlemore had finally been compromised. It was inevitable. What was surprising was that it had remained secure for so long. There were other suitable sites, many of which were already in use, but it was nonetheless a sad day in the Society's history to part company with this particular location. The history was particularly unique – especially as it related to *my people*. Father Luke was not aware of (nor particularly concerned about) the specific issues that had necessitated this relocation. He would simply move to a new parish under a different name, and continue his work there. The system, he insisted, was flawless.

The pending relocation may well have been a factor in allowing Father Luke to speak so freely. (After all, I don't want to give too much credit to my personal charms!) He asked me if my heart was in Middlemore, or if I was open to some move in the future. The question was, perhaps, a recruiting tactic, but he did not seem overly disturbed by my assertion that I was going to stay in Middlemore. There was certainly little harm that I could do here with TSD withdrawing. But this whole movement raised questions from the perspective of a lifelong citizen in this town. There was clearly an infrastructure in place – courtesy of TSD. What were the implications for the town now that TSD was leaving it to its own devices? Father Luke said that he was only guessing, but he was of the opinion that there would be some economic consequences – particularly at the George and at the chalet. If the town as a whole could weather these setbacks, then there should be relatively few social scars. It would take forever, he believed, for that police force to realize that they were now an autonomous body. Once they clued in, he suggested, there was certainly the risk of widespread corruption – *but how many towns had survived that phenomenon with their police forces?* (Father Luke posed that final question with a sardonic sort of chuckle.) As for the rest, they would probably persist to the grave in the illusion that they were serving some worthwhile function. *People like to think of themselves as being much more important than they actually are*, he said. I say: *hmmm*.

*6*

I am not sure whether Father Luke came to my way of thinking, and saw us as sworn enemies under temporary truce, or whether I succumbed to his way of thinking, a little, and saw our little encounter as little more than a relaxed fact-finding session. The truth was, however, that our enmity was no longer an issue, and that (given the lulling effects of the wine) our session had become almost pleasant by the time that it ended. He seemed satisfied with the little information that I had passed along to him, and by and large, I was happy to gain an unexpectedly broad perspective on TSD activities in Middlemore. It was only in the details of my adopted mother's role in the community that I felt cheated.

I had ventured to introduce her name to the conversation two or three times before Father Luke finally relented (out of courtesy or frustration I cannot say), and told me a little of her and her place in Middlemore. I suspected that he was being candid with me since his opening remarks simply reaffirmed much of what I had always suspected about Mrs. MacDonald. Indeed, in relating what he knew of her to me, Father Luke spoke with a distinct tone of respect. He knew that she was aware of TSD, although he did not know the extent of that awareness. For her part, she was clearly unafraid of the clout that TSD could sway, and although she was not in sympathy with what she knew about the society, her actions were never subversive. Her commitment to Anglicanism may have been the buffer, he suggested, although that commitment did not prevent her from shielding her adopted daughter from the parish church or any possible portal into TSD. Thus it was a passive relationship. She was a little like a poor rodent that I once saw caged with a boa constrictor. The snake was shedding at the time, and had no appetite, so its live meal cuddled closely, as if they were the best of friends, during the reprieve. Naturally, the food chain would not be indefinitely forestalled. I wondered, for the first time, whether or not my foster mother's passing had been so natural as it seemed. The issue, however, like Mrs. MacDonald, was long dead.

The irony in Mrs. MacDonald's life was that, in carefully extracting her Anglican faith from TSD's more expansive perspective, and in encouraging me, instead, to pursue the nature centered beliefs of my ancestors, she was actually completing TSD's cycle. The two halves, however, did not, for her, equal the society's whole. Keeping each part distinct, and playing down the role of the female, separated our family's beliefs from TSD's packaged beliefs. In this, Mrs. MacDonald was able both to gain the respect of the likes of Father Luke, and to maintain her integrity in the confused world of Middlemore. My womanhood, at least by Western definitions, was the sacrificial lamb. It was a small price to pay, however, especially in terms of how I was allowed to excel by non-Western standards of womanhood. That is to say that I was able to develop myself as a person, distinct from my gender, and yet to utilize the power of my gender for purposes other than advancing myself simply as a woman. TSD would have had trouble with this concept. *I* have trouble with this concept. But I cannot argue with the effectiveness of Mrs. MacDonald's methods in protecting me from the pervasive influence of this aggressive society.

Father Luke and I parted on friendly terms. In a way, he had been unmasked. This mysterious little rector was not nearly so threatening once the mystery of his mission was made known. The tumbledown effects of uncovering TSD activity in Middlemore had made the town relatively useless to the society, and the TSD secrets there had lost their power. To Father Luke's credit, he seemed to take this rather drastic change of order in stride, knowing I suppose, that such changes were inevitable. Still, considering his longstanding tenure in this community, he could have been a little bitter about losing his parish so close to retirement (– if, of course, Druid priests ever retire!). I swear I almost asked him for a forwarding address before I left. Fortunately, however, reason prevailed and prevented me from making such an embarrassing request. I *am* curious, though. Then again, if I did trace Father Luke to his new name and his new parish, this whole thing would start all over again. And I am quite sure that I have already had more than enough.

The changes in Middlemore have already begun. Apart from the reoccupation by unfamiliar spirits (to which I have already alluded), physical differences have become apparent to those familiar with the distinctive elements of our community. The buildings are all still intact, but the hum of construction seems to have fallen unnaturally silent. Although the George remains relatively full, and there continues to be activity at the chalet, the bustle of my little town is clearly waning. To the casual eye, Middlemore might seem to be faring rather well for such an isolated location, but the trained eye knows that the migration has already begun. Faces have been systematically airbrushed from the crowd scenes. It is just a matter of time before only the longstanding citizens remain – and those among that lot, young enough to still do so, will likely depart as well.

I am not as comfortable with the spiritual inhabitants of this town as I had expected to be. I had been convinced that my native instincts would thrive in the midst of a more earth-centered atmosphere, free of the spiritual intrusions of white culture. Either I have become unconsciously indoctrinated by the European influence, or there was something to that intrusion after all. In any case, the unexpected truth of it all is that I feel suddenly displaced, and my ties to the land have been severed. I have always prided myself on my native heritage, and my ability to detach myself from the role of the modern Western woman. Now I find myself feeling very much in tune with the typical Western woman – at least so far as my current spiritual, physical and psychological needs extend. I see *a lot* of therapy in my future. Whether the end result of the remaking of Jessica is to restore me to my roots, or to make me all right with being a woman plunked into the heart of early twenty-first century Western culture, I don't much care at this point. My main issue is personal crisis management. I have no affection for personal crises.

Although I told Father Luke that I have no intention ever to leave Middlemore, it has only been a matter of days since I have reassessed this assertion. So long as I was actively researching the spiritual activities of my ancestors, I had reason to stay. If I had ever paused to contemplate the direction of my research, I doubt that I would have anticipated such an unsatisfactory ending. My purpose was to reunite myself with my ancestors, not to dissociate myself with everything that had become important to me. For the moment, I will stay. Travel, however, has become a possibility for me for the first time in my life. I have not had the opportunity to spend much thought on where I might like to travel, but my friend, Noah Giles, should take this confession as fair warning that he is on my list. Beyond that, I have not thought – I cannot think. I am simply, suddenly, uncomfortable, both in my locale and in my own skin. The firm ground upon which I had built my defenses has suddenly shifted beneath my feet and the walls have come tumbling down.

The irony of my distress is that it is, at the same time, very liberating. I had no idea how tightly I had cocooned myself into my little world. I was always a little agoraphobic, I knew, but I had been unaware of the reaches of this ailment until all of my safety nets had been torn from me. Only then, in the realization that what I had feared had not killed me, was I free. And what *exactly* had I feared? There was no single answer to that. I had feared white men. I had feared *any* men. I had feared the spiritual world that had been woven around me – whether that involved TSD, my native tradition, my adopted mother's Anglicanism, or the demons of Western culture. I had feared ignorance, but much more, I had feared the wrong knowledge. I had feared human relationships, but I had feared the loss of my own humanity. Yet my fears had been my crutch. They made me strong in an uncertain world. And they were washed away, in an instant, like I had been blindsided by a flash flood. Now I stand naked before a merciless world, somehow confident in this change, yet with no recognizable moment of revelation supporting me. It's like a religious experience without the religion. It is up to me to remake myself, but I don't know that I am up to the task. Still, I relish the opportunity. Middlemore is my Eden, but I know that I will ultimately be cast out of the garden.

# FROM THE MEMOIRS OF DR. NOAH GILES: MID-MAY THROUGH JUNE

No man was ever so happily reunited with beast than was I with my dear Bubastes. I suspect that he wanted to remain aloof when he first saw me after my long desertion, but ultimately, he showed mercy and purred furiously as I vigorously stroked his thick coat. Lucy looked on proudly, taking deep satisfaction in having brought my feline friend safely to this point in time. She had hot tea and a light meal awaiting me upon my arrival, and served them to me in my spotless abode (in the preservation of which she had also taken great pride). In short, it was a very reassuring return, with the comforting illusion of nothing having altered during my absence. My cat, my home, and Lucy, at least, remained unchanged – and this was no small consolation considering that my mind was not coping well in restructuring its perpetual vision of Derra.

Apart from the occasional winter days of snow, and a similarly sparse number of summer days of oppressive heat, there is not much to distinguish one season in the Pacific Northwest from another. Rain is the common denominator. On the plus side, however, there is a year round lushness to the landscape the stands in stark contrast even to the pleasant spring outburst in Middlemore. It was, fortunately, late enough in the season for a few dry days to greet my arrival. The skies were overcast, and the threat of precipitation remained constant, but I was able to steal a few hours for short walks to reacquaint myself with my neighborhood. I took frequent advantage of the path beside my house that wound its way over the hill towards the cemetery to which I had followed Derra that fateful night. There was a Gothic sort of romanticism to it on those dark days, but I could not find the courage to follow the path by night. I was trying my best to tuck Derra and TSD into the back of mind, but I have been touched, as if by the finger of God, and I remain haunted by my experiences.

The process of restoring myself to my old living situation consumed my first days. A large part of that time was spent at my office, with the end result being my resignation (– or, *my early retirement,* as they tauntingly labeled my departure). So, in fact, I was not *really* restored to my old living situation. The decision to resign had actually been made well before I had arrived home, but I had not spoken it to anyone – nor even totally admitted it to myself. My first moments under the rows of florescent lights in that dull brick building, however, confirmed the brewing plan. The routine affairs of government business would have driven me crazy on the heels of my adventures, and there was no point trying to ease my way out of the organization. I tied up loose ends as best I could, but there was really no point in being thorough with it. The pile on my desk had accumulated in the time that I had been gone, and nothing short of several weeks' work could have brought my position to a satisfactory end. There was no sense of regret as I turned in my keys, and for one last time, left the premises where so many of my waking hours had been spent for so many years.

A year previous, the thought of so many free hours in my week might well have initiated some sort of a breakdown. At this point, however, it does not seem like there was time to fill. Oddly, it feels as if the weeks ahead do not contain enough hours for me to accomplish what needs to be done. There are people to see, things to learn, and books to write. There is no specific plan in my head. I have simply learned that every moment is precious, and that there are too few moments in any given lifetime. If my days consist in nothing more than long walks, then I will savor that time and count myself as blessed. Of course, I know that, for me, my days will soon fall into some sort of routine – whatever fits the situation. I will try, however, to incorporate as much flex time into my routines as possible. Opportunities are not to be wasted either. It is the means that justify the end. I feel rather confident that, by pouring my finest efforts into the means, I will arrive a most satisfactory end.

I was rather distressed by the nervous condition in which I found Detective Kennedy. His experience with TSD had most certainly altered him. Of course, my experience with him prior to this had been limited to a single lunch encounter in Middlemore. Nevertheless, the man before me in his Seattle home bore little resemblance to the professionally aggressive detective I had first met. The physical changes were obvious. He had been thin before, but in a muscular, wiry sort of way – nothing that would have drawn attention. He was now emaciated. His cheeks were hollow and there was a gray tone to his complexion that I did not recall from our previous session. He shook a little, too, as he stretched his arm towards me in greeting, though a broad smile crossed his face eerily as he reached for my hand.

The physical changes, however, did not compare to the altered state of Detective Kennedy's mind. His controlled incisiveness had struck me most at our first meeting. He had conveyed the impression of man who was constantly alert to every detail around him, as well as to the implications of many of these details. He had absorbed everything that I had told him, and had seemed extraordinarily quick in coming up to speed. There was nothing of that perception in him now – though he did seem eager to speak to me. He was wrapped in a long silk smoking-type robe when we met. I guess that the semblance of a traditional smoking jacket struck me so vividly since Detective Kennedy did carry with him a lit pipe – though he seemed to spend little time drawing on the tobacco. He informed me that it was a recent habit, but one that he had found very conducive to meditation as he occupied the hours of his recovery. He was, indeed (despite having replaced his aggressive style of conversation with a much more passive one), quite lucid in his comments. His mind had suffered a rather severe attack, but there was, I noted with some relief, hope for him. At least, the prospects of him returning to full health seemed much more likely to me as our conversation progressed than it had when I had first spoken with him.

We spent a long time re-hashing the details of what we had written to each other. I summarized some of the conclusions I had reached as a result of our respective reports, but his look remained vacant as I spoke, and I was not quite sure whether he did not hear, or whether he was disinterested in what my deductions added to the subject. Most of it, of course, the Detective Kennedy that I had first met would have deduced himself. The Detective Kennedy who sat across from me, however, was much more wrapped up in his own philosophical perspective on matters – which ranged from the accidentally insightful to the highly fanciful. Although his body remained flaccid as he spoke, there was a slight spark in his eyes when he expounded on what he thought was a particularly profound point. I did not always concur with his judgment, but I was happy to see the life stir within him.

We shared a light lunch together, but I declined the bottle of beer that he offered with it. I was not particularly hungry, but hoped that, by indulging, he might be inspired to add some nourishment to his frail frame. The beer, however, worried me when I thought beyond the calories that it could provide. His mind was much too fragile for testing with anything beyond his ill-conceived tobacco experiment. I was relieved to see that he ate his portion of food with a degree of relish, and only wished that he had served himself a little more generously. Nonetheless, the signs of potential physical recovery were soon as viable as the potential mental recovery, and I was able to relax to some degree for the remainder of our interview. Fueled by his meager repast, the good detective's mood seemed to improve as well. The agitation stilled, a little, and a semblance of normalcy settled upon him. Soon, our discourse moved into more mundane matters, totally unrelated to our Middlemore experience. I think that, if I had had some means of erasing any issue related to TSD from his mind, I would have done so. Despite his avid pursuit of the subject, as evidenced in our earlier communication, it was something that he simply needed to purge from his thoughts. Once that realization settled in, I believed, his recovery would take giant strides forward.

Thus, the final hours of our time together were spent finding areas of common interest. A lovely Persian cat that dished brief moments of affection to the detective, while studiously ignoring me, provided one point of reference. There was a fine selection of wine as well (the likes of which I had never encountered in a personal collection) that intrigued me. In fact, I toyed with the thought of allowing him to fortify himself with a strong red Cabernet that he had offered me, but decided that it was not best to encourage such indulgence at this point in time. Before I had even seen Detective Kennedy's wine cellar, I had already resolved to incorporate regular trips to Seattle into my schedule. As time progressed, I had no doubt that I would have the opportunity to enjoy some rare vintages with him, but there was no point in beginning while his health was still on the line. We also both had an affinity for nineteenth century English literature, and the unlikely musical combination of Mozart, Saint-Saëns, and both the senior and junior Johann Strauss. The most exciting discovery of all, however, was Detective Kennedy's conservatory. I did not have time to explore it any extent on that first visit, but a cursory walk through this greenhouse as I was about to depart exposed me to some of the most exotic plants that I have ever seen.

My delight in receiving the package of information from Jessica (only two days after my visit to Detective Kennedy) was tempered somewhat by the lack of details concerning Derra. It was, however, fascinating to read of the changing dynamics in both Middlemore and in Jessica herself. I suppose, too, there was value in letting Jessica's report bring my experience in that town to some sort of an end – though I had fought against such closure tooth and nail. Still, I had barely put the last page down before I realized that Middlemore no longer held any attraction for me. It had been a means to an end for me – just as it had been for TSD. Both the Society and I had harvested all that we could from that town, and it was now time to head our separate directions. I suppose that I could have chased TSD down its new paths – but to what end? I was not a news reporter out to write an exposé. I was simply a man trying to find a lost friend. And I found her – though she still remained lost.

I hoped that Jessica was serious about coming to visit me. Any regrets about leaving Middlemore behind would be resolved by the presence of that young woman on the West Coast. There was nothing else for me in Middlemore. In a warped sort of way, I missed Father Luke's services. But my life would be none the poorer without the man in my life. There had been some good talks with Tom Monroe, but I had no desire to see him in his present condition, stripped of his life's purpose – as shallow as those purposes might have been. He had been entertaining company only when was inspired by his lifestyle. When his conscience crept into his conversation, he was poor company indeed. Whether, in light of the pending changes to his inn, he transformed into a broken man, or a man haunted by conscience, he would not be the sort of man whose company I would currently seek. Jessica's pending transformations, however, had me intrigued – and there were not a lot of things in this life that would appeal to me more than a few hours in her presence.

I decided to call Jessica, to let her know that I had received her package, and perhaps, to promote the idea of her coming west to visit me. I am not, nor ever have been, a person who is comfortable with telephones. I consider the telephone to be a necessary evil, and I have remained steadfast in my boycott of such innovations as the cellular phone – though there is perhaps a future for me in texting. In the majority of my telephone conversations, I am monosyllabic – and most of vocalizations take the form of grunts. It was, then, a most extraordinary experience to find myself in conversation with Jessica for almost two hours. We ran the gambit of things, from local gossip to broad philosophical concerns. While we had had some in-depth conversations from time to time in Middlemore, they had never been so sweeping. Between my natural reserve and her defensive reserve, conversations had always come in fits and starts. On the phone, however, we talked as old friends – which, I suppose, we had become.

The gossip was entertaining, but added little to the picture of Middlemore that Jessica had painted for me in her correspondence. The most interesting bit of information actually pertained to Jessica herself. She had submitted her resignation as the director of the Middlemore library. I had realized that she was going through changes, but I had never thought that it would come down to this. She was, after all, remarkably young to hold such a prestigious post in Middlemore, and the job itself was a comfortable one. I had thought that she might venture into the world at large rather more slowly, basing herself in Middlemore, and taking more vacations – or even short leaves. From her correspondence, it was apparent that she was experiencing disorientation at several levels. The last thing that I expected her to do was to cut ties altogether with everything that she knew. Then again, I suppose she was not the type to do things by half measures. I admired the amount of courage that it must have taken her to remove the only strands of security that remained in the midst of her transitions. Surprisingly, she sounded none the worse for the effort.

Jessica spoke of a possible visit to the West Coast before I even had a chance to introduce the topic. Although she did not provide any tentative dates, it sounded like a done deal. I would have been rather dubious of the possibilities prior to our conversation, but in light of the sweeping changes in her life, I was guardedly optimistic. The idea of visitors, not really even a possibility in my past, had a sudden appeal to me. Mind you, any relatively healthy adult male would be receptive to a visit from a woman like Jessica. The only trouble was that I was no longer quite sure who now dwelt beneath that beautiful exterior.

**O**ne very pleasant change in my life (which was otherwise threatening to sink back into that old staid pattern of routines) is addition of a new neighbor and friend. Well, technically, she is not a *new* neighbor since she has lived close by, unbeknownst to me, for some time. And, she is not a *new* friend, having established our friendship some months ago in Middlemore. Nonetheless, Mandy *is* a new fixture in my home life – if such can be said so soon after my return.

The walk from my house to Mandy's apartment is, as I had deduced on the basis of the events of New Year's Eve, relatively short. It occurred to me, on one of my morning walks up the hill and through the cemetery, that it would probably be a simple matter to extend that walk a little and arrive at Mandy's apartment complex. As luck would have it, Mandy saw me approach through her window, and came outside to greet me. I most readily accepted her invitation to come inside for a cup of coffee (although my own brew was about to turn itself on automatically at my own home). The conversation was rather tentative, with neither of us wishing to turn the discussion towards Middlemore (where even our small talk had focused in the past). Yet we had no other common point of reference in our acquaintance. Nonetheless, I made so bold as to invite her to my home for dinner that night, and much to my surprise, she accepted on the spot. Again, she seemed a little awkward, I thought – perhaps in deference to the sparseness of her surroundings, and the absence of pretty much any commodity save coffee.

Although our dinner rendezvous was not a terribly relaxed meeting, I cannot say that it was, in any way, unpleasant. Both of us had made efforts to recover from our losses since our last time together. Although I had been considerably less effective in the process, I had learned to push

Derra to the dark recesses of my mind – from which she could reappear at less sensitive moments. Neither Mandy nor I was anxious to stir up old ghosts, but I think that the idea of starting up new friendships occurred to both of us even as we struggled through the conversations. We tentatively explored each other with our words, and stumbled across various points of interest. It was not, however, disjointed – as it was with Detective Kennedy. Mandy and I exploded with excitement when we surprised ourselves by landing on common ground. Still, it was a subtle thing between Mandy and me. Thrills of revelation were recorded in mental notes rather than in any overt exclamations. I cannot, of course, speak for her, but I was quite overwhelmed by the person that I discovered over this evening meal. I realized that, even over the course of long sessions with her at the George, I had not even scraped the surface of this remarkable person. Yet, at home, in a matter of hours, I had my first glimpse into the depths of the woman. My head was swirling by the time she had to leave.

Naturally, I did not allow her to walk home by herself. The route to her apartment, though very scenic and inspirational in its own way, was isolated for the most part, and not safe for a young woman to traverse on her own. There was bad history on this route for both of us as well, and I was hoping that, in each other's company, we might turn some of that around. We walked in silence, though the silence was less awkward than our conversations had been. The night was still and unusually clear. I think that the profusion of stars inspired a lot of the awe that produced the silence. Mandy, lost in her heavenward gaze, stumbled at one point. I caught her easily, but she blushed briefly in embarrassment. Taking my own eyes off of the stars at that point, I noticed the dark outline of tombstones surrounding us (for we had reached the cemetery). It was as if we had an audience watching us, wondering at the life force that we brought to this place of rest. The curiosity, however, did not seem morbid, but rather, spiritual – more of an affirmation than something sinister.

When Mandy and I reached the entrance to the apartment building, I must confess that I felt a little like a schoolboy on a first date. It was not until then that Mandy spoke – simply checking that I would be all right making my own way back home. I just laughed, suggesting that, if she were to walk *me* back home, we would be faced with the same dilemma at the other end. Again, she blushed a little – no doubt aware of the impracticalities in the situation. We remained silent again for a few long seconds. If it *were* a date, I would be using these seconds to decide whether or not to kiss her, and she to decide whether or not to invite me inside. But this was not a date. I don't think even my fantasy world stretched far enough to imagine the possibility. In an unusually bold and inspired moment, however, I did decide to break the silence by suggesting that we might share another morning cup of coffee the next day. Mandy brightened, said that she would have it brewing, and that she might like to accompany me on the second half of that walk once she had sufficiently wakened herself with the coffee. She asked me if she might expect me at any specific time, or whether I would just arrive randomly whenever I decided to begin my walk. How little she knew me!

*5*

The month of May had not yet expired when I received a package of correspond from a very unexpected source. My heart quivered nervously as I read the letter that accompanied that introduced the several pages of Derra's recollections:

*My dear Noah,*

*I fear that my first correspondence to you (was it really only a matter of months!) triggered a rather unexpected flood of events, much of which must have been very unpleasant for you. I am sorry for that. Hopefully, this material will help to unravel some of the mysteries for you, and undo, at least in some small part, some of the damage that I have done.*

*I have attached to this letter a collection of my own earlier remembrances that I thought would be useful in helping you to understand what has brought me to the state in which I now find myself irrevocably enmeshed.* [Some of these notes seemed to fit best as my fifth section, entitled: *Derra's reflections recorded at an undetermined date.* NG.] *Please don't read them as my excuse. Whatever the motivations were behind those who oversaw my education, I was well educated, and I have all the tools to make the right decisions at my disposal. The fault for not having done so rests upon me alone – though I was certainly ignorant of some very key issues. I am very comfortable with much of the religious matters, though, as they fit well into my training. I think that, given the right circumstances, you too would have been more receptive to the theologies. That is of no matter, however, as it is not my purpose to convert you, or even to discuss religion as promoted by the Society of Diana. What I do want to impress upon you is that I came to an understanding of the mechanisms that run the society only recently. Whereas the religious revelations came to me over the course of time, and seemed natural enough, nothing seemed natural in the hierarchy of the Society.*

*My religious pursuits were inspired, innocently enough, by my grandfather. I think that my friendship with you flourished because you shared many of the same thoughts. My thoughts on the feminine and on Druidry were only vaguely formed in my mind when I knew you, and we only touched briefly on such things in our discussions. I hesitated to bring too many of these ideas to you as I felt that my perspective on such things was relatively unique – though I was aware that there was an organization interested in promoting such thoughts. I think, in part, too, your own perspective on the Christian faith was broad enough to encompass such things, almost subconsciously. Part of me still wants to discuss such things with you, not to persuade you, but to listen to your insights. As neatly as the whole theological package of the Society fits into my own training, I still harbor some misgivings. Maybe it's not the theology itself so much as it is the system behind it all. It's like someone took this pure, all-encompassing religion, poured it into this incredibly corrupt vessel, shook it, and watched to see what would come out. I suppose that that's true of any religion at a certain level. It just seems too obviously true with what I have experienced.*

*What have I experienced? My dear Noah, it would take me forever to tell you what I have experienced in that seemingly short span of time since New Year's Eve. Believe me, I was totally unaware that the level of corruption in the Society extended so far as murder – though my acquaintance with Leo Mascagni should have suggested as much to me. You may have seen him dogging my heels while I was with you.*

*He was a sort of bodyguard (a* guardian angel *they called him!), sent by the Society, to watch over me. I knew that he was an unsavory sort, and not to be trusted, but I knew, too, that he was apprehensive of my status in the Society (even though the full implications of that status were not known to me at the time). I knew what he would do with other girls who suited his taste, but I selfishly didn't give it much thought – recognizing that I was safe from his advances. I like to think that the idea of him murdering someone never crossed my mind – and maybe it didn't. But I can't imagine that I would have thought him incapable of rape – and such behavior is not so terribly far removed from actually taking human life. Perhaps there is nothing that I could have done to intervene on behalf of that poor girl who was killed so shortly before I left. Still, I could have known,* anticipated, *such a likelihood. But I did not want to know.*

*I had not been in Middlemore long, however, before Society tactics became apparent to me. There was nothing specific, but even I could not miss the implications in their rhetoric. I would have left, at that point, if I could, but I was essentially their prisoner. I was free within the boundaries of the town, but they made it clear that I could not leave, and I believed that they would have no difficulty in enforcing their restrictions. My faith was of great comfort to me, but of course, the irony of that was that it was much the same faith that was being promoted by my captors. I naïvely thought that I could distance myself from their philosophy by focusing on my Anglican roots. I had no idea that Father Luke was, not only in full sympathy with the Society, but in fact, an integral part of their system there. His words, I am sure you noticed, cast a spell over his listeners. (That's typical of the Druid messages, I discovered – though you might argue that there is something of trickery about it.) Although I instinctively recognized the mechanics of his method, I was nonetheless moved by his messages – maybe* because *I could identify with them so easily. If you and I had one more conversation together, I might choose one his sermons as a launching point. I often wondered, as I sat in worship, how you would react to what he was saying. Once I knew that you were in Middlemore, I easily guessed that you would be a regular in Father Luke's church. I am curious, even now, to hear what you would have to say about his service. I realize, however, that I will never have the opportunity to discover what you think about this, or any other of the issues that this correspondence might raise.*

*My deepest regret in all of this is the way that I treated you when I saw you in England. I could argue that it was necessary for me to maintain an aura of detachment to save you – and it would not be untrue. The full, sad truth, however, is that I was detached. The corruption that distressed me, to the point of unwisely writing to you in January, had fully infiltrated my nature by the time that you saw me in May. Again, please do not read that I am excusing myself – as if I were an unwitting victim of my fate. I was neither forced nor brainwashed into making the choices that I have made. While it is true that, once I discovered who I was, and how that related to the Society, I did not feel free to leave. My mind is my own, and I have always had the option to think as I choose to think. Although mysterious deaths abound in my world, and I suspect that both my father and grandfather may have victims of the Society, I believe that, untimely as her death may have been, my mother was protected from the Society by her status. (My grandmother, though also having that same status, lived before the Society had really organized itself.) That status, in any case, makes me, in a sense, invulnerable. My excuses, therefore, are hollow. My apology is, on the other hand, sincere. If all that I have written for you accomplishes no more than to make you believe that, then I have been successful.*

*My rapid descent into my private hell need not be recounted in detail. My short weeks in Middlemore exposed me to more than enough of the inhuman side of the Society to suffice as a full warning to me of the immorality of assuming the office prepared for me. I wrote to you at the very end of my stay, in despair of the choice that I knew I would make. I knew that, by then, it was too late for you to rescue me from my choice, but I suppose, subconsciously, I had hoped that you would. (Such foolishness on my part, however, almost cost you your life.) In any case, I saw my choice as a matter of duty, and whether or not I harbored thoughts of fighting against the corruption once I was in power, I stepped into the cesspit that was the Society hierarchy. The only parallel that comes to mind is that of the heir to an unwanted throne. The power of monarchy, in such cases, is not only stripped of its appeal, but becomes an almighty stick with which the monarch-to-be is beaten into submission. One's entire life has been directed towards a single goal, and the responsibility attached to that goal makes it impossible to refuse.*

*Again, I seem to be subjugating my free will.* The human will is free within its limitations, *you used to say. I don't know that my limitations were such that I could not have chosen differently. Even so, I could have* acted *differently. Whether or not my will had limitations, my power certainly did. There was much, I admit, that I could not have changed. Nonetheless, I have always had the option of remaining truer to myself. But the overwhelming sense of isolation terrified me, and I chose, instead, simply to withdraw. While you worked away, for my sake, in Middlemore, I sat like a pampered queen across the ocean. I had access, it is true, to secrets that have traversed the centuries – so I have honed my skills as both a Druid priestess and as a disciple of Diana. You would drool at the materials at my disposal, but you might be appeased to learn that I have finally concluded that such wisdom is ultimately wasted – on me or on anyone else. My commune with the spiritual elements of this world has removed me from it. Ultimately, I can't think that such a condition is what we should hope for when we seek the Divine. Perhaps it is the common touch, that showed forth so well in you, that the Society lacks, and has taken away from me.*

*I hope that it is of some consolation to you that my apology to you is more than just a matter of words. My intervention on your behalf caused some consternation with the elders of the Society – though no one is in a position to discipline me. I have merely to turn my nose up in disgust to any admonition, like the spoiled queen that I am, and they grovel off to some distant corner. There are whispers about me, I know, but they are powerless to take action against me. I, on the other hand, still have my powers – though, through inexperience, I have allowed them to be muted. I was inspired, by your dedication to me, to actions that I would surely have not had the courage to take otherwise. Although, by position, I am irrevocably chained to the Society, their temporal powers can no longer control my physical whereabouts. It might sound unimpressive to you, but I am leaving my seat of authority and returning home. I accomplish two things in doing so. First, I strike a blow against the hierarchy of the Society. A deliberate departure by someone of my rank is unprecedented, and they do not have any plans in place for dealing with it. While they will remain confident that my spirit cannot rebel against what they promote, my physical absence will spell out a level of independence with which they will not be comfortable. Second, I am hoping against hope that, given some breathing room, I will be able to resolve some of the contradictions of spirit and mind that are tearing me apart. The truth is that I awake each morning very much surprised to find that this conflict has not yet killed me.*

*In any case, I do not expect that we will have the opportunity to be in communication again. You will remain safe, whether I live or die, and I am satisfied to have accomplished that much. Remember always that the same girl who scampered into your bedroom window late at night to ramble on about the wonders of this world to you, and your dear cat, remains alive – however well concealed she might be by outer circumstance. Our Christmas together will always be evidence that there is goodness and perfection in this world despite the constant onslaught of its enemies. Hold on to your images of me, however unpleasant and confusing they might be, as I will hold on to yours. Thank you, Noah, for being my friend. Pray for me.*

*love,*
*Derra*

*6*

It seemed natural enough to share Derra's correspondence, and accompanying notes, with Mandy. In doing so, I did not feel as if I were betraying a trust. In fact, I felt as if I owed it to both Derra and Mandy to allow Mandy to see what part Derra may have had in her friend's death. She had no part at all to my reckoning, or to Mandy's – once she had worked through the material. Besides, Mandy had become a friend. I continue to hold Derra in my thoughts, just as she requested, but it is if she has left this world. Those ghostly images of Derra that had haunted me, even on the very day that we had met, returned in the words that she wrote to me. If, for no other reason than to share my grief, I need Mandy's company, and her simple wisdom, to help me sort through the mixture of feelings that overcome me.

Re-reading Derra's words through Mandy's eyes had a healing effect. It seemed to Mandy that, despite her words, Derra had most certainly been the victim of powers beyond her control. Her life had been dictated for her years before she was even born. The remarkable thing, Mandy said, is the way that Derra has managed to battle against her fate – even when faced with overwhelming odds. In doing so, she has given herself the opportunity to become my friend, and even yet, she is like the classic mortal standing up against a pantheon of gods for the simple purpose of remaining true to herself. And that is not an easy thing, Mandy said, in light of how deeply buried the real Derra must be within the role that has been thrust upon her. I have to agree. There is, among many other things, something of a Greek tragedy in the plot of Derra's life. She has spurned the proffered ambrosia, choosing rather to starve than to partake of a tainted immortality.

We were confused, at first, of what Derra meant by returning *home.*

Her happiest times, it seems, were spent with her grandfather, and with me. Her grandfather was dead, however, and there was nothing connecting her with the home where she had spent the first years of her life. I was her friend, but nothing about where I lived could be called her home. Besides, she was pretty much convinced that our paths would never cross again. By the process of elimination, then, we assumed that she was returning to the Oregon coast – where most her childhood had been spent, and where she had grown to learn something of her destiny. *It suits her*, I think, as I reflect on my limited memories of the rough, craggy shorelines, and the moody winds that would roar up against them. Hopefully, there, she will find the solitude that she needs, and (who knows?) maybe find some resolution to the complex riddle that her life has become.

My initial reaction, once we reached this conclusion, was to head out to the Oregon coast in hope of finding Derra. Mandy, however, provided the cool voice of reason in discouraging me from this venture. From a practical point of view, of course, it is ridiculous. The Oregon coastline is not a simple walk in the park that I could traverse, in search of a solitary person, in any finite amount of time. Even if I had some sense of which part of the coast had been her home, the task would still be daunting. Without a clue, I would simply be wasting my time. Theoretically, too, it is dubious that there would be any value in intruding upon her space at this time. I had not taken offense at it, but it was clear that she had not thought that it was a good time to see me again – nor did she seem to anticipate such a time. *I have to trust*, Mandy said, *that Derra knows what is best for her. After all, she has demonstrated a strong sense of what is right in just about everything that she has done.*

I guess that another aspect of my discussion of Derra with Mandy (though not brought on by anything that Mandy specifically said) is the realization that I have to try let go of Derra. I do not mean that I am planning, in any way, to dismiss our friendship or to diminish the memories. As a flesh and blood contact, however, as someone I will see again, speak to again, or even hear from again, I know she is gone. The stresses on her are far too great to leave her in one piece, ready to pick up on friendships that she has been forced to leave behind. Her options are limited. Either she has to return to the waiting arms of those who have molded her, or she has to run in circles the rest of her life, unable to move too far away from what she has trained so thoroughly to become. Whatever resolutions she comes to in her mind, I will not be privy to them. We have shared our destinies briefly, through a freak rift in time, yet however tight the bonds we have formed, worlds separate us now. Of course, the practicalities of letting go bear no relation to how I felt about such a prospect at gut level. I could sooner surrender my life then to try to extract any part of Derra from it.

Long walks with Mandy, apart from our morning ritual, have become a part of my daily routine. She has found work in the local hospital, but her hours only extend from noon to late afternoon. It seemed reasonable enough, once we had separately concluded our morning business, for me to accompany her to work. Afterwards, too, sometimes after tending to matters downtown, I meet her, and we would take an extended walk – occasionally lasting until the late twilight hour offered by that latitude at that time of the year. I had hoped to show Derra to Mandy through my eyes, but in only a matter of one or two days' walks, I could see Derra through Mandy's eyes. The difference was, perhaps, only subtle. My Derra is a gift, to which I have unimpaired access. The Derra to whom Mandy introduced me was on loan. She was mine for a season, but unnaturally so. The life force that she showed to me was only a shadow of something that might have been. In fact, it never was – though its impact remains very real in my life. The fault is not Derra's own – though it could be said that it is the fault of her birth. She is, in her own words, an *heir to an unwanted throne.*

Mandy's words, as kindly as they fall, are of little comfort to me. It is true that, insofar as they bring a needed closure to me, they are necessary words. But there is no comfort in that closure. How could there be? Derra has evaporated. For all of her titles, she is nothing more than a wisp of wind. And even that is better than the alternatives. *Hold on to your images of me, however unpleasant and confusing they might be,* she had written. Yet the only images that I can hold in my mind are neither unpleasant nor confusing. They are distorted only by the unbearable load of sadness that weighs upon them.

**M**ost of June passed uneventfully. I had time to digest Derra's words (and Mandy's reinterpretation), but I could not chase away a pending sense of gloom. Shortly before the month drew to an end, however, Jessica Burke arrived unexpectedly at my doorstep. If ever there has been such a timely diversion in someone's life, I cannot imagine. She is certainly a beautiful sight to behold. Standing before me now, however, there is no trace of that sulking countenance as she spreads her arms to greet me. The smile softens her face, and the foreboding toughness of her past demeanor is no longer there. It is a total woman who falls into my arms, strong and vulnerable, and I am sure that I would be the envy of any man who had watches me awkwardly receive her.

"I told you I would come," she says cheerily once we separate.

"True," I acknowledge, "but you didn't exactly say when."

"If it's inconvenient, I can always stay at the local motel," she says with a wry smile.

The smile is endearing. It creeps across her face frequently in our initial conversation at times when the Jessica I had known would have resorted to her pout. It is a marked improvement. The pout, while admittedly alluring, signified a pending danger, and advertised a sort of superiority. The smile, on the other hand, is playful. It mocks, yet gently so, in a manner that most men would, I presume, find pleasantly flirtatious. Perhaps I am just generalizing from my own perspective, but on the matter of beautiful women, I have seldom found my opinions at odds with the general male populace. In any case, no healthy member of my gender would have sent this specimen of the other gender away from his doorstep to an anonymous motel. And, of course, Jessica knew that.

The smile returns as Jessica watches me rearrange the plans for my day, and listens to me plead that I as no longer a slave to routine. Perhaps most of what I cancelled did smack of daily ritual. Yet, a lot of that ritual pertains to Mandy, so I am more inclined to label it socialization than routine. Protests along this line, however, do me more harm than good. With each mention of Mandy, Jessica's wry smile expands. Ultimately, it turns into a full-fledged grin. When I question her as to its meaning, she simply shrugs her shoulders – but the grin doesn't disappear. Having little patience with sorting through those esoteric female indicators that all women (mysteriously) seem to think are so explicit, I let the matter drop. I am little annoyed, though, that Jessica is feeling so smug – thinking that she knows something about me that I don't know. But I can't be bothered to take the time to straighten out whatever it was that is running through her head.

Otherwise, settling Jessica into my home is a thoroughly pleasant experience. My last houseguest was Derra, of course, but that doesn't put a damper on introducing Jessica to my space. After all, my Christmas with Derra was magical. I didn't place such expectations on Jessica, but I am excited nonetheless. Bubastes shares in my excitement. He won't stop rubbing against Jessica's legs as she takes the short tour of the premises – almost tripping her on more than one occasion. Ultimately, as I suspect Bubastes had planned all along, she picks him up and gives him her undivided attention. He purrs vigorously in celebration of his victory. Even if I hadn't wanted Jessica to stay with me, I have no choice now. Of course, I want her to stay – I think every bit as much as does Bubastes. I call Mandy to cancel our afternoon walk (tolerating an ever-growing smile from Jessica all the while), pull some food from the freezer, and browse through my DVDs while Jessica is in the shower. My sparse mealtime offerings seem to satisfy her. We dawn pajamas, and settle together on the couch in front of the movies. The ghost of Derra dances around the room. Still, with Jessica falling gently to sleep on my shoulder, I must say that it is a friendly spirit.

I returned from my morning walk with Mandy before Jessica arose. She might have slept on indeterminately had not the smell of bacon and eggs wended its way to her room. Bubastes, who had deserted me for the night in favor of our fair visitor, follows closely at her heels. The early morning Jessica is no less alluring than was the Jessica dressed for the day. Her tanned skinned clearly requires little, if any, make-up, and the drowsy look in her eyes is simply devastating. I try not to stare as we enter discussions about the current state of Middlemore. Actually, it is more of a monologue, with Jessica excitedly relating some of the many changes that she has witnessed. I recognize some of what she is saying from the letter that she had sent me. Much to my shame, however, I must confess that, if her information went beyond what she had written, I did not notice. One would have thought that the past half-year's experience might have made me immune to the distractions of feminine beauty. No such luck.

I made arrangements with Mandy for me to come and meet her after work with Jessica. Jessica alone is enough to cause traffic accidents, but once Mandy joined us, the effect became totally lethal. I am observed with some curiosity as these beauties flank me, or as I drift behind – allowing them to exchange those more cryptic comments indigenous to their gender. It doesn't bother me that I might be seen as out of place. Womanhood itself seems to be encompassed in these two friends of mine. One dark and one fair, one softly kissed by the sun and the other having soaked the rays into her brown skin – they are the perfect circle of femininity. I cannot say for sure whether or not they detect my admiring gazes. I am not subtle – but neither is the score of humanity across whose paths we tread. On this walk, more than in anything I have read or seen in the past half year, I am more vulnerable to TSD doctrine than I imagined possible. But, then, why give something so perfect a label?

Mandy's meal is a significant upgrade from the one that I had offered Jessica the night before. I have recovered my senses to some degree (at least, as much as could be hoped surrounded by such company), and I even venture into some of the conversation. Mostly, however, I listen as the two women exchange thoughts, and seemingly, forge conspiracies. Occasionally, Jessica catches my eye, and then shifts her glance to Mandy – accentuating it with that wry smile. Mandy, too, would look at me occasionally and exchange giggles with her new friend. I would give anything to have someone interpret their unspoken gestures and whispered exchanges. Still, it is not for me to know, and I really can't complain about my lot. The end result of it all (this time announced in plain English) is that the three of us will pay a visit to Detective Kennedy the next day. It seems a rather strange choice of tourist attractions, but I think the ladies are pretty confident in assuming that I will go anywhere they lead. It doesn't take a genius to sort that one out.

isgivings about the pending visit to Detective Kennedy plagued me in the early hours of the next morning, despite my total surrender to the wishes of my lovely companions. He was receptive to the idea of a visit when I had called him in the evening, but he was not well the last time that I saw him, and at that time, mention of Middlemore or of TSD seemed to agitate him unnecessarily. I expressed my concerns to Mandy later that morning as I walked her from her apartment to my home. She reassured me that neither she nor Jessica would push matters on the detective that he would be unable to bear. *What was I thinking?* She chastised me gently for doubting them, and as I watched her express her carefully chosen words, I noticed the pink glow that the morning air had painted on her cheek. The color deepened once she realized that I was looking at her, and I quickly turned away so as not to afford her any further embarrassment.

Jessica was a vision as well. Freshly showered and made-up, her perfume blended perfectly with the sharp morning breeze that blew into my house as she opened the door to greet us. The intoxicating combination of fresh scents accentuated the pristine look that Jessica had adopted for the day's activities. I think that Mandy was as impressed as I was. I had not yet adapted to Jessica's new persona. In Middlemore, her look, though equally lethal, had seemed almost thrown together. The short skirts or jeans and tank tops, and casually brushed hair, were accessorized only by that perpetual pout. The business attire that she had dawned for our morning trip seemed to cover a different woman. The grooming had been taken up a notch, and the regular flash of white teeth, in what was once an unimaginable smile, kept drawing attention to the loveliness of her facial features. The only obvious giveaway that this was the same girl was the sight of those long dark legs extending from the short hemline of her outfit.

I drove, but spent the entire trip in silent awe. Mandy sat up front with me (at Jessica's insistence), but was twisted back towards Jessica most of the time. It really was like a vacation outing. That mood did not change once we reached our destination. A much-improved Detective Kennedy met us at the door. Forewarned of our visit, he actually seemed to have been eagerly anticipating it. His broad smile still looked a little ghostly stretched across those sallow cheeks, but the warmth of his welcome was undiminished by the effect. He still clenched his pipe tightly in his hand, but seldom put it to his lips. He had spread an elaborate lunch for us across his dining room table (not dissimilar to an English tea), and he immediately began the process by uncorking a dusty bottle of aged Cabernet. It seemed rather early in the day for such a dark drink, but the ladies and the Cabernet itself argued effectively against my protests. It slid gently down my throat, massaging life into my taste buds as it passed and sending a sweet tingle to my head once it landed. It stood in stark contrast to the heavy grog that I had experienced with Father Luke. In short order, our conversation, though focused on the sensitive issues of Middlemore and TSD, was flowing freely and lightly. Never had I imagined that an exchange of unsettling information could be so pleasant.

The endless stream of Strauss waltzes wafting throughout the house and its gardens provided the perfect backdrop to our dancing dialogues. Only when I presented Detective Kennedy with the letter that Derra had written to me did the agitation, that had been so apparent to me last time, resurface. The music, too, made a dramatic pause as the detective pondered the implications. Then, just as suddenly, the music resumed with a Saint-Saëns violin concerto, and the glint returned to Kennedy's eyes.

"She's part of the resistance," he said crisply, "– remarkable."

I think I know what he meant, but I would not presume to interpret on his behalf. He had no other comment on the letter at that time. He quickly perused the more extensive collection of notes that she had included in her packet, but seemed less impressed than he had been with the letter. He looked up at me, once he had finished, posed the word *Oregon* as a question, and waited for my nod as I waited for further comment. Instead, once I confirmed his deduction, he picked up the half empty bottle of cabernet from the table (the second or third?), topped off our glasses, and signaled for us to follow him to the greenhouse. For me, at least, this was the perfect distraction. The rare and wondrous specimens that surrounded me worked hard in a futile attempt to chase thoughts of Derra from my head. There was a mixture of exotic and wild – temperature-controlled according to their needs. It was particularly poignant to encounter the Cheddar pink (*dianthus gratianpolitanus*), that I had hoped to see in its indigenous location in Somerset, in the final stages of its bloom. Inspired by the sight, and fueled by the wine, I chattered on like a schoolgirl to my proud host. Over my shoulder I caught a glimpse of Mandy. Catching my eye, she moved her hand to her mouth in an exaggerated yawning motion. Seeing my horror at her disinterest, she quickly followed that motion with a broad smile. Jessica, too, catching this interaction flashed another of her enchanting smiles. I thought that they were both going to break out into laughter, so I returned my attention to Detective Kennedy in order that my friends might not embarrass me in front of our gracious host.

The remainder of our visit was passed in a very mellow sort of way. Each of us, in turn, drifted into a light sleep (with the notable exception of Detective Kennedy, who remained remarkably alert). Slowly, the intoxicating effects of the wine wore off and we were ready to leave. The conversation had rambled on without any discernable direction while we rested. Detective Kennedy, however, took keen interest in everything that was said, and at strange junctures, even scribbled notes in his pocketbook. His rising obsession with TSD has clearly overtaken my waning interest. Of course, our perspectives are diametrically opposite. The detective looks at things with a professional curiosity. Derra intrigues him only as she relates to TSD. My concern is purely personal. But I had stared the Society in the face and I no longer care about its functions – except, of course, in so far as they relate to Derra. Derra, however, has become more of a dream than a reality for me. In many ways, however, the dream is more potent than the reality ever was. Although her welfare is still a matter of much anxiety for me, I know that the vision, locked in my head, is all that I have left of her. This is much worse than it was wondering about her when she departed for parts unknown in the early hours of the new year.

Bidding us farewell at his front door, Detective Kennedy was in good spirits and appeared to be not at all offended by the way that we had drifted away from interaction with him at the end of our time under his roof. He shook hands vigorously with the two women, and then clasped my hand symbolically as I took my leave.

"So you think she's in Oregon?" he mused. "If she's there for any length of time, I think I can find her for you."

I am neither sure how nor why. Despite the warmth of the emotions that I still feel for her, I can distance myself enough to know that Derra is best served at this point in time by being left to her own devices.

# Editing Notes

have intermingled excerpts from my memoirs with the other first hand accounts to which I have had access, trying to remain sensitive to the chronological unfolding of events. My edits have been mostly grammatical – though there was more extensive work done piecing together the initial stages of Detective Sturgess' investigation. Detective Kennedy has been of great assistance with parts of this, and with other matters of fact, on subsequent visits.

In part, this has been a labor of love. When Derra flew into my life, she forever changed the landscape of my world. Apart from a broken heart, I am none the worse for it, but nonetheless, I carry the burden of having lived a lifetime in six short months. In fact, despite my strong feelings for Derra, and the enjoyment of my blossoming friendship with Detective Kennedy, Mandy has almost had to drag me to the detective's home, on a regular basis, so that I could work on the final editings. My problem, as best I can analyze it, is that I had taken on too much at once – mentally and emotionally – and I had found myself like someone who had overindulged in an all-you-can-eat buffet. To further the analogy: *I still love prime rib, but don't really want to see one for another month.*

The case, as far as I am concerned, is over. It is true that Detective Kennedy would like to chase down a few of the leads that he has collected, but I will not actively pursue any updates. TSD is neither the most holy nor the most evil society on the face of this earth. Their business may flourish, but I do not anticipate that their philosophy will incite any revolution in religious thought, nor do I suppose their clandestine activities will accelerate. Middlemore was a key experiment for them that ultimately failed. They may start to crumble as a result of that loss, but I suspect that it is more likely that they will rebuild – with lessons learned. Philosophically,

Derra was a greater loss to them – although they are too well invested in her life to lose her altogether. My interest could be sparked, however, by the prospect of learning how Derra resolves the dilemmas of her life. Unfortunately, I see no resolution for her, and whether she escapes the Society indefinitely or falls back into some ceremonial role, I would prefer to leave her fate to my imagination. Only there can I comfort myself with thought that the Derra with whom I spent that Christmas still exists.

Mandy and Jessica both helped with some of the revisions. Once they received copies of the proofs that Detective Kennedy and I had completed, they offered some specific comments on the parts that pertained to them. Mandy proclaimed that my descriptions of her were far too complimentary not to serve as a source of embarrassment should these records ever be made public. Jessica said that she was amused by the transformation that I allocated to her, but added, with a smile that I could see over the telephone as we spoke, that she was glad that, at my age, I could still recognize a beautiful young woman when I saw one. I will send a final copy to Detective Kennedy, too, along with these editing notes, but I will ask him not to comment. There is no end to the revising of these notes, and at this point in time, I am not open to fresh comments, as the wounds that Derra inflicted upon my heart still remain fresh. The whole thing needs to be laid to rest. I need silence on these issues now. I need to look forward, yet no further forward than my next morning walk.

# Addendum

## ADDED IN DECEMBER

It has been half of a year since I gathered, for compilation, all of the information about Derra, and the strange society that held her in its grip. As I resettled into my rather comfortable existence, enhanced by new relationships and a thoroughly altered perspective on life, I had thought that I had prepared the way to close the book on Derra once and for all. Yet the arrival of the Christmas feelings has stirred bittersweet memories of my days with her.

The pain has been somewhat softened by the constant companionship of Mandy, who herself has sad memories of this season – a New Year's Eve being the anniversary of her friend's death. My daily routines have, once again, become fixed, but I make no apologies considering that Mandy is included in most of them. It is a mellow lifestyle for me. On the surface, it probably looks like a less productive time than even the time before I met Derra. But that perception is not accurate. Although I have been more actively emptying my mind than filling it, there is a peacefulness in my existence that I had never thought possible. Companionship plays a role in this – perhaps the only significant role. I am healthier, slimmer, now. The walks have always been a mainstay for me, but a significantly improved diet (under Mandy's direction) is largely responsible for the upgrade in my condition. It has probably helped, as well, that I have (against all expectation) taken a dislike to beer when not consumed in the company of friends. Since Mandy is my main company here in town, and her urges for beer drinking are quite sporadic, the "spare tire" that was, at one point, forming around my waist has not threatened to return.

I have, however, kept to my Friday lunch routine with Lucy, after the housekeeping is done: coddled eggs, toast, watercress and a glass of beer. But I don't have the second glass anymore. I am still not immune to falling asleep afterwards with Bubastes on my lap, but the highlight of the day now is meeting Mandy after she is done with work, and sorting out our weekend plans. Happily, she has been accompanying me to the services at St. Paul's Church on a regular basis, and the simple liturgy, experienced in her company, is slowly bringing me back to terms with my faith.

The uneasiness of the season, however, was compounded by an unexpected visit from Detective Kennedy. He is back on duty, and we hadn't really been in touch with him much over recent weeks. Mandy was at my home when he arrived. He looks fit now, though much older than when I had first met him. (*Was it really only months ago?*) He was all business – and that frightened us a little. His report, though, was not entirely unexpected. It seems that Derra's body had washed ashore off the coast of Oregon. Although there was really no one to identify her, he had seen her himself, and had no doubt as to her identity once he spotted the engraved locket around her neck. Local police could discover nothing about her identity beyond that one name. Detective Kennedy could see no purpose in stirring matters up, however, so he remained silent with regard to my connection with her. No foul play was suspected. There was nothing else to say. It was truly over now. Detective Kennedy left without ever dropping his professional persona.

Upon his departure, a full year's worth of emotion welled within me, and I broke down. I don't know when, if ever, I had last cried, but I am sure that it was nothing like this. Tears gushed forth as if bursting from newly opened wounds. But the real wounds were old and varied. There was Derra, of course, and there was the world into which she had drawn me. But my own demons were there, too, chiding me for a wasted life, and taunting me with visions of the unending horrors of human existence. Yet, as I reached what I was certain must be my pain threshold, I felt Mandy's arm slip around my shoulder. Her head fell softly onto my shoulder. Soon, I was conscious of nothing more that the warmth of her breath on my cheek, and the fresh scent of her hair, that brought with it the promise of a new day.

Printed in the United States
By Bookmasters